THE HEIR OF

Alison knew she should have been wary of this English lord whose grandfather had laid waste to the highlands she loved.

She should not have listened to his words of love, or been deceived by his gentle manners, or been bedazzled by his extraordinarily handsome face and manly form.

Now as she saw him greet the beautiful Lady Deborah Willoughby from London, and heard him introduce Lady Deborah as his future bride, Alison realized how foolish it had been to think he would choose her, Alison, over an elegant society belle, so clearly one of his own kind.

Lord Ravenstoke had left her heart a wasteland—yet it was so hard to drive him out. . . .

HIGHLAND
LADY

SIGNET REGENCY ROMANCE

MARGARET SUMMERVILLE

HIGHLAND LADY

A SIGNET BOOK

NEW AMERICAN LIBRARY

NAL BOOKS ARE AVAILABLE AT QUANTITY DISCOUNTS WHEN USED TO
PROMOTE PRODUCTS OR SERVICES. FOR INFORMATION PLEASE WRITE TO
PREMIUM MARKETING DIVISION, NEW AMERICAN LIBRARY, 1633 BROADWAY,
NEW YORK, NEW YORK 10019.

SIGNET TRADEMARK REG. U.S. PAT OFF. AND FOREIGN COUNTRIES
REGISTERED TRADEMARK—MARCA REGISTRADA
HECHO EN CHICAGO, U.S.A.

SIGNET, SIGNET CLASSIC, MENTOR, PLUME, MERIDIAN AND NAL BOOKS
are published by New American Library, 1633 Broadway, New York,
New York 10019

First printing, September, 1985

1 2 3 4 5 6 7 8 9

PRINTED IN THE UNITED STATES OF AMERICA

1   Lady Alison Murray rode recklessly across the barren moor, mindless of the chill March wind. Shouting words of encouragement to her magnificent chestnut stallion, Alison urged the big horse to increase his speed. The animal's long strides propelled them swiftly across the rugged terrain and she soon found herself nearing the river that marked the western boundary of her grandfather's property.

Alison slowed her horse as she approached the river and turned southward. She continued on for some distance, and then, seeing a group of men ahead, she pulled the stallion up sharply.

It was unusual to see anyone in this part of the moor, and Alison eyed them curiously, wondering what they were doing there. There were six of them and they appeared to be busily working. As Alison drew nearer, she could see the men were constructing a stone fence.

"A fence?" Alison said aloud, quite astonished. "Why would anyone be putting a fence at the border of Grandfather's lands?" Alison frowned, and determined to discover what they were about, she urged her horse ahead.

The men glanced up as Alison approached, and eyed her appreciatively. A young woman of uncommon beauty, Alison looked striking atop her chestnut steed, her auburn hair streaming in the wind and an attractive rosy flush on her face.

Recognizing the granddaughter of the Duke of Dornach, the men smiled and respectfully pulled their caps from their heads. "Good morning, Lady Alison," said one of the men, a tall, brawny fellow with sandy-colored hair and weathered face. He addressed her in Gaelic, the lilting tongue still spoken in that part of the Highlands. "A grand horse is your Claymore. In fine form he is today."

"Aye," replied Alison. "Good day to all of you." She, too, spoke in Gaelic. Looking at the tall man, she continued, "Ranald Maxwell, why do you build a fence in this place?"

"'Tis the order o' the new laird, my lady," Maxwell replied.

"The new laird?"

"Aye, the new laird o' Glenfinnan."

A puzzled look came to Alison's face. Glenfinnan was the estate that bordered her grandfather's estate to the west. Although Alison knew that the property had been put up for sale some time ago, she was unaware that it had been sold.

So there was now a new laird of Glenfinnan? Alison was suddenly annoyed. How could she have been ignorant of so important a piece of local news?

"And what is the new laird's name?"

"Lord Ravenstoke it is," answered Ranald.

"Ravenstoke?"

"Aye." Ranald paused for effect. "An Englishman he is."

"An Englishman?" Alison regarded him in surprise. "An Englishman has taken Glenfinnan?"

Maxwell and the others nodded solemnly. "Believe it you must for true it is, Lady Alison. An Englishman now owns these lands."

"Then it is for this new English laird that you build a fence here?"

Maxwell and the others nodded.

"Never has there been a fence in this place. Why would he wish to build one?"

Maxwell shrugged. "We know not, my lady, but orders we have, and build the fence we will."

Alison frowned. "It seems eager you are to obey the orders of an Englishman, Ranald Maxwell."

Ranald bristled at the inference of her remark and paused before replying. He reminded himself that he owed Lady Alison Murray proper deference. She was, after all, the granddaughter of the Duke of Dornach, who, although not his laird, was Chieftain of the Clan. "A Scottish laird we would prefer, my lady, but no choice had we in the matter."

"Aye," said one of the other men, speaking for the first time. "No choice at all had we. But a rich man is Ravenstoke, and 'tis in gold he will pay us to build the fence."

"In gold?" replied Alison scornfully. "Aye, that is reason enough to love an Englishman."

The men regarded her with surprise and resentment. Proud Highlanders, they were unwilling to take insults even from the duke's granddaughter.

Alison regretted her words immediately and hastened to apologize. "Unfair that was," she said. "Forgive me for speaking so. It is only that I cannot bear to think of an Englishman at Glenfinnan. Rude I have been and I do apologize."

Maxwell and the others smiled, eager to forgive the young lady's rashness. They knew that she was a true Murray and, like all her family, had a hot temper and reckless streak. "Understand we do, my lady."

Alison smiled at them. "Then go I must. Good day to you all." With these words, she turned Claymore and hurried off toward home. Galloping once again across the moor, Alison wondered about the new English laird of Glenfinnan. That his first act was building a fence was most unneighborly. She imagined how he might look and conjured up a picture not unlike the present King George III, stout, elderly, and bewigged. She was certain this Ravenstoke must be a dreadful man and could hardly wait to return home and discuss the matter with her family.

Dornach Castle was a grim brooding edifice of gray stone that had been the stronghold of the Murray family for more than six hundred years. Its high walls were crowned with battlements and it was easy to envision medieval soldiers standing there ready to hurl arrows, spears, or rocks at any invaders.

Yet Alison Murray did not find the sight of her family's ancient home in any way forbidding. She had been born there and had spent almost every day of her twenty years within the castle walls, or within sight of them. No, to Alison, Dornach Castle represented home, and she loved it dearly.

Leaving Claymore with one of the grooms, Alison hurried inside. She made her way through the winding corridors of the castle toward the drawing room, which was where the family usually assembled.

The castle living quarters were not nearly so stark as the fortress's exterior. Before she had died, Alison's mother had attempted to make the castle more livable. Although the duke had not been very enthusiastic about his daughter-in-law's redecorating, he had grudgingly allowed her to purchase a few pieces of modern furniture. He had also reluctantly agreed to the banishment of several unattractive family heirlooms.

Consequently, the drawing room and parlor, as well as the main entry hall, looked quite presentable. Of course, the appearance of Dornach Castle would hardly have passed muster when compared with the elegant habitations of the well-to-do members of London society.

Lady Alison gave no thought to interior decoration as she entered the drawing room in search of her grandfather. She found him sitting in his favorite chair surrounded by her brothers, Andrew and Duncan.

All three looked up as she entered. "Allie," said Andrew, eyeing his sister's somewhat disheveled appearance in mock horror. "You might have combed your hair first."

Alison frowned at her brother. "I have no time for your foolery, Andrew. I have something I must tell you."

Andrew Murray, Earl of Culwin and Master of Dornach, raised an eyebrow and then cast a glance at his grandfather, who returned the look with a quizzical expression.

"Is something wrong, lass?" ventured the duke.

"Something is indeed wrong, Grandfather. An English laird has taken Glenfinnan."

"That is deuced bad news, Allie," said Andrew, "but

surely you knew that already. It is the Marquess of Ravenstoke."

"You mean you knew?"

"I was sure I told you," said the duke. "Or maybe I was going to tell you. Well, that does not signify, as you know now."

Alison regarded her brothers and grandfather in frustration. "I should think that I might be informed of these things."

"Och, that is like a woman, wanting to know the gossip before everyone else. I assure you that we were not hiding it from you, Allie. We have not known for long. I believe you were out riding when we were discussing it." Andrew spoke with the patronizing tone that sometimes exasperated his sister. Although two years younger than Alison, Andrew often assumed the role of the elder and wiser sibling. As heir to his grandfather's title and oldest male child, Andrew found the role appropriate. After all, Alison was a girl, and strong-willed as she was, it was he who, after their grandfather, was head of the family.

As irksome as this attitude was to Alison, it was difficult to be angry with her brother Andrew. Indeed, she was devoted to him and to her grandfather and youngest brother, Duncan. The Murrays were a very close-knit family. Since all possessed the Murray temper, they sometimes quarreled, but few families were so firmly united.

"And did you know about this Englishman, Duncan?" Alison looked expectantly at her youngest brother, who appeared a trifle sheepish.

"Aye, we would have told you this morning at breakfast, but you had gone riding. I am sorry, Allie."

Alison smiled fondly at Duncan. She loved him dearly. Only ten years old, the Hon. Duncan Murray was a mischievous but good-hearted lad. Alison had been as much a mother to him as a sister, since he had been only a tiny baby when their mother had died.

"Oh, very well, I suppose it does not matter," said Alison. "But since you are so well informed about our new neighbor, I daresay there is no need for me to tell you what I have discovered about him."

"And what is that, my girl?" asked the duke.

"Aye, tell us, Allie," said Andrew.

"It is that he is putting up a fence."

"A fence!" The duke looked startled.

"At the western edge of your lands, Grandfather, near the fork in the river."

"And why would anyone want a fence there?" said Andrew. "Are you sure it is a fence being put up?"

"You must think me a great goose, Lord Culwin. I know a fence when I see it, and Ranald Maxwell was one of the men who was building it. It seems the new laird is paying him and the others in gold."

"I don't like this," murmured his grace. "Why would the man want a fence? There has never been a fence there. Och, the Drummonds held Glenfinnan three hundred years and never put up a fence near my lands.

"I do not like this by half. I have heard no good said of this Ravenstoke, and it seems that what is said is true."

Alison looked over at her grandfather. "What is it that is being said, Grandfather?"

"That this marquess is a cold man, interested only in taking what he can from the land. I'm told he is very rich, one of the richest men in England."

"And there is more, Allie," added Andrew. "They say he is much disliked, for he is a terrible bore and a stuffy prig."

Alison shook her head. "It is a fine one we are getting, then. We may be thankful that the Dornach lands stretch so far."

Andrew nodded. "But there is no need to worry about seeing the fellow. He'll stay in London, you may be sure of that."

"Aye," agreed the duke. "I'm sure he has sent someone to oversee Glenfinnan. I know his kind, and it is very unlikely that he would ever venture north of the border. Still, lass, you had best change the path you ride, for we'll have naught to do with anyone at Glenfinnan." The duke looked thoughtful. "These are hard times for all of us, but I never thought the Drummonds would be forced to sell their lands."

Andrew nodded solemnly and Alison grew pensive. She

wondered about her own family's financial state. She knew that her grandfather would deny vehemently that the Dornach estates in any way resembled the sorry condition of the Drummonds' property. Indeed, one could barely compare the two, since the duke's holdings were so vast.

Yet, Alison found herself feeling uneasy. She knew that many of her grandfather's tenants were unable to pay their rent. She had seen too many gaunt faces staring at her from the small cottages that dotted the Dornach lands. There was too little food grown on the estate and too many hungry people depending on the often-meager harvests.

"What is the matter, Alison?" The duke's voice brought Alison out of her reverie.

"Oh, I am sorry, Grandfather. I was simply daydreaming." She tried to smile and shake the gloomy thoughts away. "If you gentlemen will excuse me, I shall be off to change." Then, having taken her leave of her brothers and grandfather, Alison left the drawing room.

2   The following morning Alison rose early and, coming down to the dining room, was surprised to find it empty. Although it was not unusual for her brother Andrew to sleep late, her grandfather and Duncan almost always arrived at breakfast before her.

Anticipating the question, the elderly serving man who had been at work in the dining room addressed his young mistress. "His grace, Lord Culwin, and Master Duncan are gone, m'lady."

"Gone, Bob?"

"Aye, tae MacGillivray Hall. His grace said tae say they would nae be back until verra late."

"I see. Thank you, Bob."

"Annie will hae your ladyship's breakfast ready soon."

Alison nodded to the servant and he left her. She watched him walk off, a thoughtful expression on her face. Bob MacPherson had been in service to the Murrays since his boyhood some seventy years ago. Alison was very fond of him and worried sometimes that he worked too hard.

Sitting down at the dining-room table, Alison propped her head on her hand in a reflective pose. Dornach Castle had too few servants now and the work fell heavily on them. Alison had often asked her grandfather if she could hire additional help, but the duke would not allow it, saying they must economize as much as possible.

It was a source of constant worry to her, for the amount of work required to maintain Dornach Castle was tremendous. Alison had closed many rooms, but still the family's living area needed much attention.

More than once Lady Alison found herself pitching in to help faithful Annie Thomson, the cook, in the kitchen or Bob MacPherson in the drawing room. That a lady did not stoop to such things did not trouble Alison overmuch. She was pragmatic, and was unafraid of work of any kind. Yet Alison knew very well that things could not continue on this way for long. She and the servants could do only so much, and very soon her grandfather would have to deal with the problem.

"Good morning tae ye, m'lady." Annie Thomson's cheery greeting brought a smile to Alison's face.

"Good morning, Annie."

Annie placed a bowl of steaming porridge before her mistress. "And what else would your ladyship be wanting?"

"This is fine, Annie. I want nothing else."

"Verra good, m'lady." Annie Thomson regarded her young mistress fondly. Alison was a good-natured girl and a considerate employer. Of course, she did have a temper and, like all the Murrays, could be very stubborn. "Then I'll be off tae finish the washing up."

"Hasn't Mary done that?"

Annie shook her head. "Mary's mother is sick again and she's gone tae look after the wee bairns."

"And what of Jean? Could she not help you in the kitchen?"

"Och, my lady, Jean and Isabelle hae enough work tae do. Ye must nae worry about me. I can do verra well myself."

Alison smiled appreciatively at the servant, who nodded and then scurried off to the kitchen. Alison shook her head and resolved to confront her grandfather once again about additional servants as soon as he returned from MacGillivray Hall.

A frown crossed Alison's lovely countenance as she thought of her brothers and grandfather in the company of Sir Ian MacGillivray. She could not abide Sir Ian and considered him to be a most unfortunate influence upon her two brothers.

Their closest neighbor and a member of a family that

had long been allied with the Murrays, MacGillivray was well-liked by both Duncan and Andrew. They thought him a great fellow and admired his skill with horses, mastery of all manner of sport, and ability to hold a prodigious amount of liquor.

Alison, however, saw in Sir Ian a host of undesirable traits, despite the fact that he was considered to be the area's most eligible bachelor. He was handsome in a rugged muscular way and quite wealthy, and, indeed, many young ladies had lost their hearts to him.

Yet Alison found nothing at all likable about the man. She considered him an uncouth bully whose conceit was unbearable. MacGillivray had a reputation as a ladies' man, and it was generally known that many a peasant lass had cause to rue her association with him.

In addition to his lamentable morals where women were concerned, Sir Ian was addicted to gaming. His chancing large sums on the toss of dice or the outcome of a horse race would not have bothered Alison save for his encouraging of the duke and Andrew to do likewise. What made the situation even worse was that Sir Ian seemed to have what was generally called the devil's own luck, while Andrew was as ill-fated a gamester as one might imagine, losing continuously and still vowing to try once more.

It was bad enough to see Andrew trying to emulate MacGillivray, but Alison worried that Duncan was also falling under his spell. She had more than once begged her grandfather to keep her youngest brother away from Sir Ian, but the duke always laughed at her fears. Indeed, his grace thought MacGillivray a true Highlander and would hear no ill said of him.

Alison looked down at the porridge, which was rapidly growing cold in the bowl. She took one more spoonful and then pushed it aside, suddenly not at all hungry.

"M'lady!" Alison's musings were interrupted by the sound of Annie Thomson's distraught voice. "'Tis Archie Fisher drunk in the kitchen! Can ye nae do something, Lady Alison?"

Alison rose from her chair and quickly followed the cook. Archie Fisher was employed by the duke as shepherd to his flock of prize ewes. He was a most unreliable man with an unfortunate tendency toward overindulging in strong spirits.

Finding Fisher sprawled out upon the kitchen floor, shepherd's crook in one hand and whiskey flask in the other, Alison lost her temper. She placed both her hands on her hips and spoke sternly in Gaelic. "Archie Fisher, drunk you are!"

The man regarded her with an inebriated grin. "Good day, m'lady."

"'Tis nothing o' the kind, man. You are to be out with the ewes. Too near lambing time it is for you to leave them alone."

"Aye, true that is, mistress," said Fisher, slurring his speech and continuing to grin up at her.

"Get to your feet," Alison shouted in English.

Fisher seemed startled at the harshness of Alison's voice. Looking momentarily confused, he tried to get up, but fell back onto the floor.

Annie glanced over at Alison. "He'll nae be any good tae anyone, m'lady."

"Did he fetch the ewes, Annie? They were to be confined here until the lambing."

Annie shook her head. "I don't know, m'lady. If only Robin Douglas was about. He could see tae the sheep. But his grace sent Robin and the other lads down tae the village wi' the horses. There is only Mr. MacPherson."

"Then I must go myself and see if the sheep are in the pen. I hope to heaven that they are, for, if not, they'll be scattered across the Highlands by now." Alison directed a look of disgust at Fisher, who had fallen quickly asleep. She reached down and took the shepherd's crook from his hand. "Might I borrow your cloak, Annie?"

"My cloak, m'lady?"

"Aye, the one on the peg."

"Ye are welcome tae it, but surely 'twould be better if I fetched your own. How would it look a lady wearing such a thing?"

"Don't be silly, Annie. I cannot care about such things now. I must hurry and see to the ewes. Get Bob MacPherson to help you with Fisher."

"Aye, m'lady."

Pulling the servant's worn cloak over her shoulders, Alison went quickly out the door. She found Fisher's little black-and-white sheep dog sitting patiently there. "At least you are not in the state your master is in, Mags," said Alison, stooping to pat the dog. The animal wagged her tail in greeting. "Come, then, girl. We'll see to the ewes ourselves."

Alison noticed the cold wind and threatening sky as she started across the castle grounds toward the sheep pen. She saw immediately that the pen was empty and she clenched her fists in anger. The missing ewes were prize animals purchased by the duke in Inverness. Her grandfather had great hopes for them and the lambs that would soon be born. Now all twenty were gone, roaming over a vast area where they might fall prey to all manner of disasters.

Pulling the cloak more tightly about her, Alison pondered the situation. It might be some time before anyone else could go after them. She looked down at the dog, who was watching her questioningly with big brown eyes. "Can you find them, Mags? Can you find the sheep?"

Mags let out one sharp bark as if in answer, and Alison laughed. "Very well, then. Find them, Mags."

The sheep dog set off and Alison followed. Seeming to understand her mission, Mags traveled briskly to the west, heading toward the rocky hills that covered so much of her grandfather's property.

After a time Alison seemed to forget her irritation at having to go off in search of the sheep. The exertion of her rapid walking warmed her quickly, and she soon began to appreciate the brisk weather and the loveliness of the familiar scenery. Alison was a passionate outdoorswoman, and although she preferred to survey the Dornach lands on horseback, she enjoyed walking well enough.

She was well-used to long walks and was thankful she was wearing her old comfortable boots. Alison had hiked many miles in them, and although not in the least stylish, they served her well.

The sheep dog continued on and Alison had to quicken her pace to keep up with the animal. Mags seemed to know exactly where she was going, and the dog's confidence encouraged Alison. She only hoped that they wouldn't have to go much farther, since the time was passing swiftly and there were so many other things requiring her attention at the castle.

Alison sighted the first sheep as she neared Loch Craidoch, a shimmering sea loch that touched both Dornach and Glenfinnan lands. There were perhaps eleven or twelve sheep placidly grazing on the banks of the lake. Alison surveyed the scene and smiled. Living her entire life in the Highlands had not diminished Alison's appreciation of their beauty. The clear still waters of Loch Craidoch reflected the craggy hills and the threatening clouds overhead. Her ladyship sighed. How she loved this land.

The sheep dog looked expectantly at Alison, who signaled for her to round up the animals. Mags eagerly went after the sheep, skillfully herding them together. The woolly animals seemed none too happy to have their seeming idyll thus cut short, but knew very well that there was no escape from the dog.

Mags' ease in handling the sheep made Alison breathe easier. It appeared that the job of bringing back the ewes would not be very difficult, after all. She searched the hills for the remaining animals and espied two more high up on the hillside. Mags seemed to sense her thoughts, and leaving the other ewes herded together, she ran off toward them.

Alison watched the agile sheep dog with admiration and reflected that she might at least be grateful that Archie Fisher had such a well-trained dog. Suddenly Alison was aware of a forlorn bleating. Looking up, she saw one ewe, high up on the hillside apart from the others. It seemed the ewe was caught on something and was struggling to break free.

Using the shepherd's crook to steady herself on the rocky ground, Alison started to climb up the hillside. The grade was steep and the footing uncertain, and she proceeded slowly.

Nearing the ewe after the difficult climb, Alison saw that the creature had entangled itself in the branches of a dead tree. The sheep looked at Alison with frightened eyes, and she tried to calm it by speaking soothingly as she approached.

"All right you are, my girl," she said in soft Gaelic. "Free you I shall." She took a step toward the frightened ewe and then stopped abruptly. Between herself and the sheep was a crevasse, a deep gash in the rocky hillside that she had not seen on her approach. Alison eyed the fissure, gauging the distance across it. It was not far and certainly she had jumped greater distances. However, getting an adult sheep back across it was a totally different matter. Of course, reasoned Alison, the ewe had found a way to get across herself and she could certainly do so again.

Alison stepped back and then, getting a running start, leapt gracefully across the crevasse. Her foot touched loose rocks on the opposite side and she felt the earth give way. Crying out in horror, Alison fell backward into the opening of the fissure and landed hard at the bottom.

A most unladylike Gaelic epithet escaped her lips as Alison picked herself up and gazed upward to assess the situation. She was not hurt, she acknowledged thankfully, but knew that her brother Andrew would think her quite muttonheaded to have got into such a situation. The opening was some four or five feet above her head and the crevasse was wider at the bottom than at the top. The walls of her cavelike enclosure sloped upward, making it impossible to climb out.

Alison searched in vain for footholds in the smooth stone, but found none. It seemed that there was nothing she could do but await rescue, and the thought was quite alarming. It could be hours before anyone began to search for her, and the Dornach property was so extensive that it could take forever to find her.

Alison heard a bark and, looking up, saw Mags at the opening above her. The dog was gazing down at Alison with a puzzled expression. "Mags," cried Alison. "Good dog! Get help! Go, Mags! Get help!"

The sheep dog barked once in reply and then was gone. Alison pulled her cloak tightly around her and sat down on the hard stone. She tried to be confident. Mags was a very smart dog and undoubtedly would return to Dornach

Castle. Certainly someone would see the sheep dog and come looking for her.

Whatever confidence Alison had began to erode after half an hour in her stone enclosure. It was very cold and the sky was darkening into an ominous blackness. She shivered and looked up once again, fearful that no one would ever come to find her.

More time passed. To Alison it seemed an eternity, but, in fact, scarcely an hour had passed when Alison heard Mags' familiar bark once more. "Mags! Good dog!" she cried in Gaelic. "Here, girl!"

Mags barked excitedly, and looking up, Alison saw the dog at the mouth of the crevasse. She waved up at Mags and shouted with joy to find a man accompanied the dog. "Oh, please, get me out," Alison called in Gaelic.

"Do you speak English, my girl?" replied her apparent rescuer.

Alison looked up at him in some surprise. She had not expected a stranger. Indeed, in this part of the Highlands, few were unknown to her. The man's question and the fact that he addressed her as "my girl" offended her. "Aye, I speak English, sir. I pray you will help me."

"Are you hurt?"

"No."

"Then reach up."

Alison stood on tiptoe and stretched her arms as far as she could. The stranger reached down into the crevasse and his two strong hands caught hers. "Careful now," he said as he began to pull her upward.

The stranger had no difficulty lifting her from her temporary prison and it was with tremendous relief that Alison once again found herself on the surface of the hillside.

"There you are," said the stranger, releasing her. "You may be thankful you were not injured."

"Aye, it was lucky, and I do thank you for helping me, sir. You cannot know how grateful I am to you." Alison smiled at the stranger, but his face remained impassive.

He picked up the shepherd's crook that had been lying at the edge of the crevasse, and handed it to her. "Here you are. And you had best get busy, for your sheep are scattered. And I suggest you be more careful in the future, my girl."

Alison fixed her enormous blue eyes on the stranger and was unsure whether to be amused or offended at his mistaking her for a shepherd girl. She did look like a shepherdess, she conceded, attired in Annie's old cloak and her old boots. Her hair was mussed and her frock soiled in the fall, and she was sure she must look a dreadful sight. Alison self-consciously brushed a strand of hair away from her forehead and wondered how to reply to this disagreeable man.

She regarded him curiously, thinking that she had never seen anyone quite like him before. He was perhaps thirty years of age, and was tall and slender. He had dark-brown hair that was carefully arranged in the latest Corinthian mode, and fine chiseled features. Alison thought that he would have been handsome but for his humorless expression, which Alison suspected bespoke an unpleasant disposition.

Although not so well-acquainted with masculine fashion, Alison was well aware that the stranger's coat and spotless riding breeches were of expensive make and that his caped cloak was quite magnificent. He was obviously a man of wealth and certainly not the sort she would have expected to find there on the barren hillside at the edge of her grandfather's lands.

The frantic bleating of a ewe caught their attention. "Oh, dear," said Alison. "The poor creature! I must help her."

The stranger eyed the sheep. "Why, she's lambing!"

"Not here?"

"Of course, here," said the man, regarding Alison as if she were an idiot. "It is clear you have much to learn about sheep." Then without another word he jumped across the crevasse and was beside the ewe in a moment. The sheep was terribly distressed. It bleated pitifully and struggled against the branches that held it fast.

Alison watched the stranger in some astonishment as he pulled off his splendid cloak and excellently cut coat and, with seeming unconcern, tossed them down on the rocky ground. He then knelt beside the ewe.

"Something is wrong here," he said as he examined the

terrified animal. "The lamb is positioned wrong. I shall have to turn it." He spoke matter-of-factly as he rolled up the sleeves of his snowy-white linen shirt. Without further comment he plunged his arm into the ewe, grasping the lamb inside the birth canal. With strong steady pressure, he expertly pulled the tiny creature from its mother. "There," he said, triumphantly raising up the lamb. He then placed it beside its mother. The sheep stared at her offspring in some confusion before tentatively licking it.

Alison thought she saw a flicker of a smile cross the stranger's face, but it quickly vanished. He pulled the tree branch away from the ewe and tossed it aside. Then, taking a handkerchief from his coat, he began to wipe his hands.

"I do thank you, sir," began Alison, quite amazed at the man's behavior. "I am so grateful and—"

Her words were cut off by a shout. "M'lord? Is something wrong?" someone asked.

"No, Mull. Come along. I need you." The stranger waved at another man who was approaching.

"My lord?" Alison repeated.

"What is it, m'lord?" said the newcomer, arriving beside Alison.

Her puzzlement at the stranger's title was superseded by her interest in the man who had just joined them. Never had she seen such an unfortunate-looking person. He was a powerfully built man of indeterminate age with graying hair and a face of remarkable ugliness. His nose twisted oddly to one side, giving him a strange unsymmetrical appearance that was made even worse by two large scars running from his right eye to his chin. Alison did not fail to notice that his right ear was curiously formed like a bulbous growth.

"Mull, I need you to help this girl."

"Aye, m'lord."

"She is taking some sheep back." He paused and looked at Alison. "That is what you are trying to do, isn't it?"

"It is . . . my lord."

"Then Mull will assist you. I fear you will have to take this sheep."

"Right, m'lord." Mull jumped across the crevasse and

picked up the ewe. The frightened animal started to squirm, but Mull held it firmly in his powerful hands. He then jumped easily back to Alison, seemingly unencumbered by the weight of the sheep.

"And the young woman can take the lamb." Putting on his coat and cloak, the stranger picked up the lamb and then leapt back across the fissure. He handed the little animal to Alison.

"You are in good hands, miss. Mull will see you get back. Now I shall be off back to Glenfinnan."

The stranger turned and began to make his way back down the hillside. Alison turned to Mull. "That man, is he . . . ?"

"Aye. That is Lord Ravenstoke and I am Jack Mull at your service."

Alison regarded the unattractive Mr. Mull warily for a moment, but then, won over by his friendly grin, Alison smiled. "I am glad to meet you, Mr. Mull. I am much indebted to you and to your master. It appears that Lord Ravenstoke is a most capable man."

"That he is, miss."

Alison watched the new laird of Glenfinnan stride quickly down along the banks of Loch Craidoch. He was certainly very different from what she expected.

"Shall we be going now, miss?"

Alison nodded, and carrying the little lamb, she and Jack Mull started back to Dornach Castle.

3   The sheep dog Mags preceded them, expertly keeping the little herd of sheep together as Alison and Mull made their way toward Dornach Castle.

"A good dog that one," said Mull approvingly as he walked alongside Alison. He carried the lamb, cradling it gently in his arms.

"Aye, she is," returned Alison. "Mags is a wonderful dog." She paused and glanced over at Mull. "It appears that Lord Ravenstoke is an unusual gentleman."

"Unusual?"

"Well, he quite astonished me. He did not seem to care one fig about his fine clothes, tossing them on the ground as he did and helping the poor ewe. And from the look of him, he knew precisely what he was doing. Whoever would have thought an English gentleman would behave in such a manner?"

Mull grinned, and although it made him look rather like a medieval gargoyle, Alison found his expression strangely endearing. "Many an English gentleman knows about farming, miss."

"Perhaps so, but Lord Ravenstoke did not appear to be the sort who would. He was dressed very grandly, was he not? Indeed, I have never seen such finery."

"His lordship is a man of wealth, miss, and dresses to fit his position. You would not expect him to have an inferior tailor, now, would you? But his lordship is no slave to

fashion like the dandy set, them what apes Brummell and
the like. If you would but see some of them in London!"
Mull rolled his eyes heavenward. "The coats some of them
wears, colorful as peacocks with enormous neckcloths
about their necks, tied in the silliest ways. Some takes half
the day fixin' them that way. And shirt points! The fops
wear them so high they can barely move their necks at all.
No, miss, Lord Ravenstoke dresses well enough but very
sensibly. He is a practical man, he is."

"A practical man, is he?" said Alison. "Then, it is
practical for an English lord to buy an estate in the
Highlands and come all this way to see to it?"

Mull grinned. "You're a shrewd one, miss. Let me say
that his lordship is a practical man most of the time."

Alison was disappointed that Mull said nothing further
and continued walking. She kept silent for a time, and
after what seemed a suitably long interval, Alison spoke
again. "No one expected the English laird of Glenfinnan
to actually come to Scotland."

"Is that so, miss? And why might that be?"

"Why, because he is English."

Mull laughed. "Then you would not wish to go to
England to see lands you had just bought?"

"I would not wish to go to England under any circumstances."

"And why not?"

Alison smiled. "Because that is where one finds the
English."

A hearty guffaw escaped Mull, and Alison laughed too.
She was finding Mull a very likable fellow despite his
unfortunate nationality.

"It seems to me, miss, that you are hard on my
countrymen. We are not all so terrible. Although I admit
that few are so kind, generous, and handsome as Jack
Mull."

Alison once again burst into laughter. "Perhaps I do
judge too harshly, Mr. Mull. It is obvious that you are an
admirable man, but indeed, it seems to me that you are
not typical of Englishmen. Now Lord Ravenstoke is more
true to type. He appears to be cold and rather haughty.
Indeed, I thought his manner toward me most unfriend-

ly." She directed a glance at Mull. "But a poor shepherd-ess cannot expect to be treated civilly by an English lord."

Mull looked closely at Alison. "But a Scottish lady might expect it, is that not right?"

"What do you mean?"

"Well, miss, I am no scholar, but then I ain't a simpleton neither. You are no more a shepherdess than I am."

Alison blushed. "I don't know what you mean, Mr. Mull."

Mull grinned. "I have spent my life with folk of all stations, miss, and know a lady when I see one. And the way you talk, miss. The Scottish folk hereabouts speak naught but Gaelic, except for them what speaks the most awful sort of English I ever heard. But you talk as well as any lady in a London drawing room."

Despite her embarrassment at being discovered, Alison was flattered. "Your master took me for a shepherdess."

"True enough, miss." Mull nodded thoughtfully. "But then a gentleman like his lordship don't have to be so observant. Oh, I do not mean that his lordship is a slow top. No, there be few so clever as Lord Ravenstoke at most things."

"You mean there are some things that his lordship is not so clever at?"

"'Tis not my place to say, miss," replied Mull with an enigmatic expression.

"But why did Lord Ravenstoke come to Scotland? Surely he cannot expect to be happy here. He will find it very different from London."

"Aye, 'tis different." Mull directed a wry smile at Alison. "For one thing, in London ladies do not herd sheep."

Alison laughed. "In Scotland, Mr. Mull, ladies do whatever circumstances oblige them to do. Fortunately, circumstances do not often oblige me to herd sheep." The two of them continued on toward Dornach Castle. "And what do you think of Scotland, Mull?"

"I, miss? Well, I have not been here long enough to form an opinion of aught but the food."

"And what do you think of that?"

"I think it best to keep that opinion to myself, miss."

"You are a true diplomat, Mull," said Alison, smiling again.

Dornach Castle came into view and Alison was not as happy to see it as she had thought she would be. She was enjoying talking to Mull, and the distance back to the castle had seemed quite short.

"And is that where you live, miss?" said Mull, staring at the gray stone walls of the ancient Murray stronghold.

"Aye, that is Dornach Castle, home of the Murrays since before the days of Robert Bruce."

Mull did not have an opportunity to express his surprise at finding the young lady's home to be a grim, brooding fortress, for a young man was running toward them. "Lady Alison, we were sae worried about ye. Where hae ye been?" The young man, who was one of the Dornach servants, stopped before them. "I was just about tae go looking for ye, m'lady. Annie thought some harm had come tae ye."

"No, Robin, as you see, I am fine. Now, you take care of the sheep so Mr. Mull can be on his way." Mull stepped forward to deposit the lamb into Robin Douglas' arms, and the young Dornach servant eyed him warily. "Mr. Mull has been kind enough to assist me." She turned to Mull. "Would you like to have some tea in the kitchen?"

"No, thank you, m'lady." Mull grinned again. "I had best get back to his lordship." He bowed slightly and started off.

"Oh, Mull?"

"Aye, m'lady?"

"Perhaps it would be best if you did not mention to Lord Ravenstoke that I am not what he thinks I am."

"Right you are, m'lady," replied Mull with an amused look. "It ain't my place to correct his lordship."

Alison smiled, and Mull turned again and walked off. Then, leaving Robin Douglas with the sheep, her ladyship proceeded to the castle.

Annie Thomson greeted her in the main hallway. "M'lady! Ye were gone sae long! What happened tae ye? I was on my way tae tell his grace and your brothers that ye were missing."

"I went all the way to Loch Craidoch and back, Annie, and had a lambing to attend to. I shall tell you all about it later. So my grandfather and brothers have returned from MacGillivray Hall?"

"Aye, they are just returned and in the drawing room."

"Then I shall go to them." Alison made her way to the drawing room and, upon entering, found the duke and her brothers engaged in spirited conversation.

"And I still say Ian's Gaisgeach cannot hold a candle to Claymore," Andrew said.

"That may be true, but after seeing Gaisgeach run this day, I fear the race between them will be closer than I had reckoned," said the duke.

"Och, Grandfather, surely you know Gaisgeach is no match for Claymore." At Alison's words, they turned toward her.

"Allie!" Duncan jumped up and, racing over to his sister, hugged her tightly. "That's what I told Ian."

"Good for you, Duncan," said Alison with a smile.

"Where have you been, lass?" said the duke.

"Aye," said Andrew. "You are a sight, Allie! You'll not ensnare a husband looking like that."

"Andrew Murray, do not try my patience." Alison directed a warning look at her brother. "Because you were not here, I had to go after Grandfather's sheep. And I was all the way to Loch Craidoch with them and was nearly killed for my trouble."

"Killed?" The duke appeared startled. "What the devil do you mean, Alison?"

"Oh, I do not mean to upset you, Grandfather. I am exaggerating. It is only that I fell into a crevasse on the hill."

"However could you be so bird-witted, Allie?" cried Andrew, but the duke silenced him with a stern look.

"And you were not hurt?"

"A few bruises, perhaps, Grandfather. I might be there still but for the Marquess of Ravenstoke."

"Ravenstoke?" said the duke.

"Aye, the new laird of Glenfinnan. It was he who pulled me out."

"Then I owe him thanks, be he Englishman or no."

"What was he like, Allie?" said Duncan, quite inter-ested.

"Well, I did not like him overmuch, and in truth he does not appear to be a likable man. Indeed, he was barely civil to me."

"Barely civil to you?" The duke looked indignant.

"You see, he took me for a shepherdess."

Andrew burst into laughter. "And so would I. Where did you find that cloak?"

"It is Annie's, and I caution you not to laugh, Lord Culwin."

"Oh, very well, but it is funny."

"You would not have thought it so, Andrew." Alison and Duncan sat down on the sofa. "And then there was the lambing."

"Lambing?" said Andrew. "Now, this does seem like an adventure. What happened?"

"Shortly after Ravenstoke rescued me, one of the ewes started to lamb. I fear the poor creature would have been lost if Ravenstoke had not helped her. The lamb was not positioned correctly and there was little I could do. However, Lord Ravenstoke very quickly managed to set things right. I must admit he appears very competent in such matters."

"Then I am heartily grateful to him," said the duke enthusiastically. "I have great hopes for those lambs, as we all know. Aye, this Ravenstoke deserves our thanks. I must repay his kindness. Who would have thought it possible that Ravenstoke would make himself so useful to me? Well, we must invite him to the Dornach Ball. Aye, that would be the very thing to show him true Highland hospitality."

"A fine idea, Grandfather," said Andrew. "Although I have no love for Englishmen, I should like to meet the fellow. Anyone bold enough to assist in a lambing and to be rude to Alison Murray in the same day deserves my admiration."

Alison laughed in spite of herself. "I would not have thought you so eager to meet an English neighbor, Andrew. Indeed, Grandfather, I do not think it wise to invite Ravenstoke to the ball. He will not wish to come, and if he does so, he will doubtlessly find everything quite beneath him."

"You are not ashamed of your kinsmen, are you, Allie?" said Andrew.

"Certainly not. It is just that I do not want this man ruining the Dornach Ball."

"Nonsense, my girl," said the duke. "After all he has done, we could do nothing less than invite him. And you know well that Ravenstoke is the object of great curiosity. Everyone will want to take a look at him. I shall send him a personal note immediately."

"Yes, Grandfather," said Alison, knowing very well that it was useless to protest any further. His grace of Dornach was not the sort of man to be swayed even by his beloved granddaughter. When the duke made a decision, there was little one could do but abide by it.

"If you gentlemen will excuse me." Alison rose from the sofa. "I shall go to my room and change. I do look a fright."

"Go with my blessing, Allie," said Andrew with a grin.

Alison cast him one last warning glance and then left the drawing room. Retreating to her bedchamber, Alison went to her wardrobe and took out the dress that she would be wearing to the ball. Two seasons old, the dress had been cunningly refashioned by the village seamstress, Mrs. Gunn. Alison had thought Mrs. Gunn's handiwork exceptionally good, but now as she looked down at the pale-blue satin gown, she was suddenly uncertain. Undoubtedly such a dress would look very shabby beside the gowns of the ladies of London society. Indeed, Lord Ravenstoke would think her very provincial.

Alison frowned and chided herself for caring what the new laird of Glenfinnan thought. He was, after all, only an arrogant Englishman. She picked up the dress and placed it back in the wardrobe. Closing the oaken doors, Alison sighed. If only she had been able to buy a new ball dress, she told herself. Then, impatient with herself for these thoughts, Alison turned her attention to the present matter and began to change her clothes.

4   Robert Manville, Fifth Marquess of Ravenstoke, sat reflectively in the library at Glenfinnan. He was enough a judge of architecture to appreciate the fine wainscoted room with its high beamed ceiling and its walls lined with bookshelves. Indeed, he found the library a pleasant place, as he did the rest of the great house.

Ravenstoke possessed four stately residences and three somewhat more modest dwellings commonly referred to as cottages. It, therefore, might have been expected that he would have been unimpressed with Glenfinnan. However, he had been delighted with it, finding the house comfortable and yet suitably baronial. It had been built during Queen Anne's reign and featured the timeless styling noteworthy of that era.

Although not so grand as his principal seat at Ravenstoke, nor so elegant as his newest house in Bath, Glenfinnan had an unmistakable charm. The marquess's practical eye did not fail to note that the place was in need of many improvements and that the grounds had been woefully neglected. Still, when his lordship had first looked upon Glenfinnan, he had been well-pleased.

Ravenstoke rose from his chair and walked to the window. Looking out on the Highland scenery, his lordship felt an unusual sense of well-being. He had ridden over this land, finding forested glens and fast-running streams filled with trout and salmon. There was also the lonely moorland, stretching to the distant mountains. It possessed a stark and desolate beauty that Ravenstoke found strangely compelling.

It seemed that Nanny MacDonald had been right. He did feel at home here in the Highlands. A rare smile crossed Ravenstoke's face. If anyone knew the true reason for his buying this remote estate and journeying all those miles from London, there would be much amusement among members of society.

He certainly had had a difficult time explaining his reasons to his family. He knew that his sisters Emily and Georgina thought it very odd indeed that he had purchased such a unprofitable property in such a far-off location. Emily and Georgina had also considered it most curious that their brother insisted on setting off on an arduous journey to see his new estate.

His lordship's motives in purchasing Glenfinnan, which he took great care to conceal, were unquestioningly sentimental. Since Ravenstoke was a decidedly unsentimental man, his behavior was most uncharacteristic.

The youngest of three children and only son, the marquess's early years had been supervised by Ellen MacDonald, a Scotswoman who was a native of the western Highlands. Among Nanny MacDonald's many talents was the ability to tell spellbinding tales of Scotland. At a very young age, Ravenstoke had felt intimately acquainted with the Highlands, and he had longed to go there himself.

Young Ravenstoke—Lord Sheffield, as he was then—had been sent away to school at age ten. After an unpleasant term, the boy had returned home on holiday, eager to see his sisters and Nanny MacDonald. It had been a severe blow to find that Nanny MacDonald was gone. His stern father had dismissed her, explaining that a nanny's services were no longer needed.

Ravenstoke never saw Nanny MacDonald again. She sent him letters for a time, the last of which informed him that she was getting married and going to America. Ravenstoke never forgot her and always knew that one day he would go to the Highlands and see Scotland for himself. It was, therefore, of great interest to his lordship when some twenty years later he espied an advertisement for Scottish properties. Shortly thereater, Glenfinnan was his and he was on his way north.

The marquess continued to stare out the window. How Deborah had protested when she had found out that he was going to Scotland. Ravenstoke frowned. He had not thought of his fiancée since arriving at Glenfinnan, and indeed, he was none too happy to find himself thinking of her at that moment.

That Lord Ravenstoke did not delight at the thought of Deborah Willoughby would have surprised a good many London gentlemen. The delectable Miss Willoughby had been the most-sought-after young lady of the past London Season. She was a beautiful girl with pale-gold locks and ivory skin, and her obvious charms were further enhanced by an impeccable pedigree and a respectable fortune.

When Miss Willoughby had accepted the tremendously rich yet decidedly dull Lord Ravonstoke, London society had been very much surprised. Still, most society matrons conceded that the lovely Deborah had made a sensible choice. Ravenstoke may be a stuffy, unlikable man, but he was so very wealthy and one could not overlook the appeal of becoming a marchioness. And if Ravenstoke was not at all dashing, the matrons noted, at least he was not a rake nor a drunkard and was moderately good-looking.

The marquess was unaware of the comments his betrothal to Deborah Willoughly had engendered. He was not at all enthusiastic about the match and often wondered why he had made her an offer. Were he completely honest with himself, his lordship might have realized that when he had extended his proposal to Miss Willoughby, he had been reasonably certain that she would refuse him. Her acceptance puzzled and rather annoyed him. Still, he could not postpone marriage forever, he told himself, and certainly Miss Willoughby would do as well as another. She would certainly look splendid standing beside him at court functions. Indeed, she had a proud nature and regal bearing. Although he found her conversation stupefying and considered her mother quite insufferable, his lordship felt that Deborah would be as good a wife as he a husband.

The marquess's thoughts turned to his meeting with the shepherd girl the day before. Remembering Alison's lovely blue eyes and auburn hair, he found himself comparing her to Deborah. Certainly the widely touted Miss Willoughby was far more attractive than the simple Scottish shepherdess. Ravenstoke knitted his eyebrows thoughtfully. No, Deborah's beauty paled beside the Highland girl. Indeed, no woman had so affected him as she had that day, and it had required all his considerable discipline to hide his interest in her. Were he a gentleman of deplorable moral values, as were so many of his contemporaries, he might have entertained unscrupulous notions about the girl. But as he was the sober and high-minded Lord Ravenstoke, his lordship forced any dishonorable thoughts from his mind.

Ravenstoke returned to his chair and absently surveyed some papers on his desk. He reflected how glad he was that he had come to Scotland. It was wonderful to avoid the usual London social engagements and spend time quietly alone amid such lovely scenery.

His lordship's musings were cut short by the arrival of Jack Mull. "Beggin' your lordship's pardon, but a messenger just arrived from the Duke of Dornach. 'Tis a letter from his grace."

"The Duke of Dornach?"

"Aye, m'lord."

Ravenstoke took the letter from the silver salver Mull extended toward him and glanced down at it with some irritation. He had hoped he might escape local society, and since he had been in residence at Glenfinnan for more than a week without receiving any calls or letters, he had been optimistic that he was going to be left in peace.

Breaking the ducal seal, Ravenstoke first saw the invitation to the ball. He frowned. He did not enjoy social functions, and he despised balls most of all. With the invitation was a note written in the duke's own barely decipherable hand. The marquess scowled as he tried to make out the words. "I am in your debt, sir, for your assistance to my . . ." Ravenstoke paused and tried to decide what the next words were. An untidy ink blot obscured a good portion of them and the few letters that were visible seemed to make no sense whatsoever. "Damn and blast," he said finally. "The man's hand is unreadable. There is something about sheep. Yes, 'and helping my sheep. The lamb and ewe are . . . both well, due to your . . .' What the devil is that word? Oh, I see, 'due to your intervention.' And there is something about gout. 'My gout prevents me from . . . calling upon you.' Thank God for that anyway."

The marquess tossed the letter on the desk. "So the shepherdess was herding the duke's sheep?"

"Aye, m'lord." Jack Mull nearly grinned, but restrained himself. "I helped the young miss back to his grace's castle, m'lord."

"Castle?" Ravenstoke's interest was suddenly peaked.

"Aye, sir. A castle it was, and not a pleasant-looking place. 'Twas the sort of place they might drop boilin' oil from, m'lord. And being an Englishman among these Scots, I felt it best to keep an eye on the parapets."

The marquess laughed. "Very prudent, Jack."

Mull grinned, delighted that he had made Ravenstoke laugh. His lordship was a very serious man, and it was known to society that few things amused him. However, Mull often succeeded in making his master laugh, a trait that greatly endeared him to Ravenstoke.

"Will you go to the ball, m'lord?"

"I don't think so, Mull. You know how much I detest such things."

"But, m'lord, would you not wish to meet the ladies and gentlemen who are your neighbors? I am sure his grace would be very disappointed if your lordship did not attend."

"Then, you think I should go, Mull?"

"It might do you good to go, m'lord. You've had no company since we've come here."

"And you think I'm becoming an eccentric recluse?"

Mull grinned again. "It is a danger, m'lord."

Ravenstoke smiled. "Perhaps you are right, Mull. Oh, very well, I shall go. It may be interesting. I should like to see this castle."

"Indeed, I know your lordship will find it very interesting," replied Mull, thinking of Alison and once again restraining himself from smiling.

"Yes, we shall see if the fabled Highland hospitality is fact or myth."

"Would you be needin' anything further, m'lord?"

The marquess shook his head and Mull left him sitting at his desk. As the servant walked down the corridor toward the kitchen, Mull reflected that it would be most amusing to witness the second meeting of his master and Lady Alison Murray.

5 Alison patted the sleek chestnut-colored withers of her horse Claymore and then leaned over to whisper a few Gaelic endearments in the big stallion's ear. Claymore whinnied in reply and Alison stroked his neck as she looked out across the moorland.

Turning her horse eastward, Alison eased Claymore into a trot and then a decorous canter. She did not give him his head for some time, but finally coming to the village road, Alison urged the stallion into a gallop. Claymore ran eagerly, his wide strides covering great distances.

Then, seeing a rider in the distance, Alison hastened to slow her fiery mount. Claymore was not at all happy to find his run cut short, but obediently reduced his speed. They continued toward the oncoming rider and Alison frowned when she recognized Sir Ian MacGillivray astride an enormous black horse.

MacGillivray pulled his horse up as he came alongside Alison. He smiled broadly at her. "Alison, my luck must be changing to meet you like this."

"I am glad to see that one of us seems to be having good luck, Sir Ian. Mine seems very ill indeed."

MacGillivray laughed and Alison regarded him coldly. He was a big man with broad shoulders, dark curly hair, and deep-brown eyes. Many thought him handsome, but Alison's distaste for the man did not allow her to see anything attractive about him.

"Gaisgeach looks well," Alison said to fill the awkward silence that had ensued.

MacGillivray nodded. "Aye, and Claymore is in good form. But let's not speak of horses."

"Sir Ian, you astonish me. Not speak of horses? I never knew that you spoke of anything else."

MacGillivray grinned. "I do say a word about something else now and again, especially when I'm in the company of a pretty woman. By God, you are beautiful, Alison Murray. How I look forward to dancing with you at the ball. I expect that you will save me several dances."

"I do not intend to save you any, Ian MacGillivray."

Sir Ian's face took on a serious unpleasant expression. "That would be most unwise, my girl. You will dance with me. I shall see to that." He grinned suddenly. "Aye, I am looking forward to the Dornach Ball. Everyone is. And I am told that the duke has invited the Englishman. Has your grandfather forgotten the Drummonds so soon?"

Alison eyed MacGillivray resentfully. "My grandfather is only thanking Lord Ravenstoke for his assistance."

"I heard all about that from your brother. So the Englishman rescued you, did he? I wish it had been me to find you, lass. I should have waited to pull you out until you promised to be suitably grateful to me." The big man leered unpleasantly at Alison and she felt an urge to strike him across the face with her riding crop.

With some difficulty, she controlled her temper. "You are no gentleman, Ian MacGillivray."

"No, but the Englishman is, I suppose."

"Aye, he is," replied Alison, and then noting the frown on MacGillivray's face, she continued, "Indeed, Lord Ravenstoke is a most charming man and I thought him very handsome." Smiling inwardly at the annoyed look her remark had solicited, Alison decided to vex the baronet further. "Perhaps the Scottish gentlemen hereabouts will benefit from the presence of such a man. He is so well-dressed and well-mannered."

"He may go to the devil!" said MacGillivray hotly. "I would not have thought a Murray girl would be so taken in by some fop of an Englishman. So you are enamored of him, are you?"

"What I think of Lord Ravenstoke is my own affair, Sir Ian."

MacGillivray scowled. "Well, we shall see if this Ravenstoke stays long at Glenfinnan. And it seems very odd to me that he has come where he is not wanted. Aye, it is very odd indeed. I would very much like to find out why such a man would take Glenfinnan. He'll find little hospitality for his kind here."

"We shall see, sir. But I do not doubt that many ladies will be willing to excuse the fact that his lordship is English. I am certain that he will be very popular and will enjoy the ball very much. I myself am looking forward to meeting Lord Ravenstoke once again."

Sir Ian looked very grim. For a moment Alison thought he was going to say something more, but he seemed to think the better of it. "Well, I shall not keep you any longer, Alison. Good day to you." He then kicked his black horse ill-temperedly and rode off.

Alison watched him go with some satisfaction. Not only had she succeeded in irritating her most unwelcome suitor, but she had made the unlikable Lord Ravenstoke a formidable enemy. Then, patting Claymore's neck once again, she continued her ride.

The following afternoon, Lord Ravenstoke decided to investigate the small village that was a distance of eight miles from Glenfinnan. It was a fine day for a carriage ride. The sun was shining brightly and the barren landscape was beginning to show the approach of spring. The marquess sat looking out the carriage window, reflecting on the beauty of the Highlands and thinking how glad he was to be there. Jack Mull, who had accompanied his lordship on the journey, noted his master's reflective mood and remained quiet.

They rode in silence for some distance and then suddenly the carriage slowed its pace to a crawl. "What is it?" asked the marquess as Mull craned his head out the window. "Why are we slowing down?"

Mull stuck his head back in the carriage and grinned. "I reckon it's because of the herd of sheep on the road up ahead, m'lord."

"Sheep?" It was Ravenstoke's turn to peer out the window. Just as Mull said, he found that a number of sheep were crossing the road in front of them. As they drew nearer to the herd, the carriage came to a halt and the marquess could hear the bleating of the sheep and the sharp barks of a dog. He espied a black-and-white sheep dog running after a recalcitrant ewe and he turned back to Mull. "It's the dog we saw the other day."

"Indeed, m'lord?" Mull repressed a smile as he thought of Lady Alison Murray. "The dog that was with the shepherd girl?"

"Yes, I'm certain of it. These must be the Duke of Dornach's sheep." Ravenstoke looked out again, thinking he would see the redhaired shepherdess, but he was strangely disappointed when there was no sign of her. The only person the marquess spotted was a somewhat disheveled-looking man dressed in a faded brown kilt and a wide-brimmed hat. The man was leaning on a shepherd's crook and was regarding the carriage with great curiosity.

Archie Fisher was quite sure that the magnificent carriage before him belonged to the new laird of Glenfinnan. The shepherd was one of the best-informed persons in the county when it came to local gossip, and he had heard much about the Englishman. He was very much pleased at the opportunity to view the stranger firsthand, and he grinned as he approached the carriage.

Fisher stared in at the occupants of the vehicle and immediately knew that he stood in the presence of the English laird. "Good day tae ye, m'lord," he said, pulling his hat from his head and eyeing the marquess with considerable interest.

"Good day," said Ravenstoke, and noting the man's silly grin and somewhat flushed expression, he decided the fellow was decidedly tipsy. The marquess wondered what connection the man had to the shepherd girl and thought it unlikely that the beautiful shepherdess could be in any way related to him.

Archie Fisher spoke again and the marquess was having some difficulty understanding the man's broad Scots accent and slurred speech. "'Tis sorry I am, m'lord, tae

trouble ye wi' stopping here. It will be but a moment and
my sheep will be oot o' your way."

"That is quite all right," said the marquess. He paused
and then motioned toward the dog that was urging the
sheep across the road. "And that is your dog?"

"Aye, 'tis my dog, Mags. A bonny dog is Mags, m'lord.
'Tis nae better sheep dog in the Highlands." A sudden
nostalgic gleam appeared in the shepherd's eyes. "Mags
puts me in mind o' another bitch I had, my dear old
Queen o' the Heather. A damn fine dog was Queenie,
m'lord. None could match her. And then, o' course, there
was Rob Roy. A quick dog was Robbie. He would learn a
command almost before ye would give it tae him."

Ravenstoke was afraid the shepherd would continue to
catalog the virtues of various sheep dogs, so he cut him off
somewhat impatiently. "And you are a shepherd for the
Duke of Dornach, are you not?"

"Aye, m'lord. I work for his grace."

"And is there not a girl who works with you?"

"A girl? Och, nay, m'lord. Archie Fisher works alone."
He grinned knowingly at the marquess. "O' course,
sometimes a lass will follow after old Archie. I'm nae
meanin' tae brag, m'lord, but I do seem taw hae a way wi'
the lassies."

Ravenstoke raised his eyebrows and regarded the shepherd with such a ludicrous expression that Mull almost
burst into laughter. No doubt his master was having a
difficult time picturing the beautiful shepherdess with the
inebriated and rather scruffy-looking Archie Fisher.

The shepherd looked back toward the sheep. "Come
on, my woolly darlin's!" he shouted. "'Tis not polite tae
keep his lordship waiting." Mags chased the last few sheep
across the road and Archie turned to the marquess. "Well,
ye can be on your way now, m'lord."

Ravenstoke nodded. "Thank you." He cast one last
quizzical look at the shepherd and then leaned out the
window and instructed his driver to continue on.

Archie Fisher lifted his hat in salute as the carriage
traveled away toward the village. The shepherd fished a
flask out his pocket and took a swig of whiskey as he
watched the departing vehicle. As he gulped down the

liquor, he was suddenly startled when a harsh voice called out to him in Gaelic.

Archie was surprised to find old Widow Brodie standing suddenly in front of him. The elderly woman was a well-known character in the area. Living like a hermit in a small cottage on the lands of Ian MacGillivray, the widow was thought by many in the community to be quite mad. Others said the eccentric widow was a witch, and indeed, there was something quite frightening about her appearance.

A black cloak covered everything but the old woman's wizened face, and her cold blue eyes sent a sudden chill through the shepherd. No one knew the widow's exact age, but it was reckoned that she was near ninety. She remained remarkably spry and quick-witted, due, according to some, to her supernatural powers.

Archie Fisher retained enough of the old Celtic superstitions to feel decidedly uncomfortable in the presence of the widow, but he managed to nod at her and address her in Gaelic. "A fine day it is, Widow Brodie."

The old woman scowled at him. "Fine for some it is."

The shepherd was reluctant to meet the ancient woman's gaze, so he turned and pointed toward the marquess's carriage which was winding slowly away from them, up a hill. "Saw you the new English laird?" he asked.

"English?" The widow spat contemptuously on the ground. "What means you by this, the new English laird?"

Archie Fisher glanced back at the widow and found she was eyeing him with a hostile expression. "Why, have you not heard?" he said. "The new English laird of Glenfinnan is he. Lord Ravenstoke is his name."

The shepherd was unprepared for the widow's reaction. "Ravenstoke?" she croaked, regarding Fisher in shocked disbelief. "His name is Ravenstoke?" She looked at the carriage, which was quickly vanishing from sight. "A young man is he?"

Archie nodded and fearfully took a few steps away from the woman. The widow stared malevolently at the carriage. Then, shaking a clawlike fist in the air, she shouted a bloodcurdling Gaelic curse at it.

Archie Fisher no longer hesitated. He ran away from the widow as fast as he could, convinced that she was a witch.

The shepherd was not the only person to observe Widow Brodie's curious and somewhat alarming behavior. Sir Ian MacGillivray had been watching the scene, perched atop his horse on a hill behind them.

The baronet had been out riding Gaisgeach when he had viewed Ravenstoke's carriage on the road below him. He had heard of the English laird's fine carriage and magnificent black horses, and he knew that the vehicle must belong to the marquess.

Sir Ian had frowned as he had watched the shepherd talking to the occupant of the carriage. Having little doubt that it was Ravenstoke in the carriage, the baronet had muttered an oath. Sir Ian was still resentful of the Englishman taking over Scottish lands, but what had especially galled him was his previous day's conversation with Lady Alison Murray. She had seemed quite charmed by the new laird of Glenfinnan, and the baronet's jealousy had made him hate Ravenstoke even more.

As the carriage drove away, the baronet espied Widow Brodie. It seemed to Ian that she had appeared from nowhere and he watched her with a mixture of suspicion and apprehension.

The widow lived in a small cottage at the edge of MacGillivray's lands, and he had many times wanted to evict the old woman. However, whenever he had tried to force her out, Sir Ian had been cowed by the widow's Gaelic curses and evil looks. Although he did not care to admit it, Sir Ian was afraid of Widow Brodie and usually took pains to avoid her.

That day, however, Sir Ian wondered why the old woman had reacted in such a vehement fashion toward Ravenstoke's carriage, so he urged his horse down the hill to find out. As he reached the road, Sir Ian saw that the widow was hobbling quickly away, in the direction of her cottage.

The baronet followed the old woman and called out to her, "Widow Brodie!"

The woman did not stop but quickened her pace. Sir Ian

cursed but continued on after her. As she approached the small thatched cottage, the widow suddenly turned around and glared at him. The baronet was somewhat intimidated by the woman's wrathful gaze, but he attempted to placate her by tipping his hat and speaking to her in Gaelic.

"A good day to you, Widow Brodie."

She stood eyeing him with a wary expression. "What brings you to my door, Ian MacGillivray?"

Sir Ian dismounted from his horse. "Saw you shout at that carriage, I did," said Sir Ian. "The carriage of the new English laird of Glenfinnan." The woman glowered at him but he continued. "Wondered, I did, why you would shout at the new laird."

The widow spat on the ground. "Cause enough that he be English, but curse him I did for another reason."

Sir Ian regarded her with great interest. "And what is that?"

"Ravenstoke," muttered the old woman. "An evil one is he. Aye, evil begets evil."

"What mean you by that?" asked the baronet.

Widow Brodie motioned MacGillivray toward her cottage. "Inside with you, then, and tell you I will."

Sir Ian was not pleased at the idea of entering the old woman's cottage, but he was so eager to hear what she had to say about Ravenstoke that he pushed his fears aside. Entering the cottage, the baronet looked around him. He was relieved to find that the small dwelling appeared much the same as any of his crofters' cottages. A huge white cat suddenly jumped up on the table, hissing at the baronet, and MacGillivray started.

The old woman gave a shrill laugh, and taking the large cat in her lap, she sat down in a rocking chair by the hearth. She stroked the cat and looked over at Sir Ian. The baronet somewhat reluctantly pulled up a chair beside her. "And what know you of this Ravenstoke?" he asked.

"Ravenstoke." The old woman spoke the marquess's name as if it were a curse. She closed her eyes for a moment and then opened them and stared at MacGillivray. "Know you of my Alec?"

The baronet looked somewhat puzzled. "Alec?"

"Aye. My husband he was. Married we were in 1745. 'Twas a year of much joy and sorrow." The widow shook her head and her eyes held a faraway look in them. "The year Prince Charlie landed in Scotland. Och, there were few who could look on the bonny face of our prince and not follow him. So joined the prince's army did my Alec. Newly married we were, and being apart from him was so hard to bear."

Sir Ian tapped his knee impatiently. "But what of Ravenstoke?"

Widow Brodie fixed an angry eye upon him. "Quiet you will be, Ian MacGillivray, or the rats shall feast on your tongue!"

The baronet looked from the widow to the large white cat in her lap. The cat's giant green eyes seemed to regard him menacingly, and Sir Ian drew in a nervous breath. "Sorry I am, Widow. Go on if you will."

The old woman closed her eyes again and then suddenly shuddered. "Followed the prince all the way to Culloden did my Alec!" The widow opened her eyes and her expression was one of horror. "Forget that day I never shall! Cut down like sheep were our Highlanders. Slaughtered by the English butchers! May they all burn in hell!"

The widow rocked silently for a few moments. "My poor Alec, hacked to pieces was he under the orders of that foul fiend from hell, the Duke of Cumberland." She looked at the baronet. "Aye, eager to carry out his orders were the English murderers. And worst of all was Cumberland's officer, Baron Wicklow. Called him 'Bloody Wicklow' we did. 'Kill every one of the Highland swine,' said Wicklow, and when it was over, Culloden moor was red with Scottish blood."

Sir Ian nodded. "Infamous it was, what the English devils did that day. Not a soul in the Highlands will ever forget Culloden or the vile deeds of Cumberland and Bloody Wicklow." The baronet paused. "But what of Ravenstoke? What has he to do with this?"

"Ravenstoke! The grandson of the accursed Baron Wicklow is he," cried the Widow Brodie.

Sir Ian eyed her incredulously. "Grandson of Bloody Wicklow? But how know you that?"

The widow got up from her chair, and depositing her cat on the floor, she walked over to a large chest. Opening it, she searched through the chest and finally pulled out a yellowed piece of paper. She handed it to the baronet. "'Tis all there. From an English newspaper it is, sent to me by the son of an old friend. It told of Bloody Wicklow's death, and much comfort it was to know that he was in hell. One heir had he, the Viscount Sheffield, the son of the Marquess of Ravenstoke. Ay, Ravenstoke. Forget that name I never shall!"

Sir Ian read through the obituary of Baron Wicklow and then looked up. "So grandson to Bloody Wicklow, is he. How dare he show his face here." MacGillivray reread the newspaper article and then handed it back to the widow. "Do not fear, soon will this Ravenstoke regret his coming."

Then, eager to be gone from the widow's company, Sir Ian left the cottage. He mounted his horse and started off. As he rode away, he thought about what he had discovered about Ravenstoke and could not wait to divulge the news.

There would be few in the Highlands who would not despise the grandson of Bloody Wicklow. Sir Ian paused. Perhaps he would wait to reveal the secret rather than go carrying the tale about like some gossip. MacGillivray nodded thoughtfully and a smile appeared on his face. Aye, he would wait for the appropriate moment to disclose the marquess's infamous ancestry. Sir Ian smiled again and wondered what the Lady Alison Murray would think of her charming English laird now.

6 The Marquess of Ravenstoke looked grim as he studied himself in the mirror. He had suffered Mull's attentions in preparation for the Dornach Ball ill-humoredly, and the worthy servant had taken the first opportunity to depart from the room.

Continuing to scrutinize his appearance in the mirror, Ravenstoke frowned. The evening clothes he was wearing had been made by one of London's most exclusive tailoring establishments, and the coat and breeches of black superfine fitted his lean frame admirably. His snowy neckcloth had been expertly tied in an unostentatious but fashionable style, and his white silk stockings and shiny black evening slippers looked very splendid indeed. Although he looked quite handsome, Ravenstoke took no pleasure in his modish attire.

He did not wish to attend the Dornach Ball that evening and was most unhappy with himself for submitting to what would undoubtedly be a most unpleasant ordeal. The marquess was not a social animal and did not enjoy such occasions. The idea of appearing at the home of a man he had never met and being civil to a host of new people did not please him. Ravenstoke also suspected that those attending the ball would have little reason to welcome him, a foreigner to their company.

His lordship frowned again and turned away from the mirror. Perhaps he would not go, after all. It would be a simple thing to send a servant with his regrets.

"Granger has brought 'round your carriage, m'lord."
Mull's words made the marquess look over at the door.
Jack Mull was standing expectantly, his master's cloak and
hat in his arms.

"All right, Mull," said Ravenstoke, dismissing any
further thoughts of avoiding the Dornach Ball. A gentleman had many duties to perform, and his lordship knew
very well that this was one of them.

While Lord Ravenstoke was unhappily contemplating
attending the Dornach Ball, Lady Alison Murray was
viewing the same prospect with a similar lack of enthusiasm. The annual ball had always been a source of great joy
to the Murray family, and Alison in past years had always
looked forward to it.

Now, as her maid worked on the final adjustments to
her coiffure, Alison was filled with misgivings. She was
certain that the ball would be a disaster, but was unsure as
to why she felt that way. Perhaps it was knowing that Ian
MacGillivray would be there, attempting to monopolize
her attention. Alison suppressed a sigh. Whatever the
reason, she was beginning to dread the ball.

"Och, your ladyship looks verra beautiful."

"Thank you, Mary," said Alison with polite disinterest.
In truth, she did not share her maid's opinion. Glancing
into the mirror, Alison acknowledged that her hair looked
well enough. It was dressed in tight ringlets in front while
the long hair in back had been braided and neatly coiled.
A single satin ribbon of Murray tartan was all that
ornamented her auburn tresses, and the effect was quite
elegant.

It was her ball dress that made Alison have doubts
about her appearance. She rose from her chair and
studied it critically, wondering if anyone would recognize
it. Certainly, it had been cleverly altered, and the result
was not unattractive. The skirt of the pale-blue satin gown
had been trimmed with a deep flounce of rich ivory-
colored lace. The seamstress had also added lace along the
neckline and sleeves.

Alison frowned. It was the same dress, nevertheless,
and undeniably provincial. Chiding herself for caring

about such matters, Alison took up her gloves and fan from the dressing table.

Alison thought of Ravenstoke and wondered how he would react to finding that she was Lady Alison Murray and not some poor shepherdess. The idea was quite funny, but how much better the joke would be if she were wearing a very grand dress like the ones worn by the great ladies of London.

"I fancy that I am ready, Mary."

The maid nodded. "And truly ye look sae verra bonny, m'lady. His grace is down already wi' Lord Culwin. The guests will be arriving soon."

"I know," replied Alison. Then, thanking her servant for her good work, she proceeded from the room.

As Alison walked down the hallway, she heard a shout. She turned back and saw her brother Duncan rushing toward her. He was clad in his nightshirt and his red hair was sticking out of his nightcap in wild disarray.

"Duncan! You shouldn't run about dressed like that," said Alison sternly. "You shall catch a cold. Now back to your room, young man."

"Och, Allie," protested Duncan. "I don't want to go to my room. I want to watch the guests for the ball."

"I see. And do you plan to greet them in your nightshirt, Master Duncan?"

Her brother grinned. "Don't be silly, Allie. I was going to hide at the top of the stairs and spy down on them. Oh, please say I may, Allie!"

Alison smiled and remembered that when she was a girl, she had also perched at the top of the stairs to watch the guests arrive for the Dornach Ball. Duncan looked pleadingly at her and Alison laughingly relented. "Oh, I suppose it would be all right. But just for a little while. You are too young to stay up so late."

Duncan shook his head disgustedly. "It is dashed unfair, Allie. I am always too young for things."

Alison smiled sympathetically. "I know. But it won't be very long before you'll be attending the Dornach Ball yourself."

"I wish I was going tonight," said Duncan regretfully. "I should like to get a look at the new English laird of Glenfinnan."

"And why is that?" asked Alison.

"I've never seen an Englishman before, Allie." Duncan looked thoughtful. "I think it might be interesting to see one."

"Indeed? Well, perhaps I shall tell Lord Ravenstoke to go upstairs and you two can have a chat."

"Och, don't do that, Allie," said Duncan, somewhat alarmed. "I've heard he is a mean one. He probably doesn't like children overmuch."

Alison laughed. "All right, Duncan, I shan't send him up, then. Now, go fetch your dressing gown and you may watch the guests arrive in all their finery."

Duncan looked admiringly at his sister. "I'm sure none of the ladies will be as pretty as you, Allie."

"Why, thank you, Duncan. I'm sure none of the gentlemen will be as handsome or charming as you."

Her brother grinned and made an exaggerated bow. "And would you allow me the first dance, Lady Alison?"

Alison curtsied. "That would be lovely, Master Duncan." She hummed a tune, and she and Duncan danced about the hallway in a lively reel. They were interrupted by the appearance of their brother Andrew. "Allie! There you are! You must come down now. The guests are beginning to arrive. Ian's already here and asking for you."

Alison frowned. She had no desire to see Sir Ian MacGillivray, and for a moment she wished she were a girl again. How much more fun it would be to sit at the top of the stairs with Duncan, spying down at the guests. "Och, all right, Andrew." Alison turned and hugged Duncan. "I must be going."

"You'll tell me all about the ball tomorrow, won't you, Allie?" he asked hopefully.

"Of course, Duncan. And I told Annie to bring you up a special treat tonight . . . a piece of Dundee cake."

Duncan seemed somewhat consoled by this information and hurried back to his room to get his dressing gown.

Alison watched him with a smile, and then, taking Andrew's arm, she proceeded downstairs to join her grandfather.

7

The rain started just as Ravenstoke entered his carriage, and by the time he neared Dornach Castle, great torrents were beating down upon the carriage roof. The dismal weather intensified his lordship's unhappy mood, and as he caught sight of the grim fortress, he had an urge to direct his driver to turn back to Glenfinnan. Although the brooding stone edifice was only barely discernible in the darkness, it appeared to Ravenstoke to be a most forbidding place.

A liveried servant opened Ravenstoke's carriage door and, holding an umbrella over the marquess's head, escorted him inside. Ravenstoke then shed his cloak and hat, depositing them with a woman servant who, in his lordship's opinion, eyed him far too boldly.

Entering the ballroom, the marquess was first struck by the vastness of it and then by the great crowd of people already inside. He had arrived late, as was his custom, and had some satisfaction in knowing that he was perhaps the last guest to appear.

Surveying the assembly, Ravenstoke noted that most of the gentlemen were attired in Highland dress and that his fashionable evening clothes seemed strangely out of place amid the sea of tartan kilts now confronting him. He stood there feeling conspicuous and decidedly uncomfortable.

The herald announced his arrival, and as expected, all those within hearing turned toward him with expressions of undisguised curiosity. Ravenstoke reacted to this unwanted interest by adopting a look he hoped would be interpreted as careless indifference.

As he entered the ballroom, Ravenstoke was met by an elderly gentleman dressed in splendid Highland regalia. He wore a handsome kilt of green plaid, an old-fashioned coat of black velvet, and a snowy linen shirt that featured rows of lace at the throat and cuffs. He had such a look of authority that the marquess knew immediately that he was facing his host, the Duke of Dornach.

"How good of you to come, Ravenstoke. I am Dornach."

"How do you do, your grace?" said the marquess politely. He extended his hand to the duke, who shook it vigorously.

The duke gestured toward a young gentleman standing beside him. "Ravenstoke, may I present my grandson, Andrew, Earl of Culwin and Master of Dornach?"

The marquess shook the hand of the young man, who was regarding him with a cool appraising look. "How do you do, Lord Culwin?"

"Lord Ravenstoke." Andrew nodded and continued to scrutinize the marquess. The young earl was dressed in a kilt and velvet coat nearly identical to that worn by the duke. Although thinking the costume quaint and rather barbarous, Ravenstoke found himself noting that Lord Culwin looked quite dashing in it.

"Everyone is eager to meet you, Ravenstoke," said the duke.

"Aye," said Andrew, "they speak of nothing else."

Ravenstoke was not pleased at this information but replied civilly, "I am most obliged to you for inviting me, Duke."

" 'Twas the least I could do for a man who has done me the great service you have, sir." The duke looked out across the ballroom. "My granddaughter is likewise obligated to you, sir."

"Your granddaughter, sir?" said Ravenstoke, slightly confused.

"Aye, and she did not have the opportunity to thank you properly for your assistance. Andrew, where is your sister?"

"I shall fetch her at once, Grandfather." Andrew directed a grin at Ravenstoke and his mirthful expression further confused the marquess.

"Aye, you were good to help my granddaughter, Ravenstoke," continued the duke. "And you did so most ably. I was glad to see that, Englishman or no, you're a man who knows sheep."

Now thoroughly perplexed, Ravenstoke regarded the duke strangely. Before he could reply, the duke spoke again. "There she is, my granddaughter, Lady Alison Murray. Lass, this is Lord Ravenstoke, but then, you have met, have you not?"

The marquess turned to greet his host's granddaughter and was utterly dumbfounded. There standing before him was the lovely shepherdess he had rescued from the crevasse. The realization that the young woman was the duke's granddaughter made Ravenstoke feel utterly ridiculous. Dressed in her blue gown trimmed with ivory lace, Alison looked startlingly beautiful. She carried herself like a princess, and seeing her now, he wondered how he could ever have taken her for anything but the lady she so obviously was.

"Actually, we were not properly introduced, Grandfather." Alison looked up at the marquess and was not disappointed by the expression on his face. He was regarding her with a mixture of embarrassment and astonishment, and she smiled mischievously. "I do not think that I had opportunity to thank you properly, my lord. I shall do so now. You were most kind to assist me."

"Lady Alison . . . I . . . that is . . ." Ravenstoke looked completely flustered. Attributing the marquess's incoherence to his granddaughter's presence, the duke smiled. Some men did not know what to say to a pretty woman, and Ravenstoke was obviously one of them. His grace of Dornach experienced some satisfaction at the thought of this wealthy Englishman becoming tongue-tied beside Alison. Of course, Murray women had been known to have that effect on men.

"I told my grandfather how well you handled sheep," said Alison. "I fear you do not have a similar view of my abilities." She turned to the duke. "Indeed, Grandfather,

I fancy Lord Ravenstoke thought me the most goose-capped of shepherdesses."

Looking quite discomfited, the marquess managed to reply, "Lady Alison, I assure you I thought no such thing."

"You are too kind, my lord," said Alison. "But do not fear for the sheep, for I shall try to avoid sheepherding in the future."

Her blue eyes sparkled with amusement and Ravenstoke knew that she was making sport of him. He was relieved when the duke spoke.

"Well, Ravenstoke, I fear I cannot allow my grand-daughter to monopolize your attention. There are so many here who wish to meet you, sir, and everyone would take it very ill if I did not start introducing you about. Do excuse us, Alison, but we must give the others the opportunity to meet his lordship."

"Very well, Grandfather," said Alison in such a disap-pointed voice that Ravenstoke suspected she was being sarcastic. He allowed himself to be led away, glad at not having to talk anymore to the young lady.

Alison watched him go with a bemused expression. How confused he had been and how different he seemed from the gruff gentleman she had met before.

"There you are, lass. You have been avoiding me all evening."

Alison looked up to find Ian MacGillivray standing before her. He looked strong and handsome in his elabo-rate Highland finery, a fact that even Alison had to admit. "I have not been avoiding you, Sir Ian."

"No? Well, it appears to me you have."

"The ball has just begun, sir."

"Aye, it has just begun now that your Englishman has arrived. I saw how you were looking at him, Alison, and I think it shameless that you should throw yourself at the man."

"Throw myself?" Alison regarded MacGillivray incred-ulously. "Whatever are you talking about? I scarcely spoke to Lord Ravenstoke."

"Aye, but words aren't necessary, are they? I'll warn you, lass, that you need not trouble yourself with the likes of him when a better man stands before you."

"A better man?" Alison looked beyond Sir Ian. "I would be grateful if you would point the gentleman out to me."

MacGillivray scowled. "I'm warning you, Alison, I'm not a patient man."

"You need not tell me that, Sir Ian, for it is obvious to anyone who is in the least acquainted with you. Now, do excuse me."

MacGillivray reached out and grabbed Alison by the wrist. "Not so fast. I wish to say something more to you."

Alison angrily pulled her arm away. "And I do not wish to hear it!" She hurried away from him, leaving the baronet frowning ominously at her retreating form.

As Lord Ravenstoke made his rounds of the guests, scores of eyes followed his every move. There was hardly a soul in attendance that night who had not heard of the Englishman who had taken Glenfinnan, and there was tremendous curiosity about him. The guests thought it odd that a London gentleman would come to their remote corner of the Highlands.

None of the guests were predisposed to liking an Englishman, especially one who had taken the ancestral property of one of their own. Ravenstoke's reserved manner made him appear aloof and haughty and did little to ensure his popularity.

In truth, the marquess was trying his best to be sociable. Ill-at-ease at such functions, Ravenstoke had never been good at making small talk. To make matters worse, some of the guests spoke in broad Scots dialect and he had difficulty understanding them. As a result, he did not always smile at appropriate moments, and many of the guests deemed him humorless and a cold fish.

One of the area's most redoubtable matrons, Lady MacIntosh was among the many ladies introduced to Ravenstoke. After exchanging a few words with him, Lady MacIntosh hurried about, informing those who had not been fortunate enough to have met the marquess of her estimation of his character.

"I did not like him overmuch," Lady MacIntosh confided to one of her friends. "He barely condescended to speak to me. He is quite arrogant and I am certain he thinks our society beneath him. Why ever did such a man come here? I do hope he returns to England soon."

These thoughts were shared by many of the company, and most of all by Sir Ian MacGillivray. The baronet was somewhat heartened by the uniformly negative reactions to Ravenstoke. Having spent much time watching the duke lead the Englishman around the ballroom, Sir Ian was sure that Ravenstoke's stony visage would not endear him to his new Highland neighbors.

Thus reassured that the marquess was suitably unpopular, MacGillivray concentrated on his pursuit of Lady Alison Murray. That young lady was doing her best to elude him, remaining with her friends and several elderly kinswomen. Realizing that she was avoiding him, the baronet grew increasingly irked and withdrew to the company of gentlemen who were stationed around the whiskey punch.

Among the jovial throng clustered near the punch bowl was Andrew Murray. Andrew downed another glass of punch and grinned at Sir Ian as the small orchestra struck up a spirited reel. "And why aren't you dancing, Ian?"

"And why aren't you?"

Andrew laughed. "I hate to break the lassies' hearts. Since I can dance with only one at a time, 'tis cruel to disappoint the others."

Sir Ian laughed and slapped his friend on the back. He took a drink of punch and then his face grew serious. "That sister of yours is driving me mad."

"Alison?"

"Aye, 'tis the only sister you have, my chowder-headed friend. She has been avoiding me all evening."

"Och, Ian, you know the games the lasses play. I'll wager she only wants you to give her a bit of a chase."

"You may be right," returned Ian, somewhat mollified. "Look, Ian, there she is." Andrew gestured across the room. "Go ask her to dance. She'll not refuse you."

"We'll see," muttered MacGillivray, and then, putting down his glass, he went off toward Alison.

Alison saw Sir Ian coming toward her and knew by his expression that he was in a foul humor. She was standing with two of her Murray cousins, Elizabeth and Margaret

Murray, young ladies attending their first ball. As he neared, Alison looked quickly about for a means of escape, but Sir Ian was upon them before she could do anything.

"I hope you ladies are enjoying yourselves," said he, smiling broadly at Alison's cousins. It was ovious that her companions did not share Alison's aversion to MacGillivray, for Elizabeth and Margaret both blushed and looked quite delighted at his attention.

"Aye, Sir Ian," said Elizabeth. "It is a lovely ball."

"Lovely it is, but only for the presence of beautiful ladies like yourselves."

Elizabeth and Margaret giggled and exchanged glances, and Alison frowned and cast a disapproving look at Sir Ian.

The big man grinned down at her. "I believe, Alison, that you have promised me the next dance."

"I fear you are mistaken, sir."

MacGillivray's face clouded. "The next dance is mine. I see no other man here to claim you."

Alison looked from MacGillivray to her cousins, who were regarding her curiously. "I have promised the next dance to someone else."

"And who might that be?"

Alison hesitated and looked quickly across the ballroom. Her eyes alighted on Ravenstoke, who was not too far away and still being taken in tow by the duke. "I have promised Lord Ravenstoke the next dance."

"Lord Ravenstoke?" said Margaret Murray. "Why, cousin, how could you wish to dance with him?"

"Indeed," said Elizabeth, clearly surprised. "He does not appear to be in the least dashing and he is so very . . . English."

"He is a guest of my grandfather's and we must be civil. Now, do excuse me, Sir Ian. But surely you must dance with one of my cousins!" She turned to the young ladies. "Would not one of you oblige Sir Ian with a dance?"

Margaret and Elizabeth seemed thrilled at the prospect. "Oh, aye, Sir Ian," said Elizabeth, "but you must dance with both of us!"

"That is only fair," said Alison with a smile. "So you

are well-occupied for the next two dances, Sir Ian. Now, do excuse me."

Alison hurried away, feeling rather pleased with herself. Glancing back over her shoulder, she saw MacGillivray's scowling face and could not help but smile. However, her smile vanished when she saw Sir Ian abandon her cousins and come after her.

"Alison," he called loudly, and several heads turned in his direction.

Alison rushed to the side of her grandfather and Ravenstoke. "Och, there you are," she said a trifle breathlessly. "Lord Ravenstoke, his grace has been keeping you so busy that I must remind you that you promised me a dance."

"What?" said the duke. "A dance? Did you, Ravenstoke?"

The marquess looked at Alison in some surprise. Before he could reply, MacGillivray arrived beside them. His face was angry and flushed with drink. "It is my dance, Alison," he said. "I'll have no more tomfoolery."

Ravenstoke took his cue from Alison's expression and did not hesitate further. "I am sorry, sir," said the marquess. "Lady Alison has promised to be my partner."

"Then you'll have to take your turn, Ian," said the duke.

Even in his slightly inebriated state, MacGillivray knew better than to argue with the Murray of Dornach in his own home. He only frowned as Ravenstoke led Alison away.

"I do thank you, Lord Ravenstoke," said Alison, taking his lordship's arm. "You have done me a service."

"You should withhold judgment on that, I think."

Alison looked over at Ravenstoke, who was regarding her with the serious expression that seemed to be the only one he had. "And why is that, my lord?"

"Because, Lady Alison, I am a terrible dancer."

Alison burst into laughter and the marquess smiled slightly. "Lord Ravenstoke, you do have a sense of humor!"

"I have never been known to possess one. Nor do I have any other such qualities that would endear me to

society. You may be certain that I have not charmed
anyone here tonight."

"But surely, Lord Ravenstoke, that was not your intention."

"No, perhaps not." The marquess smiled again, and
Alison was struck by how his smile transformed his
countenance, making him appear far more handsome.
Despite his self-deprecating remarks, Alison realized that
Ravenstoke was not without charm.

"And you must be having a miserable time, sir, being
pulled about by my grandfather and now being tricked
into dancing with me. I am sorry to involve you with my
problem."

"And your problem is the robust gentleman?"

"You are a perceptive man, Lord Ravenstoke."

"So perceptive that I took you for a shepherdess."

Alison cast an impish look at the marquess. "I do admit
that I was none too pleased at that, for it was not very
flattering to be taken for a shepherdess. And then to be
chided for doing the job poorly was quite vexatious."

"I am sorry. You must have thought me quite boorish."

"Well, my lord, I did not form an entirely favorable
opinion of you. However, I am beginning to alter it. After
all, you have rescued me twice now. Once from the
crevasse and once from even greater peril, Sir Ian Mac-
Gillivray."

Ravenstoke smiled and found unfamiliar feelings stir-
ring within him. He had been immune to the charms of so
many pretty women, knowing well that they were out to
ensnare his fortune. Indeed, he had become very cynical
about the female sex and had thought notions of love and
romance utterly preposterous. His relationship with his
fiancée was devoid of any fond feelings on either of their
parts, and the marquess had prided himself on his calm
businesslike approach to marriage. Now, however, looking into the fine blue eyes of the lovely Lady Alison, his
lordship was finding himself strangely confused.

The music began just as Alison and Ravenstoke joined
the other dancers, and the marquess was soon involved in
a lively Highland reel. He was totally unfamiliar with the
steps and tried without great success to follow the other
gentlemen.

The Marquess of Ravenstoke's attempts to dance were noted with a mixture of surprise and approval by the ladies and gentlemen at the ball. The Highlanders were glad to see that the Englishman was willing to attempt a reel. That he was failing miserably did not matter at all, and a number of the guests acknowledged that at least the new laird of Glenfinnan was finally taking part in the festivities.

Ian MacGillivray watched Ravenstoke and Alison with increasing rancor. After drinking one more glass of whiskey punch, he made his way to the dancers and then stood there glowering, his beefy hands resting on his hips in a threatening posture. Alison was so involved in the dance and in giving Ravenstoke encouraging looks that she did not notice MacGillivray standing there watching them.

"I would not have thought Alison Murray would dance with the descendant of the man responsible for butchering so many of her kinsmen." Sir Ian's booming voice startled everyone and brought the dancing to an abrupt halt. "Aye, it is true." MacGillivray pointed menacingly at Ravenstoke. "This Englishman, this new laird of Glenfinnan, is the grandson of Bloody Wicklow!"

A collective gasp escaped the assembly and all turned to stare at Ravenstoke, who was regarding Sir Ian with a bewildered expression.

"Aye, he will not deny it. His mother was Wicklow's only daughter and he is heir to his estates! Heir to the man who was Cumberland's right hand. Aye, none of us can forget that it was Bloody Wicklow who hunted down the survivors of Culloden, slaughtering them like sheep."

Alison listened to MacGillivray's words in shocked silence and then turned to Ravenstoke. "Is it true, Lord Ravenstoke? Are you the grandson of Baron Wicklow?"

The marquess frowned. "My grandfather was John, Baron Wicklow and he was an officer under the Duke of Cumberland's command. But I know very little of his Scottish campaign. Why, these events happened seventy years ago."

"We have long memories in the Highlands, Ravenstoke," said the duke, a grim expression on his face.

"Aye," said Andrew Murray hotly. "We will never forget Bloody Wicklow and his infamous deeds."

Sir Ian nodded. "And the Englishman has returned to the scene of his grandfather's crimes."

Ravenstoke looked from Sir Ian to the sea of hostile faces now surrounding him. He turned toward Alison. "Truly, I knew nothing of this."

"That does not signify," said the duke. "The grandson of Bloody Wicklow is not welcome here. I wish you to leave my house and never again will you be welcome here or anywhere in the Highlands."

"Grandfather!" Alison came forward to stand beside the marquess. "Surely Lord Ravenstoke cannot be held accountable for the sins of his grandfather."

"That is enough, my girl!" The duke spoke sharply and was visibly upset. "I'll not have a descendent of Bloody Wicklow at Dornach Castle. You had best be gone, sir."

Ravenstoke thought it best to say nothing further. He cast a quick glance at Alison and then turned and walked off. There were excited murmurings and indignant looks as he made his way through the ballroom. Alison directed an angry look at MacGillivray, but the baronet only smiled and looked well-satisfied with himself.

8 Jack Mull had not expected his master home for several hours. Therefore, he was quite surprised when one of the Scottish maidservants informed him that Ravenstoke had returned and was in a "deevil o' a mood."

Thus forewarned, Mull entered the marquess's rooms. He found his lordship sitting glumly in an armchair by the fireplace. "Shall I attend to the fire, m'lord?"

"What?" Ravenstoke had been deep in thought and he looked up at Mull.

"The fire, m'lord. 'Tis almost out."

"Oh, yes, thank you, Mull. I think I shall be up for a time."

Mull tended to the fire, adjusting the draft and adding some wood until it came to life once more. "That should do you, m'lord," said Mull, rising from the massive fireplace and looking expectantly at the marquess.

"That will be all, Mull. You go on to bed."

"Very good, m'lord." Mull turned to go.

"Mull?"

"Aye, m'lord?"

"Have you heard of Bloody Wicklow?"

"Bloody Wicklow?" Mull regarded Ravenstoke thoughtfully. "No, I have not. Was he a highwayman?"

Ravenstoke smiled slightly. "Worse than that, it seems. He was one of Cumberland's officers at Culloden. I am

61

told he ruthlessly ordered the slaughter of the retreating Highlanders, and his memory is hated here." Mull made no reply and the marquess looked for a moment into the fire and then back at his servant. "Bloody Wicklow was my grandfather, Jack."

"Your grandfather, m'lord?"

Ravenstoke nodded. "I knew he had helped put down the Young Pretender's rebellion, but I had no idea he was so hated. Good God, I shall never forget the looks on their faces when they heard I was his grandson. They looked at me as if I was some sort of monster."

"You mean at the ball, m'lord?"

"Yes, at the ball. While I was dancing with a very charming lady, a certain oafish fellow, a loudmouthed giant called MacGillivray, spoke up and told the assembly that I was descended from the infamous Baron Wicklow."

"But, m'lord, no matter what sort of man your grandfather was, that was many years ago."

"It does not signify how long ago, Jack. A thousand years may go by and still the descendants of Bloody Wicklow will be unwelcome here."

"Will we return to England, m'lord?"

"Return to England? Certainly not. I would not give MacGillivray the satisfaction. I shall stay at Glenfinnan for a time anyway. Indeed, even before knowing of my notorious ancestor, the Highlanders were hardly disposed to like me."

"Then you were right in thinkin' the ball a bad idea, m'lord. 'Twould have been better had you stayed away."

"Perhaps," murmured his lordship, thinking of Alison. "But then, I did have the opportunity to become reacquainted with a young lady whom we both met once."

Mull tried to keep a straight face. "A lady, m'lord?"

"Lady Alison Murray, the granddaughter of the Duke of Dornach. You had the honor of escorting her home, I believe."

"Did I, m'lord?" Jack Mull could no longer keep from grinning. "Not the young lady with the sheep, m'lord?"

"Of course, the lady with the sheep! I can see from your expression that you knew all along she was no shepherdess." Ravenstoke looked exasperated with his servant. "Why didn't you tell me? I felt like such a fool."

"I am sorry, m'lord," said Mull, not looking in the least contrite, "but her ladyship asked me not to say anything to you. I knew that you would want me to honor her wishes."

The marquess's irritation turned to amusement. "You are a rogue, Jack Mull. And I am an idiot. How could I have taken her for a simple shepherdess?" An unusual reflective look came to Ravenstoke's face. "You should have seen her, Jack. She was the most beautiful . . ." Realizing suddenly that he was being indiscreet, revealing himself in this way to a servant, the marquess stopped abruptly. "You may go, Mull. I shall take care of myself."

Jack Mull nodded and left his master. As he made his way down to the servants' quarters, he wondered about Ravenstoke and Lady Alison. It seemed the young lady had got through his lordship's usually impervious defenses. Pity that he is engaged to Miss Willoughby, thought Mull, thinking of his lordship's fiancée with disfavor. He did not like the lady and thought her unworthy to be Marchioness of Ravenstoke. Mull knew very well that it was not his place to judge his master's future wife, and yet he could not help but compare the haughty Deborah with Lady Alison, a girl who had charmed him from the first. "Pity," said Mull aloud, and then he vanished into the servants' hall.

The following morning Andrew Murray hurried to catch up with his sister as she strode across the stableyard. "Do wait, Allie!"

Alison stopped and frowned at her brother. "I don't know why I should. You have been completely insufferable since the ball, Lord Culwin."

"I? Just because I defend Ian? By heaven, he said what had to be said."

"Andrew, we have gone over this time and again. I see no need to discuss it further. In your view Ian MacGillivray can do no wrong."

"Come, now, Allie, let us cease this quarreling. It has gone on too long."

Alison regarded her brother with a serious gaze. "And so it has, Andrew. But both you and Grandfather see no ill in Ian MacGillivray, and I see nothing else in him. It was ungentlemanly to act as he did at the ball, and I cannot believe otherwise."

"But surely we have a right to know about this Ravenstoke. By God, the man has gall coming here."

"Andrew, I see no purpose in saying anything more." She turned away from him. "I am going riding, so I pray you excuse me."

"I shall go with you."

"No, I shall go alone or not at all."

"As you wish, Lady Alison." Andrew was visibly irritated. He had not expected his sister to rebuff his attempt to put an end to their quarreling, and she seemed totally unreasonable. "Go off and pine for your Englishman."

Alison stopped instantly and stared indignantly at her brother. "And what do you mean by that, Andrew Murray?"

"I mean that it is clear you have a *tendre* for Ravenstoke."

"You know very well that is nonsense."

"Do I? Well, I hope it isn't true, for I will not allow a sister of mine to have anything to do with such a man."

"You will not allow? Andrew Murray, you cannot tell me what to do!"

"Can't I? I am your brother and Master of Dornach! After Grandfather I am head of the family and you must do as I wish."

"I will do as I please, Master of Dornach," replied Alison hotly. "How dare you speak to me so!" Not trusting herself to say anything more, Alison walked quickly away from her brother. She found Claymore saddled and ready, and as she rode away from the castle, she did not even glance at Andrew, who stood there sullenly, watching her go.

Alison's anger did not abate until she had traveled some distance across the Dornach lands. She directed the chestnut horse toward the river and pulled him up short as she reached it. She then turned Claymore and rode in the direction of Glenfinnan.

Although she did not actually expect to see Ravenstoke, Alison knew that she would not at all mind seeing the marquess again. Certainly Andrew's insinuation that she had lost her heart to the Englishman was absurd, and yet there was something about the new laird of Glenfinnan that was undeniably appealing. Alison smiled as she thought of Ravenstoke's expression upon seeing her at the ball.

It was odd, she reflected, how her impression of him had changed so quickly. She had disliked him at first, finding him cold and arrogant, but at the ball, she had discovered that there was much more to his lordship's character than was readily apparent.

After a short time, Alison crossed onto Glenfinnan lands. She proceeded on toward the manor house, but then halted Claymore. There, sitting atop the tall stallion, she surveyed Ravenstoke's property and decided to turn back. Even if her grandfather approved of any further association with the marquess, it was hardly proper for a lone young lady to call upon a gentleman. Indeed, she did not doubt that Ravenstoke would think her remarkably forward if she showed up on his doorstep. Therefore, Alison turned her horse around and started back to Dornach Castle.

She had not gone very far when she caught sight of Ravenstoke astride a fine bay horse. He waved to her and then cantered up beside her. "Lady Alison, how good it is to see you." Ravenstoke lifted his tall beaver hat politely.

"Good day, Lord Ravenstoke," said Alison, somewhat embarrassed at meeting the marquess on his own property. If Ravenstoke found it curious to find her riding on Glenfinnan lands, he showed no sign of it. Instead, his lordship seemed genuinely happy to see her, and Alison was suddenly very glad she had come.

"I am relieved that you are willing to talk to me, ma'am. I had supposed that I was to be completely ostracized."

"I am sorry for what happened. I think it was horrid of Sir Ian to say such things."

"It was certainly a revelation to me to discover how much my grandfather is hated in the Highlands. I should have been more interested in his military exploits. Indeed, he died when I was a very small boy and I never knew much about him." Ravenstoke smiled slightly. "I do know that my father did not like him, nor any of my mother's family, and I daresay the feeling was mutual."

The marquess shrugged. "I did not expect to be loved here in Scotland, but then I did not expect to be detested either. Perhaps it was a mistake to come. Perhaps I should go back to England."

"Is that what you want to do?"

The marquess shook his head. "I have been here scarcely a fortnight and yet I have never felt more at home. I came here searching out a childhood dream and was not for a moment disappointed in anything I found."

"A childhood dream?"

Ravenstoke nodded. "My old nanny was from the Highlands and she was always telling me about them. Many times I thought of coming here, and when I learned of this property, I found myself compelled to have it." A smile crossed his countenance. "My solicitor thought I was mad. He did not think it a wise investment, but I could not let go of the idea of having my own home in the Highlands."

"Then, that is why you have come here?"

"Yes, I know it must sound utterly foolish that memories from the nursery would cause me to take such action. Be assured I did not explain my motives to my solicitor. Indeed, I have not explained this to anyone but you, Lady Alison, and I daresay you must think me quite odd."

Alison patted Claymore, who was growing restless at the prolonged stay. "I see nothing odd about it, my lord. This land has cast a spell on many who have seen it, and those born here, though they may go to the far reaches of the earth, can never forget it. I know that is how it is with me."

"And you would never wish to leave it?"

"Och, no, it is where I belong. Of course, I cannot say that I have never entertained the notion of traveling to exotic foreign lands."

"Indeed? And where have you thought of going? Rome? Or perhaps Egypt? It seems quite vogue to talk of going to Egypt."

Alison laughed. "London is quite exotic and foreign enough to me, my lord."

"Then, you would like to see London?"

"I had not thought so before." Alison directed a mischievous look at the marquess. "I have formerly not held a very high opinion of the English, my lord, but now, having for the first time formed an acquaintance with an Englishman, I am adjusting my views."

"I am flattered that you don't think me so very dreadful."

"You, my lord? Oh, dear. I was actually referring to your Mr. Mull."

Ravenstoke burst into laughter and Alison joined him. "So Mull has charmed you?"

"He is a most admirable fellow. One cannot help but like him."

"And he is a dashed sight more perceptive than I. I expect it did not take him very long to know that you were no shepherdess."

"That is true, but as Mull told me, 'a gentleman like his lordship don't have to be so observant.'"

Ravenstoke grinned. "I am gratified to see that my servant was prepared to make excuses for me."

"Indeed. He also assured me that you were no 'slow top.'"

His lordship laughed again. "I am even more indebted to him."

Alison smiled at the marquess. She was finding herself very much attracted to him, and the words of her brother Andrew suddenly came back to her with disquieting effect. "I do think I should be going, Lord Ravenstoke."

The marquess was visibly disappointed. "You will not come to the house for tea?"

"Oh, no, thank you. I really must be going. Good-bye, my lord."

Ravenstoke lifted his hat once more. "Good-bye, Lady Alison." He watched her turn her stallion and ride quickly off, and then he cursed himself for offering tea. He knew very well that she could not take tea with him. He was, after all, the heir of Bloody Wicklow, and he knew that her grandfather would be furious to know she had even been talking to him. The marquess gazed once more at Alison's retreating form and then turned his own horse and headed back toward his house.

9 The morning following her meeting with Ravenstoke, Alison sat in the drawing room, working on her embroidery. Highly skilled at such work, she deftly added a few stitches to the delicate pattern of roses and thistles that was emerging from the canvas. Then, looking up from the needlework, Alison sighed.

She should not be thinking so much of Lord Ravenstoke, she told herself. Indeed, since seeing him on the Glenfinnan lands, he had been constantly in her thoughts. If only he could call on them here at Dornach, but no, that was impossible and certainly it would be very forward of her to ride off to see him again. No, it would be better to forget the marquess.

"Allie! There you are!" Duncan Murray came into the drawing room and hurried over to his sister.

Alison regarded her youngest brother with an affectionate look. His red hair was tousled and there was a merry grin on his freckled face. "And what mischief have you got yourself into, Duncan Murray?"

"None at all. I am being very good."

"And why aren't you in the schoolroom with Mr. Ferguson?"

"Mr. Ferguson had a very bad headache and said that he must go home to bed. He wished me to say he did not know when he would be able to return."

"Duncan." Alison tried to look stern. "And what did you do to upset Mr. Ferguson?"

"I did nothing, Allie. Of course, he did not seem very pleased with my sums and he did not much like my Latin declensions."

"Poor man," murmured Alison. She knew very well that Duncan was no scholar and poor Mr. Ferguson, a hardworking and studious man, was constantly frustrated by his pupil.

"Could we not go walking, Alison? The weather is good."

"I think, young man, that you should not abandon your studies despite Mr. Ferguson's indisposition. Surely he has left you some work you might do."

Duncan's face fell. "Oh, please, Allie."

Alison hesitated, and then, recognizing her failure as a disciplinarian, she finally nodded. "Very well, but allow me to finish this leaf. I shall only be a minute."

Duncan sat down beside his sister and watched her for a few moments. "That is very nice."

"Thank you."

Duncan glanced about the room and looked rather restless. "Allie, Andrew said that you like the Englishman, Lord Ravenstoke."

Alison looked over at her brother. "Andrew is exaggerating in order to vex me. Of course, I do not dislike Lord Ravenstoke. He seems to be a well-mannered gentleman."

Duncan looked disappointed. "They say he is a cruel man like his grandfather, Bloody Wicklow. Ian says Bloody Wicklow was a bad one and all his kin are cursed. He says we must beware of Lord Ravenstoke, for he is a treacherous Englishman."

"What nonsense! You must not believe everything that Ian says. Lord Ravenstoke is a very nice man and not all Englishmen are evil."

Duncan looked skeptical, but made no reply. They were interrupted by the arrival of the elderly servant Bob MacPherson.

" 'Tis Sir Ian MacGillivray to see ye, m'lady."

"Ian! Oh, do show him in, Bob," cried Duncan. "What luck for him to call."

"Wait just a minute, Bob," said Alison, but MacPherson was somewhat hard-of-hearing and did not attend her.

A few moments later Ian MacGillivray appeared at the door. He was dressed carelessly in mud-spattered riding clothes, and his curly black hair was wild. "Ah, Alison. And young Master Duncan. How are you, my lad?"

"Very well, sir. Mr. Ferguson was taken ill and I cannot have my lessons."

"What good fortune, lad. I've no fondness for books myself. They're of no use to a gentleman."

"In any case, they are of no use to you, sir," said Alison coldly.

MacGillivray grinned. "And have I your leave to sit down, Lady Alison?"

"You have not."

The big man grinned again and sat down on a chair across from Alison and Duncan.

"Andrew and the duke are not here." Alison eyed MacGillivray distastefully.

"Oh, your man told me that. 'Tis you I came to see anyway."

Duncan was regarding Sir Ian with undisguised admiration. "Ian, do tell Allie that Lord Ravenstoke is a cruel man. She does not believe it."

"Your sister is not a lady who can be told much of anything, lad. She'll think as she will. You'll make a difficult wife, Alison Murray, but I'll warrant you'd be worth the effort."

"Will you marry Allie, then?" said Duncan. "Och, I do hope you will. Then we would be brothers!"

"You are a wee lad close to my heart. Do you hear, Alison? Duncan approves of me."

"And I do not, so that is the end of it."

Duncan looked from Sir Ian to his sister and noted the unhappy expression on her face. He decided to change the subject and turned it once again to Ravenstoke. "Old Mattie Robinson told me Bloody Wicklow killed more than a thousand men."

"Duncan! I will have no more of this talk. You will not mention Lord Wicklow again."

MacGillivray smiled over at Duncan. "Ladies do not

enjoy talking about such things. We must not upset your
sister's delicate sensibilities."

"Oh," said Duncan, regarding his sister sympathetically.

Alison frowned at Sir Ian and was greatly relieved when
her brother Andrew appeared at the door. "Ian! Bob told
me you were here."

"And where is the duke?"

"Och, he stayed at the village. So, how is Gaisgeach?
You had said he had some tenderness on the right front
leg."

"Aye, but that is gone now. He's right enough."

"Glad I am to hear it," returned Andrew.

Alison rose from her chair. "Do excuse me. I am sure
you two have much to discuss. Come, Duncan."

"No, do stay, Allie," said Andrew.

"No, I shall leave you. Come, Duncan."

Duncan reluctantly followed his sister from the drawing
room, and Andrew and Ian were left alone. Sir Ian did not
take his eyes off Alison until she vanished from sight.
"You've a bonny sister, Andrew Murray, but a stubborn
one."

"Aye," said Andrew. "Of late she has been most
headstrong. She will hear no ill said of the Englishman,
and I feel she has some girlish fondness for him."

"Damn him," muttered MacGillivray. "Would that he
never came to Scotland. And why he should turn her head
is a puzzlement. But then he is a very rich man."

Andrew looked insulted. "You cannot think my sister
would care for a man's wealth."

"Och, I know not what she cares for, but you had best
keep a watch on her. I did not like the way she looked at
Ravenstoke at the ball, and the way the fellow looked at
her made me want to murder him. I hope to God that he
will soon tire of playing the laird of Glenfinnan and go
back to London, where he belongs."

"Do not fear," said Andrew boldly. "He'll come nowhere near my sister. You can be sure of that."

Ian slapped his friend on the back and the two men
turned the subject once again to horses.

10 As young Duncan Murray crossed from his grandfather's lands into those of Lord Ravenstoke, he was filled with a sense of adventure. He felt as though he was one lone Highland soldier on a dangerous mission in enemy territory, and his pulse quickened with excitement. Duncan hid himself behind a scrubby tree and surveyed the area. Seeing no enemy troops, he proceeded stealthily in the direction of the manor house.

After catching sight of Glenfinnan, he stopped once more and planned his strategy. He could see no one about the house, but could hear some voices from the direction of the stables. He therefore advanced cautiously, hiding behind shrubbery until he made his way to the side of the house. There he peered into one large window, hoping for a sight of the foe, Ravenstoke, heir to Bloody Wicklow.

To his great disappointment, the room was empty, and Duncan frowned. He had hoped to get a glimpse of the monstrous Englishman, but there was not a soul to be seen. Moving along the house to the next room's windows, the boy heard a noise and froze against the stone wall of the house. A man was approaching, walking briskly. As Duncan caught sight of the man's face, he caught his breath in shock. It was a most hideous face, badly scarred and with a nose that twisted to one side in a grotesque manner.

Duncan fervently prayed that this horrible creature would not detect him, and he breathed a sigh of relief when the man passed by and then vanished behind the house. Turning his attention once again to the window, Duncan looked into the next room. Again he was disappointed, for it, too, was empty. The room itself was somewhat interesting, however, for upon its walls was a collection of antique weapons: swords and claymores and ancient pistols. Duncan stared into the room, so intrigued by the weapons that he temporarily forgot his desire to see Ravenstoke.

"What are you doing there, boy?" A man's gruff voice startled Duncan, and he turned around quickly. Duncan gasped as he found himself facing the hideous man, who was now even more frightful, since upon his misshapen face was a decidedly unfriendly scowl. "I said what are you doing?"

Duncan did not reply. For a brief moment he was terrorized into immobility.

"Come away from there," said the horrible man, reaching forward to grasp his arm.

Duncan pulled away in horror and, dodging the man, raced off as fast as he could go. His heart pounding wildly, the boy dashed across the grounds. He heard the horrible man shout something and knew that he was being pursued. He ran madly, not caring which direction he was heading and only hoping that he could outdistance his adversary. He saw that he was heading toward the river, but did not recognize it as a barrier until he was almost upon it. The sight of the rapidly flowing water made Duncan stop. He looked in both directions and behind him and knew immediately that he was trapped. His pursuer was advancing and he had nowhere to go. The boy eyed his antagonist and then looked back at the swollen icy waters. Without any further hesitation, Duncan Murray jumped into the river.

Jack Mull watched the frightened boy vanish into the water and shouted an oath. He reached the riverbank within seconds and dived in. The coldness of the water gave Mull a jolt, but he recovered quickly. He could not see the boy and was gripped with a terrible fear that the child was already lost. Indeed, the swiftness of the current made him wonder whether he, expert swimmer though he was, could survive.

Battling against the icy water, Mull flailed his arms about, searching vainly for the boy. As he thrust his head above the water and took a gulp of air, Mull thought he heard a cry, and there, several yards beyond him, was the boy's head. It vanished seconds later beneath the water and Mull made a desperate attempt to reach him.

Finally touching the boy, Mull clutched wildly at him, lifting Duncan with Herculean effort above the water. Then, grasping him firmly about the neck, Mull started for land.

It was with tremendous relief that Mull felt the ground beneath his feet, and although exhausted, he managed to pull the unconscious boy onto the riverbank. Kneeling beside the child, Mull slapped his face gently. "Please, lad, come on now."

There was no sign of life from the boy for a moment, and then a gasp escaped Duncan. He coughed and expelled a great quantity of water. "Thank God!" cried Mull, tears coming to his eyes. "We'd best get you to the house before you freeze to death."

Duncan Murray looked gratefully at his rescuer and former adversary and made no protest when Mull picked him up and carried him off toward the house.

Ravenstoke was reading in the library when one of the Scottish servants, a hulking lad in his late teens, rushed in. "M'lord, Mr. Mull hae rescued young Master Duncan Murray frae the river!"

"What the devil!"

"Aye. 'Tis true. Nearly drowned he was. And Mr. Mull too."

"Where are they?"

"In the old laird's bedroom, m'lord. Mrs. Brown is seeing tae them."

Ravenstoke hurried off, and arriving inside the room, he found Mrs. Brown, the housekeeper, in command. A redhaired boy, attired in one of the marquess's nightshirts, was in the bed and the housekeeper was forcing some sort of potion into him. One of the other servants

was tending to the fire and Mull was standing there
soaking wet, eyeing the lad with a worried expression.

"Is the boy all right?"

"Aye, m'lord," said Mrs. Brown, a stout middle-aged
woman with gray hair and a stern disposition. "He'll be
fine. 'Tis rest he needs." She looked at Mull. "'Tis Mr.
Mull who needs looking after. He'll nae do as I say,
m'lord. He must get those wet things off or he will take a
chill."

"What happened, Jack?"

"It was my fault, m'lord. I found the boy peering in the
window and I chased him off. He jumped into the river,
m'lord, before I could stop him."

"Into the river? Good God!"

"And Mr. Mull was a hero, m'lord," said Mrs. Brown.
"James Gowan saw everything and Mr. Mull saved the
wee lad."

"I am sorry, m'lord," muttered Mull.

"Sorry? Don't be ridiculous, man." The marquess
placed a hand on Mull's shoulder. "Get some rest, Jack.
You're exhausted, and get out of those wet clothes immediately."

"Aye, m'lord." Mull cast one last look at Duncan and
left the room.

Ravenstoke gazed down at the boy. Duncan was wide
awake and regarded the marquess with big blue eyes, not
unlike those of Lady Alison. "How do you feel, young
man?"

"Well enough, sir."

The marquess looked over at Mrs. Brown. "Should the
physician be called?"

"I don't think that will be necessary, m'lord. Not for the
lad. But I worry more about Mr. Mull."

"See to him, then, Mrs. Brown."

"Aye, m'lord."

The housekeeper left the room, leaving Ravenstoke to
watch over Duncan. "You are Master Duncan Murray?"

"Aye, my lord."

"And Lady Alison is your sister?"

"Aye, my lord."

"Are you well enough, Master Duncan Murray, to
explain how this happened? What ever were you doing

here peering in my window? Is that a proper way for a gentleman to come calling?"

"No, sir." Duncan looked very sheepish. "I am sorry. It is only that I did not know you were—"

"That I am what?"

"A regular gentleman, my lord. Alison said you were a nice man, but everyone else said you were—"

"What? Some sort of monster?"

Duncan hesitated and then nodded. "I wanted to see for myself."

Ravenstoke allowed a slight smile to form on his lips. "Did you think I would have two heads? Or one eye like a cyclops?"

"No, sir, but I did think you might look more . . . well, more evil."

The marquess laughed. "And don't I look evil enough for you?"

Duncan smiled. "Indeed not, my lord."

"Then I fear I have disappointed you. But remember, young man, that one need not look evil to be evil."

The boy nodded thoughtfully. "And one who looks evil may not be so. Your man, for instance. I was so very afraid of him and yet he saved me."

"Mull? My young friend, there is not a better man in the kingdom than Jack Mull."

"But his face, sir, it is quite fearful."

"That is because of Mull's unfortunate former profession."

"Profession, sir?"

"Yes, Mull was a prizefighter."

Duncan's eyes grew wide. "A prizefighter? Was he famous?"

"For a time. Indeed, he was widely known. But that was many years ago. In fact, I was scarcely older than you when I first saw Jack Mull exhibit his pugilistic skill."

"And that is why his face is that way."

Ravenstoke nodded. "Mull fought many times over many years. It is a miracle he is still alive. Prizefighting takes a high toll on those who engage in it. It is a pity that gentlemen seem to enjoy it so much."

Duncan did not necessarily share this view, but he kept silent and the marquess continued. "Now, get some rest and we will see what is to be done with you. If you are well enough, I shall drive you back to Dornach Castle. If not, I shall send a note to your family that you are staying the night."

"Thank you, my lord," said Duncan, thinking either prospect quite exciting. He had heard one of the castle servants comment on the fine carriage that had brought the English lord to the ball, and the idea of riding in such a splendid equipage was certainly thrilling. The thought of staying overnight at Glenfinnan was likewise appealing, for Duncan wished to learn all he could about the marquess. He was also hopeful that he might see the interesting Mr. Mull once more. "I do thank you," repeated Duncan, and the marquess smiled and then quietly left the room.

Alison entered the drawing room and, seeing the duke comfortably ensconced in his favorite chair, greeted him cheerfully. "There you are, Grandfather. How are you feeling?"

"Better than I have for some time," said his grace, regarding Alison fondly.

"Good." Alison went over to her grandfather and placed an affectionate kiss on his cheek. "You must take care, sir, that you do not overtire yourself."

"I am no invalid, my girl," said the duke. "It is only that this blasted gout plagues me at times. Now, sit down and keep an old man company."

Alison obediently sat down.

"And where is that young scamp Duncan?"

"I don't really know, Grandfather. He has been gone all afternoon."

"Gone? Where is Ferguson and why doesn't the man keep the boy at his lessons?"

Alison frowned. "I fear that Mr. Ferguson finds the task of teaching Duncan more than he can bear. The poor man went home with a headache."

"A headache! Och, Ferguson is a weak-willed fellow. I shall have a word with Duncan, Alison. He has driven off his other tutors and I'll not tolerate him driving off this one. And it grows late. The lad should be home."

Seeing that this news of Duncan was making his grace

decidedly ill-humored, Alison changed the subject to a more pleasant topic, her stallion Claymore. The duke was soon discoursing on the merits of this excellent steed and after a time forgot his wayward grandson.

Just as the duke was speculating on Claymore's chances of beating Sir Ian's horse Gaisgeach, Duncan burst into the room. "Grandfather! Wait until I tell you about my adventure!"

Alison noted her brother's disheveled appearance. "Good heavens, Duncan! What mischief have you got yourself into?"

Duncan grinned, but before he could reply, the Marquess of Ravenstoke entered the room.

"What the deuce!" The duke regarded his lordship in astonishment. "Ravenstoke, what are you doing here?"

Ravenstoke looked first at Alison, who met his gaze with a questioning look. He then turned to the duke. "I know well, Dornach, that I am unwelcome here. I only wanted to make sure the boy got back safely."

As the marquess turned to leave, Duncan rushed over to his grandfather. "But, Grandfather, will you not thank Lord Ravenstoke? He brought me back from Glenfinnan in his carriage. And his man Mull saved my life!"

"What?" cried the duke, quite befuddled. "Saved your life?"

"Aye! Pulled me from the river he did! I nearly drowned!"

"Wait, Ravenstoke," called the duke as the marquess retreated toward the door. "What is the lad talking about?"

"Yes, please, Lord Ravenstoke," said Alison. "Whatever happened?"

His lordship turned and approached them. "It is as the boy says. He fell in the river at Glenfinnan and my man was fortunately there to rescue him."

"Och, it was terrifying," Duncan said dramatically. "The water was so cold and the current so fast. I remembered going under the water and fighting to come up again. The next thing I knew I was on the banks! Mull had saved me! He was a boxer, you know."

Alison knew well how treacherous the river could be in

the early spring, when melting snow from the mountains turned it into a raging torrent. She looked gratefully at the marquess. "Lord Ravenstoke, you must thank Mull. We owe him a great deal."

"Aye, it appears we do," said the duke. He turned to his grandson. "And what were you doing at Glenfinnan, my lad?"

Duncan looked down.

"Out with it, boy! What devilment were you at that caused you to fall into the river?"

"Och, Grandfather, it was my fault. Mull is a frightening person—that is, before you have made his acquaintance—and when he caught me looking in the window . . ."

"The window?" The duke eyed his grandson sternly. "You were looking in the window at Glenfinnan?"

"Aye." Duncan hung his head. "I wanted to see Lord Ravenstoke."

"Duncan, a gentleman does not peer into windows," cried Alison. "Why ever would you do such a thing?"

Duncan looked shamefacedly at Ravenstoke and then at his sister. "I heard such terrible things about Lord Ravenstoke that I wanted to see him for myself. But you were right, Allie. He is a nice gentleman and one would never know he is kin to Bloody Wicklow."

"Duncan!" Alison looked over at Ravenstoke, quite embarrassed.

To her surprise, the marquess laughed. "The poor lad was sorely disappointed to find that I had neither horns nor a forked tail."

Alison and her grandfather burst into laughter and Duncan grinned. "You are quizzing me, Lord Ravenstoke! I did not expect that, but I did think you might be more fearsome. Of course, Mull appears more formidable. He was a boxer and was once famous."

"You mentioned Mull's unfortunate pugilistic career already, Duncan," said Alison.

Not sharing his granddaughter's distaste for fisticuffs, the duke was quite interested. "Not Jumpin' Jack Mull?"

Ravenstoke nodded. "The very same."

"You know of him, Grandfather?" asked Duncan.

"Aye, lad, anyone with a taste for the sport has heard of Jumpin' Jack Mull. But it was a good many years ago. I saw him myself once. 'Twas in Edinburgh. He fought Malcolm McGraw, who was much the worse for it. Aye, I lost my guineas that day, and though it was galling to see Scotland's finest take a drubbing, I had to admit I'd never seen a better fighter."

Duncan's eyes grew wide. "Wait until I tell Andrew! Och, perhaps Mull might teach me how to box."

"Duncan," cried Alison, "if you but approached your studies with half as much enthusiasm!"

Duncan looked over at Ravenstoke. "Do you think, my lord, that I might come to Glenfinnan and see Mull?"

The marquess smiled. "You are welcome at Glenfinnan, Duncan." He paused and looked over at the duke. "But it is up to his grace to allow it."

Duncan looked eagerly at his grandfather. The duke hesitated and then replied, "It seems that my debt to you, Ravenstoke, is so great that I must put your ancestry aside. Duncan has my permission to visit you and you are welcome at Dornach Castle. Indeed, you will stay for tea."

Ravenstoke looked over at Alison. "I should like that very much, Duke."

Duncan grinned and happily escorted the marquess to a chair.

11 Two days after Ravenstoke's visit, Alison, her brothers, and her grandfather were seated at breakfast. Between mouthfuls of kipper, Duncan began to once again recount his adventures at Glenfinnan.

"As I live, Duncan!" exclaimed Andrew. "How many times must you tell this tale? I am heartily sick of hearing about Ravenstoke and his noble servant."

Duncan looked crestfallen and Alison and the duke came quickly to his defense. "Where are your manners, Andrew?" cried Alison.

"Aye," said his grace. "You'll not speak to your brother in that way!"

Andrew was unrepentant. "Perhaps you have all forgotten who Ravenstoke is, but I have not. It may be true that his servant saved Duncan, but one deed cannot erase the memory of his damned ancestor. And what of an Englishman taking lands always held by Scottish lairds?" The young man looked indignantly at his grandfather. "I would not have thought the Murray of Dornach would so quickly abandon his Scottish heritage. Thank God there are some true Scots left like Ian MacGillivray!"

Alison gasped and the duke grew livid with rage. "How dare you," he sputtered. "How dare you speak so to me! Get out! Get out!"

Andrew rose from the table, and angrily tossing his

napkin down like a gauntlet, he stormed out of the dining room.

Worried at her grandfather's expression, Alison tried to calm him. "It is only the Murray temper, Grandfather. He'll soon come to his senses."

"Murray temper or no," said his grace, "I have never borne such insolence. What has come over the lad?"

"I fear it is Ian's influence."

"Ian? What has he got to do with it?"

Alison frowned. "He hates Ravenstoke and can speak only ill of him. He has so swayed Andrew that my brother forgets himself."

"Indeed he has," muttered the duke. He rose from the table. "And I have lost my appetite. I am going to my rooms."

His grace's gout seemed to be bothering him and he limped slowly away. Neither Alison nor Duncan spoke until the duke was gone. "How could Andrew have spoken to Grandfather in such an infamous manner?" said Alison.

Duncan, who held his grandfather in awe and esteemed his brother only slightly less, nodded sadly. "It is my fault, Allie. I shouldn't have mentioned Glenfinnan again. I know that Andrew has been ill-tempered ever since he learned that Grandfather had Ravenstoke stay for tea."

"You are in no way responsible, Duncan, for Andrew's display of rudeness. Do not be so glum. Andrew will make things right with Grandfather as soon as his temper cools. Now, go ahead and eat your breakfast."

Duncan looked down at the kipper on his plate. "I am not hungry, Allie."

Alison smiled. "That is certainly uncommon for you, Duncan. Come, then, why don't you and I go for a walk? The weather is quite fine."

Duncan brightened. "Aye, I would like that."

"Good, then fetch your cloak and hat." The boy hurried to do so and Alison returned to her room to put on her well-worn pelisse. The garment was fashioned from fine gray woolen fabric and trimmed with rose-colored velvet. It had once been very fashionable and had long been Alison's favorite. Although it still looked well enough, Alison was aware of its outdated styling. Then, putting on her bonnet of matching rose-colored velvet adorned with gray satin ribbons, Alison went to join her brother.

Once outside in the castle yard, Duncan's spirits were lifted. The sun was shining brightly, and although a bit brisk, the weather was pleasant for walking. "Allie, could we not walk to Glenfinnan? I should like to see Mull. After all, I have never thanked him."

"It is a very long way to Glenfinnan, Duncan, although not far enough to have deterred you. It would take all morning to walk there, and in any case, I do not think we should call on Lord Ravenstoke so soon. No, I thought we might go to the village. It is but an hour's walk. I need some new ribbon and some lace." Duncan did not look overly enthused at this, but Alison continued. "Of course, we might also stop at the confectioner's shop. That is, if you would not mind doing so."

Duncan grinned and they started along the road to the village. After walking about a mile, they espied an approaching carriage. Duncan readily recognized the vehicle, which was pulled by four magnificent black horses. "Allie! It is Lord Ravenstoke! I told you about those horses. Aren't they grand?"

"Aye," replied Alison, taking little note of the horses coming toward them. The knowledge that she might once again see the marquess caused a strange quiver of excitement to pass over her.

The carriage slowed and came to a halt beside them. "Lord Ravenstoke! Good morning, sir," said Duncan eagerly.

The marquess smiled and then opened the carriage door. Alighting from the vehicle, he tipped his hat to Alison. "Good morning, Lady Alison, and to you, Duncan. I see you are taking advantage of the weather."

"Aye, sir," said Duncan. "Indeed, I wanted to call upon you at Glenfinnan, but Allie said it was too far to walk. It is rather far to walk, but not far in a carriage."

"Duncan!" cried Alison, much embarrassed.

Ravenstoke laughed. "I would be honored if you would ride with me back to Glenfinnan."

Duncan looked expectantly at his sister. "Could we, Allie? Lord Ravenstoke has invited us!"

"I fear the poor man has had little choice." She smiled at Ravenstoke. "Really, my lord, I do not think—"

"Do say you'll come. You would do me a great service, Lady Alison. The house is filled with so many curious items and I know a Highland lady such as yourself would be well able to explain them to me."

"I think Mr. Ferguson would be better able to advise you on such things, Lord Ravenstoke. He is so well-versed in Highland history."

"Mr. Ferguson!" cried Duncan. "Truly, my lord, you would not want to have him at Glenfinnan. He is such a dull fellow."

"Duncan!"

Ravenstoke smiled. "And who is this Mr. Ferguson, young man?"

"He is my tutor, sir."

"And a most long-suffering gentleman," added Alison.

"But he is indisposed, Lord Ravenstoke. He suffers from headaches," said Duncan.

Ravenstoke and Alison exchanged an amused glance. "Lady Alison, since Mr. Ferguson is not available, surely you will do me this service and come with me to Glenfinnan."

Alison hesitated before replying. "Oh, very well. We should be very happy to accompany you."

Duncan looked overjoyed and scrambled up into the carriage. Ravenstoke extended his hand to Alison and assisted her into the well-sprung traveling coach. As she took his hand, their eyes met and Alison blushed, confused at the unusual sensation his touch had engendered.

She was grateful when Duncan created a distraction. "What a bang-up carriage, Lord Ravenstoke," he said, running his hand appreciatively along the leather seat. "And bang-up horses, too."

"Thank you, Duncan," said the marquess with a faint smile. "I am gratified that you approve of them."

"I do indeed," said Duncan. "I'll wager this is as fine a carriage as the Prince Regent has."

"Yes," returned Ravenstoke, "I suspect it is."

Duncan was clearly impressed. "Do you know the Prince?"

"We are slightly acquainted."

Alison regarded the marquess with interest. "I imagine you see the Prince often in London."

"Often is something of an exaggeration. I have viewed the royal personage many times, but am scarcely a member of the Carlton House set."

"But you have met the Prince?" asked Alison.

"Yes, indeed. I have had the privilege of speaking to His Royal Highness three times and he has spoken a total of twenty-two words to me."

"Twenty-two words each time, Lord Ravenstoke?"

An ironic smile crossed his lordship's face. "No, Lady Alison, a grand total of twenty-two words. I have committed them to memory. Let me see. 'Ravenstoke, eh? How do? Sad about your father.' That was the first occasion. 'Fine weather, what? Good day.' And finally the most memorable, 'Ravenstoke, is it? Oh, yes. Nicely done cravat, what?'"

Alison burst into laughter and Duncan regarded Ravenstoke strangely. "Then, he is not a good friend of yours, my lord?"

The marquess exchanged a look with Alison and replied with a smile. "I can scarcely claim such a friendship."

"Good," said Duncan gravely. "I am glad of it, for Prince George is not the rightful heir. A Stuart should sit on the throne."

"Mind your tongue, Duncan," said Alison with mock severity. "You will shock Lord Ravenstoke with such treasonous words."

Duncan looked rather alarmed. "You'll not report me to the Prince, will you, sir?"

"I don't know, Master Duncan. After all, I am sorely in need of topics for discussion with His Royal Highness." Ravenstoke then broke into a grin and Duncan appeared relieved.

"You are quizzing me again, aren't you, sir?"

"I am indeed, young Jacobite. But your sister is right. It is best not to speak against royal George, especially to an Englishman."

"Oh, of course, sir. I suppose I had forgotten."

"Forgotten?"

"That you are an Englishman, sir."

Ravenstoke smiled. "I take that as a compliment, Duncan."

Duncan nodded vigorously and the marquess and Alison both laughed as the carriage continued on toward Glenfinnan.

Seeing Glenfinnan from the window of Ravenstoke's carriage, Alison was struck by its beauty and how the manor fit so harmoniously into the landscape. Nestled in a glen between the rugged Highland mountains, the great house seemed perfectly suited to its surroundings. West of the house the river cut its way through the rocky terrain, and in the distance, the waters of Lake Craidoch glistened in the sun.

Ravenstoke was seated across from Alison and he noted the expression on the young woman's face. "The view from this direction is quite grand, isn't it?" he said.

Alison looked over at him. "Aye, there are few lovelier sights than Glenfinnan."

"There are a few lovelier sights, Lady Alison," said the marquess, regarding her with a meaningful glance that quite disconcerted her.

Duncan was unaware of his sister's discomfiture. "It is a nice house, Lord Ravenstoke, but it is rather small when one is used to Dornach Castle. Of course, it would be rather nice to live in a modern house like Glenfinnan, don't you think, Allie?"

This comment brought a smile to Alison, for although the house at Glenfinnan was young in relationship to Dornach Castle's great antiquity, it was more than one hundred years old. "Indeed, medieval castles do have their disadvantages. Yes, Glenfinnan appears to be a much more comfortable house. Do you not find it so, my lord?"

"I find it quite comfortable. In truth, of my houses, I think I like it best."

"And how many houses do you have, sir?" asked Duncan curiously.

"Duncan," said Alison, "you must not ask Lord Ravenstoke such things."

"Oh, I don't mind, Lady Alison. I have five houses altogether."

"Five?" Duncan regarded him in astonishment. "Do you live in all of them, my lord?"

"From time to time," replied his lordship.

"That is a great many houses," said Duncan, clearly impressed. "Are you as rich as Croesus, then, my lord?"

"Duncan!" cried Alison, horrified. "I am sorry, Lord Ravenstoke."

The marquess only smiled the slight smile that was now so characteristic of him. "It is all right. You are an inquisitive fellow, Duncan. No, young man, I do not believe I am as rich as Croesus, for, according to legend, he was very rich indeed. But I am not a poor man."

Taking the marquess's last answer to mean that he was a very wealthy man, Duncan seemed well-satisfied. Worried that her brother might cause her any further embarrassment, Alison was relieved when the carriage arrived at the door of Glenfinnan.

Once inside, Duncan lost no time asking the marquess if he might see Jack Mull. Ravenstoke agreed and sent one of his other servants to fetch him. Mull arrived shortly afterward, joining them in the drawing room. "Mull," said his lordship, "Master Duncan is eager to see you."

"Is he, m'lord?" The servant grinned down at Duncan and his merry smile gave his unfortunate visage an elfin quality. "Good mornin' to you, young sir. I am glad to see you lookin' so well."

"I did not have the opportunity to thank you, Mull," said Duncan, extending his hand to the servant.

Mull glanced over at Alison, grinning again, and then shook the boy's hand. "You are most welcome, Master Duncan."

"And I am so very grateful to you, Mull," said Alison. "From Duncan's account, you are a brave man indeed."

"Of course he is, Allie," exclaimed Duncan. "After all, he is Jumpin' Jack Mull!"

The servant appeared surprised and turned to the marquess. "Your fame has preceded you, Mull," said Ravenstoke.

"Aye!" said Duncan. "My grandfather saw you fight in Edinburgh against Malcolm McGraw."

"Did he, now?" said Mull. "His grace must have a good memory, for that was many years ago."

"Oh, he remembered it well enough, Mull," said Duncan. "He lost too many guineas on that bout to forget it."

Ravenstoke's dark eyebrows arched in amusement. "Beware, Mull. It seems the duke has little cause to remember you fondly."

"Don't worry, Mull," said Duncan, having taken his lordship's remark seriously. "My grandfather does not hold such things against anyone. Why, last year he lost more than that when he bet against Sir Alec Ramsay's horse Merlin in a match race. He still likes Merlin very much and said he was a fine horse."

"I am sure that Mull is much relieved, Duncan," said Alison, smiling at the servant.

Mull grinned. "That I am, m'lady."

Duncan regarded Mull with admiration. "Do you think I could be a boxer?"

"If you wasn't a gentleman, Master Duncan," replied Mull, "it would not surprise me."

"Did you hear that, Allie?" said Duncan. "Mull thinks I could be a boxer!"

"But since you are a gentleman," interjected Alison, "you must leave that sport to others."

Duncan looked disappointed but then brightened. "But even a gentleman must know how to fight." He looked over at the servant. "Would you teach me a few pointers, Mull?"

"I don't know, young sir," said Mull, looking over at the marquess.

Ravenstoke turned toward Alison. "It is up to your sister, Duncan."

"May I, Allie? Oh, do say yes!"

Alison hesitated, but looking into her brother's excited face, she found it impossible to refuse. "Oh, very well. But do be careful, Duncan."

"I shall," said Duncan. A mischievous smile crossed his freckled face. "I promise I shall not hurt Mull."

They all laughed. "Very well, then," said Ravenstoke. "Mull, take Master Duncan outside."

Mull nodded and led an eager Duncan from the room.

Alison watched them go, a faint smile on her face. "He is such a rascal," she said fondly. Turning to Ravenstoke, she found him gazing intently at her. Her eyes met his and a silent communication seemed to pass between them. Alison colored and quickly looked away. "You said, Lord Ravenstoke, that there were certain household things you wished me to explain to you."

"Oh?" said Ravenstoke, looking faintly perplexed. "Oh, yes, of course. There are quite a number of things. This painting, for example." He gestured toward a landscape painting in a heavy gilt frame that was hanging on the wall. "I suspect it portrays an area nearby."

Alison crossed the room and stood in front of the picture. "This is Glen Donwyn. It is on the northern boundary of my grandfather's lands. Glen Donwyn is such a lovely place and the artist has caught its spirit so well."

"I should like to see it," said Lord Ravenstoke. "Perhaps you might show it to me one day."

Alison looked up into his lordship's gray eyes. "Aye, I know you would appreciate the view."

"I should appreciate any view with you in it," said Ravenstoke, surprising himself by the boldness of the remark. He had never been one to make such compliments to ladies, and in the past he had always dismissed such talk as nonsensical flummery. Hoping he had not embarrassed her, the marquess hastened to continue. "I did wish to show you a most curious collection of things. They are in the library."

As Ravenstoke led Alison from the drawing room to the library, she glanced over at him and reflected that she was becoming dangerously fond of the Englishman. She had been sincerely flattered and faintly amused by his last remarks, knowing that such gallantry was uncharacteristic of the staid and sober marquess.

"I do like this room," said Ravenstoke as they entered the library. "It has a certain atmosphere. And from the west windows one can see Loch Craidoch." The marquess was suddenly feeling rather awkward, for he was finding the presence of the lovely Lady Alison strangely disquieting. Looking over at her, he was filled with a tremendous urge to take Alison into his arms and cover her lovely

mouth with his own. Calling upon his self-control, Ravenstoke looked again toward the windows. "Yes, I do enjoy
that view."

Alison walked over to the windows and gazed out.
"Aye, it is lovely. How nice it must be to sit at your desk
and be able to look out at such a view." Alison glanced
over at the desk, which was situated nearby, and found it
cluttered with papers and books. "It appears, my lord,
you spend much time working here."

"Oh, I fear my desk is quite untidy. I have been going
over my plans for improvements at Glenfinnan."

"Improvements, Lord Ravenstoke?"

The marquess nodded and took up one of the books.
"Yes, this book describes some new agricultural methods
that I hope to try here. I feel there are many things that
could be done to improve the land's productivity and
ensure a better living for the tenants." Ravenstoke looked
suddenly apologetic. "I fear I bore you with such things."

"Not at all, my lord. I am very much interested, for we
have a great need to make Dornach lands more productive. And I do think it admirable that you wish to improve
the lot of your tenants. I am sure my grandfather would
want to hear all of your ideas."

"I shall be happy to discuss them with him at any time."
Turning the discussion away from agriculture, the marquess gestured toward an old curio cabinet in the corner of
the room. "This is what I was referring to previously,
Lady Alison. There are some very strange objects inside,
relics of some kind."

"Oh, I remember seeing this when I was a girl." Alison
went over to the cabinet and peered through its glass
doors. "I cannot imagine why the Drummonds did not
take these things with them. They meant so much to Sir
Ronald, but then his sons were not so sentimental."

The marquess opened the doors of the cabinet and
extracted a rusted metal object. "I wonder at the signifi-
cance of this. It appears to be some sort of dagger."

Alison took the object and nodded. "It is the dirk of
Roderick Drummond, who was called Roderick the Iron
Hand. He was quite a hero in the time of Wallace. My
grandfather often told us about him." She handed the

dagger back to the marquess, who regarded it with interest.

"I suspect this weapon was put to good use then." He smiled. "I imagine it found its way into quite a few English hearts."

Alison laughed. "I fear so."

"It is surprising that no ghosts have come to haunt me, taking this house as I did," said Ravenstoke.

"I suspect they know that you mean no harm, despite being English." Alison directed her blue eyes at him and smiled. "Are you certain that you have no Scottish blood, my lord?"

"Not that I know of, but I have never been overly concerned with genealogy. Perhaps if I dug deeply enough, I might find some. I shall endeavor to do so at first opportunity, Lady Alison." He smiled at her and once again had the urge to take her into his arms. Exhibiting admirable restraint, he turned his attention to the curio cabinet. "And what of this?" He took out a tiny porcelain box and opened it. "It seems to be a bit of ribbon and a lock of hair."

"Oh, I cannot imagine that even the most heartless of men would have abandoned this," cried Alison, taking the tiny box and studying the lock of faded blond hair.

"What on earth is it?"

"It is Bonnie Prince Charlie's hair!"

"By God, is it, indeed? You mean this is a lock of the Young Pretender's hair?"

"I should not call him that in the Highlands, my lord," laughed Alison. "Aye, that is what it is. Oh, my grandfather will not believe it is here. He was so envious of the Drummonds for having it. You see, Prince Charles Edward stayed here a night with the Drummonds during the Forty-Five. If only he had stayed at Dornach Castle! But, no, the honor went to Glenfinnan. Prince Charles was most generous in leaving mementos behind him. So many houses in the Highland can boast a handkerchief or lock of his hair."

A slight smile came to Alison's face. "Poor Grandfather. We have not one souvenir of the prince at Dornach Castle. But then the duke's father had no part in the

Forty-Five, having died of fever some months before Charles landed. Grandfather himself was born in 1745 on the very day of the prince's victory at Prestonpans." Alison handed the relic back to the marquess. "How my grandfather will envy you, Lord Ravenstoke."

"I had no idea this was a thing of such importance," replied his lordship gravely. He looked down at the little decorative box and then at Alison. "Would you give it to the duke, Lady Alison? I think it more fitting that he have it than I."

"Oh, that is so good of you, sir, but you must not give such a thing away lightly."

"I do not give it lightly, Lady Alison."

"No," said Alison, looking up at the marquess, "I don't think you do." She accepted the relic from him, and as she did so, her hand met his. She regarded him questioningly.

His lordship's praiseworthy restraint crumbled as he gazed into her blue eyes. "Alison," he said, and leaning toward her, started to place his arms around her.

"There you are, Allie!" An exuberant childish voice startled both Alison and Ravenstoke, who came to his senses and stepped back quickly. "You must see what Mull has taught me." Duncan rushed over to them and got into a fighting stance. "No ruffian will best Duncan Murray."

"I pray you do not forget where you are, Duncan," said Alison a trifle severely. As much as she loved her youngest brother, she felt his interruption most untimely.

"Oh." Duncan looked over at Ravenstoke. "I am sorry, Lord Ravenstoke. I did forget. But Mull was wonderful. Would you like me to show you what he taught me?"

The marquess looked regretfully at Alison, who returned his glance and then placed a restraining hand on Duncan's shoulder. "Perhaps you might show his lordship at some other time. It grows late and we must be getting back home."

Duncan looked disappointed. "I did have a bang-up time, sir."

"I am gratified to hear it."

"And I had a lovely time, Lord Ravenstoke," said Alison, extending her hand to the marquess.

He took it and held it longer than custom dictated. "I hope you will call upon me again soon."

Alison nodded. "And you must come and see us at Dornach Castle. And thank you so much for the gift."

Duncan regarded her questioningly, and when Alison explained what was inside the porcelain box, Duncan could not contain his delight. The marquess called for his carriage, but to Alison's great disappointment, Ravenstoke was prevented from accompanying them by the appearance of a distraught servant who begged he attend a household matter of great importance.

His lordship, therefore, could only escort Alison and her brother to the carriage and watch the well-sprung vehicle start off toward the Dornach lands.

When Glenfinnan and the marquess had vanished from view, Alison sat back on the plush seat and reflected that she was undeniably in love with Ravenstoke. If only Duncan had not appeared, thought Alison, suppressing a sigh.

Unaware of how unwelcome he had been, Duncan talked excitedly about how thrilled the duke would be to accept Ravenstoke's gift. While her brother prattled on about Bonnie Prince Charlie, Alison scarcely listened. All that occupied her mind as the carriage made its way toward Dornach Castle were her feelings for Ravenstoke and the delightful suspicion that the marquess returned them.

12   His grace of Dornach had been so moved by
Ravenstoke's generosity that tears had come
to his eyes when he had taken the lock of Prince Charles
Edward's hair from his granddaughter. Andrew, who had
come to an uneasy peace with his grandfather, seemed less
enthused but examined the relic with great interest none-
theless.

The morning after receiving this exceptional gift, the
duke, with Andrew in tow, set out to call upon Mr.
Ferguson. That hapless scholar was an expert on Jacobite
history and was devoted to the memory of Bonnie Prince
Charlie. His grace had no doubt that Mr. Ferguson would
know of a fitting way to display the relic at the castle and
was eager to discuss the matter with him.

After the duke and Andrew had left, Alison tried to
concentrate on a number of different tasks. She examined
the household accounts, discussed menus with Annie
Thomson, and read through some of her grandfather's
correspondence. As duke and head of the Murrays of
Dornach, his grace received many letters, and when
financial problems had forced the duke's secretary to give
notice, it was Alison who had largely taken on his duties.

Attending to her grandfather's affairs usually interested
Alison, but that morning she was finding it very difficult to
think of anything but the Marquess of Ravenstoke. If only
he would call on them at Dornach Castle, she thought.
She so wanted to see him again.

Finally abandoning the correspondence, Alison retired to the drawing room, where she sat down before her embroidery and began to work. She was soon joined by Duncan, who was in exceptionally high spirits. "Do you think Lord Ravenstoke will call today?" he asked. "I could show him what Mull taught me."

"I think Lord Ravenstoke saw enough of that yesterday, Duncan. And since we just called upon him, he may not return our visit for a time."

"But maybe he will come," said the boy hopefully.

"Perhaps," said Alison, trying to sound disinterested. Changing the subject, she started to ask her brother about his studies. Fortunately for Duncan, this unpleasant discussion was cut short by the arrival of MacPherson, the butler.

"You've a visitor, m'lady."

"A visitor?"

"Aye, Sir Ian MacGillivray."

"Oh," replied Alison glumly. She had hoped that it was Ravenstoke. "Do tell him that I am not receiving anyone, Bob."

The elderly servant nodded, but before he could even turn to leave the room, MacGillivray appeared in the drawing room. "Good morning, Ian," said Duncan, hurrying to greet the big man.

"Sir Ian." Alison eyed him icily. "Are you in the habit of entering homes without leave?"

"Your pardon," he said, casting an ironic look at her.

Bob MacPherson looked questioningly at his mistress and seemed relieved when she motioned him to go.

MacGillivray sat down on the sofa next to Alison, and Duncan hurried to take a seat in the armchair across from him. "Oh, Ian, you will never guess where Allie and I went yesterday."

"Then tell me, lad."

"We went to visit Lord Ravenstoke at Glenfinnan, and his servant Mull taught me how to box. But that was not the best thing that happened. Lord Ravenstoke gave Alison a little box from Glenfinnan and inside . . ." Duncan paused for effect. "Inside was a lock of Prince Charles' hair! The Drummonds left it and Lord Ravenstoke thought Grandfather should have it. Was that not good of him, Ian? Oh, I know you do not like him, but he is a good fellow. Isn't he, Allie?"

Ian MacGillivray listened to the boy and frowned ominously. He turned to Alison. "So, you called upon Ravenstoke?"

Alison tried to appear unconcerned. She added a stitch to her embroidery. "We did."

"And he is not at all what you said he was," said Duncan. "He is not like Bloody Wicklow in the least. And he gave Grandfather the—"

Ian cut him off impatiently. "I've heard enough from you, boy. So he gave the duke a lock of sainted Prince Charlie's hair? And what did that mean to him, an Englishman? Aye, 'tis easy to give away that which means nothing to you. Och, I warrant he is now laughing at you, thinking you daft to think so much of a dead man's hair."

"That is not so," cried Duncan, very much insulted.

"Keep quiet!" shouted MacGillivray, his face growing angry. "I'll suffer no more of your drivel, whelp. Get out with you. Go back to the nursery and leave me in peace."

"How dare you speak to my brother in that infamous way," cried Alison, rising from her seat. "You had better leave now, Sir Ian."

"Aye," said Duncan, jumping up and glaring at his former idol. "You had best go, sir."

MacGillivray looked from Duncan to Alison and then got slowly to his feet. His lumbering form towered over Alison and her brother, and she feared for a moment that he would refuse to depart. "Very well," he said. Then, pointing a finger threateningly at them, he continued, "Alison Murray, I warn you not to get too friendly with the Englishman. If you do, you shall have cause to rue it. And you, Master Duncan, you are no friend of mine, nor are you a true Scot."

"And you are a bully and no gentleman," said Duncan hotly.

MacGillivray clenched his fists and took a step toward Duncan, who, rather than retreat, went into his now-familiar fighting stance.

Alison hurried to place herself between Sir Ian and her brother. "Ian! He is but a boy!"

MacGillivray growled. "Your sister had best protect you, cub. You're in need of a sound thrashing." He looked over at Alison. "And so are you, my girl." Her shocked expression caused Sir Ian to grin unpleasantly. Then without another word, he stalked off.

When he was gone, Duncan frowned. "I used to think he was a good man. I thought he liked me."

Alison put her arm around the boy's shoulders. "I know," she said sympathetically. "It is hard to find that someone is not all we thought him to be. Come, perhaps Mrs. Thomson can find you a bit of cake." The two of them set off for the kitchen, and as angry as she was at MacGillivray, she was also grateful to him for showing his true colors and allowing Duncan to see him as he truly was.

A short time later Alison left her brother with Mrs. Thomson in the kitchen and returned to the drawing room. She had scarcely sat down at her embroidery when Bob MacPherson once again entered the room. "M'lady, Lord Ravenstoke's man is here with a parcel for you."

"Lord Ravenstoke's man? Mull?"

"Aye."

"Bring him in here, then, Bob."

The elderly man nodded and left. A few minutes later he returned, followed by Mull. "Thank you, Bob," said Alison, dismissing the butler, who eyed Mull on his way out and made it clear to his mistress that he did not approve of such persons in the drawing room.

"Good morning, Mull."

"Good morning, m'lady," said Ravenstoke's servant, grinning impishly at her. He extended the parcel he was carrying toward her. "'Tis from his lordship. He wished to call himself, m'lady, but there be many problems at Glenfinnan needin' his lordship's attention. 'Tis a painting. I shall unwrap it if you like."

"That would be good of you, Mull."

The servant took off the brown paper that covered the painting to reveal the landscape of Glen Donwyn she had seen at Glenfinnan. "His lordship said you liked it very much and he wanted you to have it."

"That is extremely kind of him, but he should not have done it," said Alison. "Do thank him for me and tell him that the duke was so very pleased with his other gift."

"I shall, m'lady." Mull bowed slightly and, thinking himself dismissed, started for the door.

"Mull?"

"Aye, m'lady?"

"I did not thank you for your efforts with my brother."

"Master Duncan?" Mull grinned. "He is a fine young gentleman, and a quick one. I enjoyed workin' with him." The servant scratched his head thoughtfully. "Helpin' that young pup put me in mind of another time I helped a young gentleman what needed to learn a few pointers. He wasn't much older than Master Duncan at the time." Mull grinned again. "That young gentleman was his lordship."

"Lord Ravenstoke?" Alison regarded the servant in some surprise.

"Aye," replied Mull. "That was how I first met his lordship. It was some fifteen years ago, m'lady. I was in my prime then and winnin' all my bouts. In Windsor it was, and I shall never forget it. I had won two fights and was little the worse for them. Quite cocky I was, too, in those days, m'lady.

"Well, I was roamin' about the town the day after the bouts, havin' a bit of time before we was to leave for London, when a young gentleman comes up to me. He was about twelve years old but looked younger. Small and scrawny he was, but with a serious look on his face like all the problems of the world was upon him. He asked if I was Jack Mull, and of course, I thought he ought to know very well that I was. I asked him his name and he said it was Sheffield.

"He asked me if I might be interested in a business propositon. Indeed, that is how he put it, speakin' in a most solemn sort of way. He said he would pay me if I would teach a few things that would help him fight off certain bully boys at the school. Eton it was, of course.

"I was not particularly interested, bein' set with blunt after the two bouts and not wishin' to waste my time on some grim-lookin' little gentleman, but I could not resist askin' him what he intended to pay me. 'A guinea,' he says, and I could hardly refuse that. So, m'lady, I says I would show him a thing or two, and we went off to find a place to get to business." Mull paused and smiled. "I'd never seen a more determined young fellow, m'lady. Oh, he knew nothin' about fightin' and I had my work cut out for me.

"I earned my money that day. When we were done, he had learned enough to defend himself. He gave me the money and then he smiled for the first time. I figured he wasn't much used to smilin' by the way he done it. But he run off, happy as a lark, and of course, I never thought I'd see him again."

Alison was listening intently to this story and regarded Mull expectantly. "And then what happened?"

"Well, a fortnight later I got a note signed Sheffield. He was Lord Sheffield then and his father was Lord Ravenstoke. Anyway, I was very surprised to get a letter from the likes of him. He said that he would always be grateful to me and that I did him a great service. I kept that note. In fact, I have it to this day, and glad I am that I saved it.

"Well, then, m'lady, many years passed. I was slowin' down and the other lads was gettin' younger every day. I started to take some beatings, bad ones as you can see by this face of mine. I went from town to town tryin' to earn enough with my fists to make a livin', but I was almost never winnin' anymore. I kept at it, for boxin' was all I knew.

"Then, finally, it was hard to get any bouts at all. I went to London and had to beg to get my last bout. There was a big crowd there. I remember thinkin' it was like old times, and I knew I would make good again." Mull cast a rueful smile at Alison. "The Irish lad I was fightin' nearly killed me. I don't remember much about it, except how he kept at me, with fists like sledgehammers. I woke up two days later in a strange bed in a big room. I had no idea where I was.

"A gentleman came into the room. I couldn't see him very well, for my eyes was still so swollen. 'You don't remember me, do you, Jack Mull?' he says. 'No, sir,' I says, and he askes me if I remembered a boy named Sheffield. Well, m'lady, I knew then who he was and told him so. His lordship seemed glad to see I remembered him. He said he wanted to help me, for he still owed me a debt. I reminded him he paid me a guinea, and his lordship laughed and said that was hardly payment enough. He said bein' able to fight some bullies at school had made his life tolerable.

"And so I stayed there until I got better. Then his lordship asked me if I wanted to work for him. I had never been in service, m'lady, and didn't know if it was the life for me, but havin' little choice, I agreed. That was nearly four years ago and I have not regretted it for a moment."

"You are fond of Lord Ravenstoke, aren't you, Mull?"

"Fond of his lordship? Well, m'lady, I can say this: if he asked me to, I'd go back into the ring with that same Irish lad tomorrow." The now-familiar elfin grin crossed Mull's unsightly countenance. "Of course, knowin' that his lordship is a sensible man, I'm sure he'd never ask me to do any such thing."

Alison laughed. "Lord Ravenstoke is lucky to have you, Mull. And that is a wonderful story. Now, I shan't keep you any longer. Give my thanks to his lordship for the painting."

"I shall, m'lady." Mull turned to go.

"And Mull?"

"M'lady?"

"Thank you for telling me about how you met Lord Ravenstoke."

Mull nodded and, smiling once more, turned and left her.

Alison looked at the picture of Glen Donwyn and then sat down on the sofa and thought about what Mull had just told her. She tried to imagine the marquess as a boy at Eton, being bullied by some of the other students, but she found it terribly difficult. So he had need of fisticuffs to survive his school days? Thinking of Duncan and his fighting poses, Alison smiled and returned to her embroidery.

13   That afternoon Alison resigned herself to working on the ducal correspondence. She sat at a heavy carved oak desk in the library and penned a response to one of her grandfather's numerous letters. After a time, she put her quill pen down, and looking at the newly hung painting of Glen Donwyn, Alison sighed.

It was so hard to concentrate. The castle seemed unusually quiet, for the duke and Andrew had not yet returned from visiting Mr. Ferguson. Alison suspected that they had stopped off at the village pub to boast of Castle Dornach's new relic. Alison picked up another letter, but after a brief study of its contents, put it down. Deciding that it was impossible to get any more work done, she rose from the desk and left the library.

Alison walked through the cavernous hallways of Dornach Castle and, finding no one else about, wondered if the place were completely deserted. The thought of being alone in the castle was suddenly disquieting, and Alison made her way to the servants' hall in search of company. As she neared the kitchen, she heard the sound of Duncan's laughter.

Entering the kitchen, Alison found a pleasant domestic scene. The fire burned brightly in the hearth while the servants Jean and Isabella busily kneaded bread dough. Duncan sat at the kitchen table beside the cook, Annie Thomson, who was telling him a story as she finished mixing a batch of shortbread.

Duncan looked up and grinned. "Allie! You have come just in time to hear how the knight broke the witch's spell and saved the princess!"

"Indeed? I should like to hear it."

"Och, m'lady," said Annie with a grin, "ye hae heard the tale sae many times ever since ye were a wee bairn."

"Aye, Annie, but I never tire of it."

"Then do go on, Annie," said Duncan, but before the cook could oblige him, a loud masculine voice interrupted them.

"What hae ye tae feed a hungry man?"

The women and Duncan looked over to see Archie Fisher enter the kitchen. The shepherd looked disheveled, and Alison eyed him with disfavor, wondering whether the redness of his nose was due to the coldness of the weather or some recent imbibing. He was followed by the faithful dog, Mags, and the little animal hurried over to Alison, greeting her with a happy bark and furiously wagging tail.

Alison reached down to stroke the dog's head. "I am always glad to see you, Mags, but your master is a very different matter."

Fisher seemed to see Alison for the first time. "Your ladyship! I did nae expect tae find ye here." He looked over at Duncan and grinned. "Nor ye, Master Duncan."

"And I did not expect to see you here, Archie Fisher," said Alison severely. "Why are you not out with the sheep?"

"Och, m'lady, I been wi' them most o' the week and watchin' them like a mither. But I wanted tae tell ye the news!"

"And how do you have news, Archie," said Duncan with a wry grin, "if you have been with the sheep all the time? Or is it the sheep that told you?"

The shepherd laughed and wagged a bony finger at the boy. "The sheep tell me many things, lad, but this I heard frae young Randolph Cowan frae o'er Glenfinnan way."

"Och, Archie Fisher," said Annie Thomson impatiently, "will ye tell the news or won't ye?"

"Very well, old woman. 'Tis that Agnes Gunn hae given birth tae a bonnie wee laddie."

"That is good news," said Alison.

"Aye," returned Fisher, "and Agnes is fine. 'Tis hard tae picture the lass wi' a bairn o' her own."

Annie Thomson nodded. "I remember the day she came tae work here at the castle. She was a scrawny wee thing and sae shy she would nae speak a word tae anyone."

"Well," said Fisher, "ye can no say that o' her now. She's like the rest of ye women, cacklin' like hens all the day long."

Annie raised a wooden spoon threateningly at the man. "Who are ye tae talk, Archie Fisher? No one gabbles like ye in all the Highlands! Now ye hae told your news, get oot wi' ye!"

The shepherd grinned at Annie and then turned to Alison. "Hae pity on a hungry man, m'lady. I've nae eaten all day. Can I be blamed for wishin' a bit o' bread frae the best cook in the county?"

Annie appeared somewhat placated by this remark, and in spite of herself, Alison smiled. "Oh, very well, Archie. Jean, bring some bread and meat for Archie and then he will be on his way."

"And a nice bone for Mags, too," said Duncan, who was scratching the sheep dog behind the ears.

Fisher thanked Alison effusively and then, after the food was brought to him, began to eat noisily. Alison then turned to Annie Thomson. "I think I shall go and visit Agnes. Would you prepare a basket of food for her?"

"Aye, m'lady."

"Good. Then I shall leave you." Alison left the kitchen and proceeded to her rooms. She thought about Agnes Gunn and smiled, happy at the news that her former servant was well and delivered of a healthy child. Agnes had always been one of her favorites, and Alison remembered how she had missed her after she left the duke's employ and married John Gunn, a farmer who was a Glenfinnan tenant.

Entering her dressing room, Alison opened the doors of the massive wardrobe and took out her green riding habit. She dressed quickly and then paused briefly in front of the mirror. Thank goodness, she reflected, that the sea-green velvet wore so well. Indeed, the garment, although several seasons old, was very attractive and hugged her admirable figure to perfection.

Alison put on her hat and wondered what she might bring to Agnes as a gift for the new baby. She left her rooms and walked down the long corridor to the nursery. It had been some time since she had been inside this now-abandoned room, and entering it once again, she was filled with nostalgia. There were all of Duncan's toys along with some of her own. Alison noted the toy soliders, dolls, and Duncan's prize hobbyhorse, all of them standing a lonely vigil in the dimly lit room.

"Why, poor Jemima," she said aloud, picking up a raven-haired doll. "You have been sorely neglected." The doll's porcelain face seemed to regard her reproachfully and Alison laughed. "How dull it must be for you, but you do have company."

She set the doll down and went over to a chest of drawers in which most of Duncan's baby things had been stored. Alison found a tiny blanket and a cap and booties, and remembered that she had knitted them herself for Duncan when she had been but a girl of ten and her brother a new baby.

These should do nicely for Agnes, thought Alison, folding the baby things neatly and thinking again about her former servant. It was strange to reflect that Agnes was now a married woman with her own child. Indeed, she and Agnes had been born in the same year, although Alison had always thought herself much older and wiser than her maid.

Alison sighed and hoped that Agnes was happy. She had heard that John Gunn was a dour man, but a good one at heart, and certainly life as a farmer's wife was preferable to a lifetime in service at Dornach Castle. Alison remembered the afternoon Agnes told her she would marry John Gunn. The maid had been so happy and excited at the prospect that Alison had been thrilled for her.

Alison looked thoughtfully down at the baby things in her hand. It was funny that she had never thought that much about getting married, although it had always been understood that she would do so. She had had numerous suitors since coming out in society at seventeen, but the idea of marrying any of them had not appealed to her. Indeed, foremost among her suitors was Sir Ian MacGillivray, and the idea of being wed to him was utterly repellent.

She thought of Ravenstoke and a slight smile crossed her face. The idea of being married to the English lord was far from repellent. In truth, she had never before had such an appealing notion than that of sharing her life with Ravenstoke. She conjured up the picture of the two of them alone at Glenfinnan and envisioned the marquess taking her into his arms and kissing her passionately. How she would love to be in his arms and in his bed. Alison blushed deeply and chided herself for such unseemly thoughts.

"Allie! Here you are!" Duncan stood at the door to the nursery and Alison started at the unexpected interruption.

"Oh, Duncan, you startled me. I have found a few things to take to Agnes. You have no further use for them."

"Good," said Duncan, looking about the room. "Och, there are my soldiers. I have not played with them for ages."

"Then you may reacquaint yourself with them. I shall go and visit Agnes."

"Could I not go with you?"

"Not today. The baby is so very young. But later I shall take you."

Duncan seemed satisfied and entered the nursery and picked up his soldiers. "Annie has the basket ready for you in the main hall."

Alison nodded and left her brother. She found Annie Thomson waiting for her, and taking up the basket of food, she headed for the stables. Claymore snorted with anticipation as she approached and Alison patted his sleek neck. A groom quickly saddled the stallion, and moments later, Alison was on her way to the Gunn farm.

She was too lost in her own thoughts to appreciate the scenery or the unseasonably warm weather and bright sunshine. When she came to the border of her grandfather's lands, Alison noted how far she had come with some surprise. It was not much farther to the home of John and Agnes Gunn, and a short time later, she espied the crofter's cottage where she knew Agnes resided. It was a picturesque little house, neat and trim with stone walls and thatched roof, and the sheds and fences nearby were well kept up, testifying to John Gunn's industry.

A few shaggy Highland cattle grazed nearby and they lifted their heads as Alison and Claymore came near. A spotted dog barked in warning at them and a man came out of the cottage and watched Alison's approach.

"Good day to you, John Gunn," said Alison with a bright smile. She had only spoken to him once before, on the day of his wedding, but she had seen him in the village many other times. He was a big man with sandy-colored hair and light freckled complexion.

"Lady Alison Murray." Gunn took off his cap respectfully. " 'Tis an honor, m'lady."

"I have come to wish you and Agnes well and to see the baby."

Gunn nodded. "Agnes will be sae verra glad tae see ye." He held Claymore's head as Alison dismounted and then took the basket from her. "Go on in, m'lady. I'll see tae the horse."

After tapping lightly on the door of the cottage, Alison opened the door and entered. "Agnes?"

"Is that ye, Lady Alison?" Agnes Gunn's voice came from the back room of the cottage, and Alison proceeded from the tiny main room to the bedroom where Agnes lay.

"Hello, Agnes."

"M'lady, how good it is o' ye tae come."

Alison smiled warmly and reflected that her former servant looked very well. Motherhood seemed to agree with Agnes Gunn. Her round face radiated happiness and her brown eyes sparkled.

"How well you look, Agnes," said Alison.

"Och, m'lady, I doubt that." She pushed a strand of black hair from her forehead and into the tidy cap she was wearing. "But ye look like a fairy princess, as usual."

Alison laughed. "How I miss you, Agnes. And there is the wee bairn!" A tiny creature lay sleeping soundly in a cradle next to the bed.

"Aye, m'lady."

"He is a beautiful little boy. What did you name him?"

Agnes beamed. "Charles. That is John's father's name."

Alison smiled down at the baby. "I expect that your father is very proud of you, young Charlie."

"Aye, that I am, m'lady." John Gunn appeared at the bedroom door. He handed the basket back to Alison.

"I have brought you a few things, Agnes."

Her former servant seemed quite thrilled with the baby gifts and the food from Dornach Castle, and she and her husband thanked Alison heartily. John Gunn brought a chair in so that Alison might sit down beside Agnes and then he left the two women to chat. Agnes was much interested in how all the Murrays were doing. She had always been especially fond of Duncan and laughed as Alison related his struggles with the hapless Mr. Ferguson. She then inquired after all the servants and Alison talked for some time, informing Agnes of how each one was faring.

After concluding her report on the servants, Alison suspected it was time to be going. She did not want to overtire the new mother and started to take her leave. "Oh, could ye nae stay a while longer, your ladyship? I've had no time tae tell ye—that is, tae ask ye—"

"What is it, Agnes?"

Agnes looked suddenly serious. "'Tis about the new laird o' Glenfinnan. They say ye hae visited him, ye and Master Duncan."

"Indeed I have, and I think he is a very pleasant gentleman."

"Is he, m'lady?"

"Why, yes. Och, I know it is hard having an Englishman come in and take Glenfinnan. And perhaps Lord Ravenstoke appears to be a cold man, but I do believe he has the interests of his tenants at heart. If everyone would but give him a chance, I think they would find him a fair man, and a good one."

Agnes regarded her former mistress thoughtfully. "Do ye think, m'lady, that ye could tell that tae John? He is sae unhappy wi' having an English laird, and since he heard o' his lordship being grandson tae Bloody Wicklow, he can't speak o' little else."

Before Alison could reply, John Gunn appeared once again at the door. "Och, John," said Agnes, "her ladyship says she thinks Lord Ravenstoke a good man."

Gunn frowned and troubled lines appeared on his forehead. "Meaning no disrespect, m'lady, but I dinnae know if ye would be a good judge o' that."

"John!"

"Nay, woman, her ladyship knows verra well I mean no offense tae her."

Alison nodded. "But why are you so unhappy with Lord Ravenstoke? What has he done?"

"Nothing tae me, m'lady."

"Truly, John Gunn, it seems to me you must not allow prejudice to cloud your judgment. You can not hold his lordship responsible for things his grandfather did."

"Aye," said Agnes, "her ladyship is right."

John Gunn regarded his wife sullenly, and Alison felt it best to say nothing further. She rose to take her leave. "I really must be going. It was so good to see you and I shall call again in a few days."

Agnes thanked her for calling and then Gunn escorted Alison out. He said nothing to her as he opened the door of the cottage and she suspected that he was irritated with her for speaking well of Ravenstoke. Once outside, Gunn started off to fetch Claymore, but the sound of an approaching horseman made him stop and look out across the moor. Alison followed his gaze and immediately recognized the tall form of Ravenstoke. "Why, it is Lord Ravenstoke."

John Gunn frowned, thinking it a most unhappy coincidence that the object of their discussion some moments earlier would now appear. He had not yet met his new landlord and did not seem at all pleased with the prospect.

The marquess was surprised to see Alison Murray standing there in front of the modest crofter's cottage. Noting that John Gunn was eyeing his approach with a grim expression, Ravenstoke masked his delight at seeing Alison and adopted a reserved, disinterested expression. Pulling his horse up in front of Alison and Gunn, the marquess tipped his hat. "Lady Alison, this is an unexpected pleasure."

"Indeed, Lord Ravenstoke, I am surprised to see you." Their eyes met for a brief moment and Alison was temporarily disconcerted. She found it necessary to make some explanation for her presence there. "I was visiting Mr. Gunn's wife, Agnes. She once was employed at Dornach Castle and she has just had a baby boy."

Ravenstoke looked from Alison to John Gunn. "Gunn?"

The man nodded and, with seeming reluctance, pulled his cap from his head. "Your lordship."

"My congratulations, Gunn, and to your wife. I hope she and your new son are well."

"They are, m'lord."

Alison looked over at John Gunn and then back at the marquess. She wished that Ravenstoke did not appear so cool and formidable, and knew that his manner was too aloof to endear him to a Highlander like John Gunn. "Perhaps you would like to meet Agnes, Lord Ravenstoke," said Alison, regarding the marquess hopefully.

Ravenstoke looked into her blue eyes for a moment and then turned to Gunn. "I should like that, Gunn. If your wife is able to receive me, of course."

John Gunn had not expected this response and was caught off guard. "Aye, m'lord. If ye would allow me tae tell Agnes ye are coming first." He hurried off, and Ravenstoke dismounted.

"I am glad you agreed to see Agnes, Lord Ravenstoke. You will find the baby quite adorable."

A faint smile came to the marquess's face. "I do not generally find infants adorable, Lady Alison, but shall make an attempt for your sake."

Alison smiled up at him. "I must take this opportunity to thank you for the painting. I do love it. And, my lord, my grandfather has not yet got over the thrill of receiving your gift of Prince Charlie's hair. If you had but seen his face when I gave it to him!"

"I am glad he liked it," replied Ravenstoke. Alison Murray's presence was once again exerting a most unsettling influence upon him, and the marquess found himself thinking how well the riding habit she was wearing revealed her admirably curved figure.

"My wife would be sae verra honored if your lordship would come in."

"What?" Ravenstoke looked at Gunn with a slightly puzzled look. "Oh, yes. Would you accompany me, Lady Alison?"

Alison smiled and, taking his lordship's arm, went back into the little cottage. Agnes was sitting up in bed, her cap straightened and the baby in her arms. "Your lordship, this is my wife." Gunn made the introduction and then regarded the marquess warily.

"How do you do, Mrs. Gunn?" said the marquess, nodding to Agnes. "My congratulations to you. That is a fine son you have there. He looks to be a strong young fellow."

"That he is, m'lord," said Agnes proudly. "Would your lordship and Lady Alison like tae sit down?"

Alison expected Ravenstoke to decline this offer, but he nodded. "I should like that very much, Mrs. Gunn."

John Gunn hurried to fetch another chair and Alison and the marquess sat down.

"Do you think I might hold the baby, Agnes?" said Alison. Agnes seemed delighted and Alison took up the baby and cradled him in her arms. "He is a darling, is he not, my lord?"

"Indeed," said the marquess, looking at Alison and thinking what a charming picture she presented sitting there with the baby in her arms.

John Gunn was a perceptive man and he did not fail to note the way Ravenstoke was looking at Lady Alison Murray. He frowned.

Alison continued to gaze down at the baby. "He is a sweet wee thing, Agnes. Dear wee Charlie."

"Charlie," repeated the marquess, glancing over at Agnes. "So that is the baby's name?"

"Aye," interjected John Gunn. "Charles Edward."

Ravenstoke looked over at Alison, who feared she would burst into laughter at his lordship's quizzical expression. "An admirable name," commented Ravenstoke, turning to Gunn. He then abruptly changed the subject.

"I did have a purpose in coming here today, Gunn. I am eager to meet all my tenants, but I am especially glad to make your acquaintance. By all accounts you are a good farmer and a hardworking man. I value such men highly."

Agnes smiled proudly at her husband, who regarded the marquess doubtfully. Ravenstoke continued. "I am very much interested in making the small farms of Glenfinnan more productive. I have given the matter considerable thought and believe I have some ideas that will improve productivity. I would like your cooperation in putting some of these ideas to work."

Gunn's doubtful look turned into one of suspicion. "And what ideas might your lordship be thinking of?" he said.

"My plan involves converting a substantial portion of crop land to sheep. Your land would do admirably for this purpose."

Alison noted that John Gunn's reaction to Ravenstoke's idea was decidedly unenthusiastic. The man frowned. "I am nae a sheep man, m'lord."

"Of course not, but you can become one. I have some fine stock being brought up from Edinburgh. I shall give you half and the rest to your neighbor, Scott."

"Does your lordship mean tae order me tae abandon my crops, then?"

The question took Ravenstoke by surprise. He had thought Gunn would be eager to accept his idea. "Of course, I shall not force you to do so, Gunn."

"No, certainly not," said Alison, hurriedly entering the conversation. From Gunn's expression she feared he might say something he would later regret. "But really, John, I cannot understand why you do not like his lordship's idea. Sheep are well-suited to this land. I am sure you know of our Dornach sheep. The duke himself is very enthused about them." Alison glanced over at Ravenstoke and smiled. "Indeed, I, too, have taken a certain interest in them, and my grandfather's herd is doing quite nicely." She rocked the baby gently. "Aye, John Gunn, you must think of your wee son and Agnes and be willing to try something new."

Although still skeptical, Gunn appeared a little more

receptive to the idea. "Then his grace is going tae raise more sheep?"

Alison nodded.

John Gunn looked over at his wife, who looked encouragingly at him. "Verra well, m'lord. I will try it."

"Good. When the stock arrives I shall contact you. And now I do think I must be going."

"And I must go, too," said Alison, rising from the chair, and depositing the baby back into his mother's arms, she bade farewell to Agnes. Alison and the marquess then left the cottage, and once outside, John Gunn wordlessly brought them their horses.

Ravenstoke lifted Alison up into Claymore's sidesaddle and then mounted his own horse, a handsome bay gelding. "May I ride with you, Lady Alison? I am heading in your direction. There is another tenant I must see."

"Certainly, my lord." The two of them set off in the direction of Dornach lands and Alison was aware that John Gunn was watching them closely.

"I am obliged to you, ma'am, for your assistance," said Ravenstoke. "Indeed, the man Gunn was quite hostile to the idea of raising sheep here. I was told he is an intelligent man. It seems he is not one to attempt anything new."

Claymore pulled at the bit, unhappy at the decorous pace, and Alison firmly checked him. "Change does not come easily here, sir, but I suspect John Gunn is worried that you will force him and the other small crofters off your land."

The marquess regarded her in surprise. "Why would he think that?"

"Perhaps you have not heard that some landowners are doing so, and not so very far from here. The Duke of Sutherland has driven many of his tenants off his lands. He has ordered their cottages burned and has forced them into rude huts by the sea where they are expected to become fishermen." Alison smiled ruefully. "Highlanders who have for generations been farmers are now expected to completely alter their way of life. It is barbarously cruel." Alison looked over at the marquess. "And it was done because Sutherland thought sheep would be more profitable. He wanted to make room for them."

"Good God," said his lordship. "No wonder the man looked at me so! What a great idiot I am. But I assure you, Lady Alison, it is not my intention to displace any of these people."

"I know, my lord," said Alison, smiling over at him. "You would never be so unfeeling as that. And in time, your tenants will realize it. I know they will come to know and appreciate you." The look Ravenstoke now directed at her caused Alison to color, and she looked down and patted her horse. "I was so very glad to see Agnes looking so well. I am very fond of her. And the baby was so sweet."

"Charles Edward?" Both the marquess and Alison laughed and Ravenstoke shook his head. "It seems I am constantly reminded of royal Charlie. I am certain His Late Royal Highness would be much gratified by his namesake."

Alison nodded. "Indeed he would, although Agnes told me the baby was named for John Gunn's father."

Ravenstoke laughed again. "And not the Pretender?"

"Probably for them both." Alison smiled at the marquess and they continued on. After what seemed to both of them a very short time, they reached the edge of the Glenfinnan property. They stopped to make their farewells. Alison then started off toward Dornach Castle, and looking back, she found Ravenstoke watching her. She waved and he returned the gesture. Alison smiled and, filled with thoughts of Ravenstoke, continued on.

14   The following morning Alison sat in her sitting room, reading a book. Although the novel, entitled *The Pirate Prince,* was a most exciting tale, Alison was finding it very difficult to concentrate on the story. Finding her mind wandering, she sighed and then closed the book.

"Allie, are you busy?"

Turning toward the door, Alison saw her brother Duncan.

"Not really, Duncan. What is it?"

"Mr. Ferguson would like a word with you."

"Och, Duncan, you have not vexed Mr. Ferguson again, have you?"

Duncan looked a bit sheepish. "I fancy I have, but, indeed, Allie, I am trying to be better. It is only that everything is so dashed dull."

"Dull or no, Duncan Murray, you must try harder. Very well, I shall speak to Mr. Ferguson and I do hope he does not intend to give up entirely on you."

"He is in the drawing room."

"Then I shall go down to him. You had best wait in your room, young man."

Duncan nodded and discreetly withdrew. Alison shook her head and wondered what she was going to do with the boy. He was, indeed, the most reluctant of scholars, detesting books and schoolwork. Like all the Murrays,

Duncan loved action and was happiest on horseback or running about with lads his own age. Sitting inside with a book was agony to him, especially on a spring day. A slight smile came to Alison's face, for she realized that she was not so unlike her brother. She did enjoy reading, but what she loved most of all was being out of doors.

Rising from her chair, Alison went over to the mirror to check her appearance. She was wearing a simple frock of heather-colored muslin and she noted with approval the garment's modestly high neck and long sleeves. Even the puritanical Mr. Ferguson could not fault such a dress, she decided. Alison glanced quickly at her hair, and after patting one wayward curl into place, went off to see him.

She found her brother's tutor standing inside the drawing room. He was looking into the carved oak case that displayed the newly acquired relic of Bonnie Prince Charlie's hair. Alison could not help but smile at Mr. Ferguson's far away look, knowing that he was doubtlessly thinking of those glorious days when the royal Stuart raised a Highland army and marched to England.

A slight balding man of middle years, Mr. Ferguson was a stern and seemingly humorless bachelor. His clear blue eyes were framed with spectacles that gave him an owlish appearance, and he had a habit of staring at a person with such intensity that Alison sometimes found him rather daunting.

"Mr. Ferguson?"

"Lady Alison Murray. Good morning tae ye, ma'am."

"Good morning, sir. Duncan has told me you wish to speak to me."

"Aye, I do." Mr. Ferguson nodded gravely.

"Do sit down, Mr. Ferguson."

The man nodded, and then, after waiting for Alison to sit down, he flipped up the tails of his old-fashioned coat and lowered his lean frame into an armchair. "I expect ye know what I am about tae say."

Alison nodded wearily. "Duncan has been doing poorly."

"Och, that he has." Ferguson shook his head. "I hae said before that I hae never seen a boy wi' less aptitude. He is never accurate in doing his sums, and his writing is most times illegible. His French is verra poor and his Latin disgraceful. The lad hae no interest in geography and can no tell Paris frae Constantinople. I fear I can do little wi' the lad, and 'tis not right tae take your money and produce sae little result."

"Och, I know it must be so very trying for you, sir, but do you not see any improvement at all?"

Ferguson shrugged. "Perhaps a wee bit."

"Then could you stay on for even a few more days. Mr. Ferguson? Unlikely as it may seem, perhaps Duncan would do better. I know the duke would be most grateful to you if you did not leave us."

"Verra well, Lady Alison. Like Robert Bruce's spider, I shall try again. I must say that of late Master Duncan hae shown great interest in learning about Prince Charles Edward."

"That is a good sign, is it not? And no one knows more about the prince than you do, Mr. Ferguson."

Pleased at the compliment, Ferguson modestly brushed it aside. "I do know a wee bit."

"A wee bit? Why, sir, the duke has often said there is not a man in the Highlands who knows more about history than Mr. Ferguson."

"His grace said that?"

"Aye, sir."

"His grace flatters me," said Ferguson, obviously well pleased, for as Alison knew very well, the man held the duke in the highest esteem.

At the moment Bob MacPherson appeared inside the drawing room to announce a caller. "Lord Ravenstoke is here, m'lady."

"Lord Ravenstoke?" Alison tried hard to appear indifferent. "Do show him in." She turned to Ferguson as the servant retreated. "I do not believe you have met Lord Ravenstoke."

"I nae hae met him," said Ferguson, his cool tone expressing clearly that he had no desire to alter the situation.

Ravenstoke appeared at the door. He smiled at Alison and looked questioningly at Ferguson, who rose stiffly to his feet as the marquess entered.

"Good morning, Lord Ravenstoke. Do come in. You

have not met this gentleman. May I present Mr. Ferguson? Mr. Ferguson this is Lord Ravenstoke."

The Scotsman took Ravenstoke's outstretched hand with seeming reluctance and eyed the marquess warily. Ravenstoke did not fail to note this and directed slightly raised eyebrows toward Alison.

"I have told the marquess about you, Mr. Ferguson," said Alison.

"That she has," said Ravenstoke. "Lady Alison has proclaimed you to be the best authority on Highland history. Indeed, I am glad to meet you, sir, and hope that you will call upon me at Glenfinnan. There are so many things I wish to learn from you."

Ferguson had not expected to be so complimented by this English lord and could not help being flattered. He had heard all about Ravenstoke and, being a fervent Jacobite, was prepared to dislike him. After all, an Englishman, especially the grandson of Bloody Wicklow, had no business in the Highlands. Still, Mr. Ferguson was a man very much impressed by the nobility and having been so civilly addressed by the marquess, he decided to withhold his judgment.

"Your lordship has an interest in Highland history?"

"I do, Mr. Ferguson. You cannot imagine how pleased I was to learn that Prince Charles Edward was at Glenfinnan." Seeming to anticipate the Scotsman's thoughts, Ravenstoke continued. "You must think it very odd that I should think so, being as I am the grandson of the Baron Wicklow, so despised in this area. But I have great admiration for the prince's conduct in the Forty-Five. Indeed, I must admit I knew little of the subject before coming here, but I found an excellent book in the library at Glenfinnan. It was written by a Mr. Montgomery and a dashed fine account it was."

"Does your lordship mean *Heroic Days of the Forty-Five?*"

"That is the title, Mr. Ferguson."

Ferguson seemed to stand taller. "The author of that book is my grandfather, Alexander Montgomery."

"Indeed, Mr. Ferguson?" Alison was quite interested. "I did not know that you had a grandfather who was a distinguished author. I, too, have read this book. Why have you not let it be known that Mr. Montgomery is your grandfather?"

"Och, no one wants tae hear o' the deeds o' a man's grandfather."

"If only no one wished to hear of the misdeeds of one's grandfather," commented Ravenstoke.

This remark brought a rare smile to the face of Mr. Ferguson, and Alison knew that the marquess had won him over. "Gentlemen, do sit down, both of you."

Ravenstoke sat down on the sofa beside Alison and looked across at Ferguson. "I expect you are very familiar with all the historical locations in the area."

"Aye, my lord. 'Tis an interest o' mine."

"Mr. Ferguson is our local expert," said Alison. "I don't think anyone knows more about the history of Daingneach Dubh than he."

"Daingneach Dubh?" repeated his lordship.

"Aye," said Ferguson. "It means Black Fortress in Gaelic. It is in ruins now, but was the home o' the Murrays before Dornach Castle."

"And it is so lovely," said Alison. "It overlooks the sea. There is something about the place . . . But one has to see it for oneself."

"I would very much like to do that. Is it far?" said the marquess.

"More than an hour's ride," replied Alison.

"Can one get there by carriage?"

Alison regarded Ravenstoke curiously. "Aye."

"Then why don't we go? I have my carriage. Mr. Ferguson, you could explain the history."

The suggestion took Mr. Ferguson by surprise, but Alison could tell the idea appealed to him. It certainly appealed to her, for she could think of nothing she would rather do than accompany Ravenstoke to Daingneach Dubh. "I dinnae know, my lord. Master Duncan is nae done wi' his lessons."

"Could not Duncan come with us?" said the marquess. "Surely he could learn much by doing so."

"What a splendid idea, Lord Ravenstoke," said Alison. "Do say you will come, Mr. Ferguson."

The Scotsman looked thoughtful for a moment and then

nodded. "It would be good for the lad tae hear about the early home o' his ancestors. Verra well. I shall be most happy tae come."

"Good," said Alison. "Then why don't you go and inform Duncan, Mr. Ferguson? He is in his room."

Ferguson nodded. "Aye, I shall fetch the lad."

"Then we will leave as soon as possible," said Ravenstoke, realizing that he was very much enthused about the outing. He usually did not care for sight-seeing, but the idea of visiting a ruined castle with Lady Alison Murray was a most enjoyable prospect.

After the tutor had left them, Alison turned to the marquess. "It seems you have charmed Mr. Ferguson."

Ravenstoke smiled. "In truth, Lady Alison, I do not usually charm those I meet."

Alison laughed. "You did very well with Mr. Ferguson."

The marquess looked thoughtful. "It is odd, but I very much wanted him to like me. I don't usually care what others think of me, and here I was, flattering the fellow shamelessly."

"And what a coincidence that you mentioned the book by his grandfather."

"Oh, that," said the marquess. "An amazing coincidence to be sure." Ravenstoke turned to Alison and suddenly broke into a smile. "Of course, to be honest, I must admit that I did have some inkling of the relationship."

"Lord Ravenstoke! You mean you knew all along?"

"Well, one of the servants, who had been dusting the library, saw that I was reading the book and mentioned to Mull that the gentleman who wrote the book was related to Mr. Ferguson. Mull, of course, informed me of the connection."

"My lord, you were quite devious." They both burst into laughter and then Alison excused herself and hurried to make ready for the excursion.

The ride over a rather bumpy road to the old Murray stronghold proved to be most enjoyable for all four of the occupants of Ravenstoke's carriage. Duncan had been overjoyed to learn of his good fortune. Instead of the expected scolding, he found himself going out to Daingneach Dubh, a spot with which he was well familiar, but under the circumstances, was quite eager to see once again.

Mr. Ferguson could not help but be pleased to find himself seated in a fine carriage with such illustrious company. It was indeed an honor to be there beside the beautiful Alison Murray, granddaughter of the duke and possessor of the bluest of Highland blood. And sitting across from him was an English nobleman of august rank, who was a most pleasant and intelligent gentleman and clearly little tainted by the connection with Bloody Wicklow. Mr. Ferguson made a mental note to check into his lordship's pedigree, for he suspected that a gentleman of Lord Ravenstoke's obvious merit must have some Scottish ancestry.

His lordship was also enjoying the ride. It was a great pleasure to be seated directly across from Alison, and he could hardly bear to take his eyes from her. Attired in a pale-yellow pelisse of twilled silk and wearing a charming bonnet that suited her lovely face to perfection, Alison looked beautiful. Every so often she would smile at the marquess and he found himself completely enchanted.

The conversation never lagged as Duncan asked numerous questions of the marquess and Mr. Ferguson. He had a great interest in his lordship's horses and, after this topic was exhausted, turned his attention to Mr. Ferguson. He asked that gentleman all about the ruined castle toward which they were speedily heading, and the tutor was quite happy to discuss the history of the early Murrays. As the subject matter included all manner of medieval warfare and featured some notable and very bloody battles, Duncan was enthralled.

It did not seem very long until they neared Daingneach Dubh. Alison had informed Ravenstoke that the carriage would not be able to go the entire way, as the road ended, and they would have to walk a short distance up the hill to the ruin. When the vehicle came to a halt, Ravenstoke looked at Alison. "Can we be here already?"

She nodded. "It did seem a short ride, did it not?"

Ravenstoke felt like replying the journey seemed far too short, but instead, he merely nodded.

Looking out the carriage window, Duncan pointed enthusiastically. "There it is. There is Daingneach Dubh!"

The coachman opened the carriage door and assisted Alison out. Ravenstoke and the others followed, and once outside the carriage, Alison motioned toward the ruin. "Is it not wonderful? Daingneach Dubh! What a lovely place. How I wish that it was still our home."

Ravenstoke viewed the ruined castle for the first time and was struck by the beauty of its setting. It stood high on a hill overlooking the sea, the lone evidence of human occupation of this remote portion of Dornach lands. Although little remained of the ancient fortress save one wall and part of one tower, there was a stately grandeur about the ruin.

"It is marvelous," said Ravenstoke.

Alison smiled "I knew you would think so."

Mr. Ferguson nodded toward the castle. "There is Daingneach Dubh, Lord Ravenstoke. There is nae older structure in this part o' the Highlands."

"It is quite remarkable, Mr. Ferguson." The marquess looked over at Alison. "Shall we go on?"

"Aye, my lord. The view from the hill is splendid." They started on up the hill. It was a steep and difficult climb, but Duncan raced up the incline, agile as a mountain goat. Mr. Ferguson surprised Ravenstoke by his ability to follow quickly after the boy. The wiry Scotsman appeared to have no trouble on the sharply sloping ground and soon left Alison and him far behind.

"Good heavens," said his lordship as they picked their way slowly and carefully up the hill, "the fellow makes me feel like a doddering old man."

Alison smiled. "Mr. Ferguson does very well for a man of two and forty."

"Two and forty? He does well for a man of twenty." The marquess looked over at Alison and offered his arm to her. "Do be careful, Lady Alison. There may be a dangerous crevasse or two ahead." He broke into a smile and Alison laughed.

"I pray you do not remind me of that," she said, taking his arm. "I assure you there is no need to worry that I shall repeat that earlier disaster."

"I should hope not," said the marquess. They exchanged smiles and then proceeded.

When they arrived at the top, Alison and Ravenstoke stood there silently admiring the panorama of Highland scenery. In one direction the bracken-covered moor stretched toward distant rugged mountains. In the other direction was the vast blueness of the sea. Sea gulls glided across the sky, their strident calls filling the air.

Ravenstoke was strangely moved as he stood there beside Alison and reflected that he had never before seen anything so beautiful.

Alison looked over at him and seemed to sense his thoughts. "I am certain that there is no place lovelier than this in the entire world," she said.

He glanced over at her. "Aye," he said softly. "There could be no place lovelier."

Alison looked up into Ravenstoke's eyes and feared for a moment she had lost all sense of propriety. She wanted nothing more than to find herself in his lordship's embrace, to feel his strong arms around her tightly and his lips upon hers.

The marquess was experiencing similar feelings, and so intent was he upon Alison that he seemed to forget that they were not alone. He was, therefore, surprised to find himself addressed by Mr. Ferguson. "And what does your lordship think o' Daingneach Dubh?"

Ravenstoke looked over at the man. "Oh, it is splendid, Mr. Ferguson. Simply splendid."

"Aye," said Ferguson, nodding. "That it is." The tutor then began to relate numerous facts about the old castle's history, and although his lordship would have much preferred being alone with Alison in this romantic spot, he found himself very much interested.

With Ferguson as guide, the four of them walked along the old castle wall. The Scotsman told of the building of the fortress and its later destruction at the hands of a rival clan.

Duncan listened as the tutor then described what life

was like at Daingneach Dubh. "Mr. Ferguson," he asked, "would you have liked to have lived in those days?"

"Och, nay, lad," said Ferguson, launching into a discussion of the superiority of modern times. He and Duncan walked on ahead, leaving Alison and Ravenstoke to stroll slowly along behind them.

Alison looked over at the marquess and smiled mischievously. "I suspect that you would have liked to have lived in those days, my lord."

"And why do you think that? Do I seem so medieval to you?"

"Well, it is rather easy to picture you in armor."

Ravenstoke laughed. "You may find this surprising, Lady Alison, but I assure you I have never had the urge to participate in a joust or the siege of a castle. I am content to live in the present age."

"And so am I. Of course, I suppose living at Dornach Castle is scarcely the height of modernity."

They both laughed again and continued on slowly, seemingly unconcerned that Mr. Ferguson and Duncan were far ahead.

15   The duke and Andrew Murray returned home to Dornach Castle late in the afternoon. Entering the drawing room, they found Alison seated on the sofa working on her embroidery. Beside her was Duncan, intent upon the pages of a book. Since the youngest Murray had never been known to have an interest in literature, his grace and Andrew thought it very curious to see Duncan thus engaged.

"Good Lord!" cried Andrew, regarding his brother in astonishment. "Whatever has happened to you, Duncan? Either my eyes deceive me or you are reading a book!"

Duncan looked up at his brother and grinned. "I am reading a book, Andrew." He held up the bulky volume. "It is called *Heroic Days of the Forty-Five*. And it is a bang-up good book, too."

"It was written by Mr. Ferguson's grandfather," added Alison.

"The devil!" cried Andrew. "No wonder it is so dashed fascinating."

"Do not make jests about a book such as that, Andrew," said the duke sternly. He looked over at Duncan. "Well, I am heartily glad to see you reading a book like that one. It will do you good to learn of the Forty-Five. After all, my own uncle died at Culloden as well as scores of Murray kinsmen. You should read the book, too, Andrew, when your brother is done with it."

Since reading was not one of Andrew's favorite activities, he was not altogether pleased at the idea. However, he dutifully nodded and told his grandfather that he would be certain to do so at first opportunity.

The duke sat down in his chair. "Och, what a day we had. We bought a fine ram from Ian."

"Knowing him," said Alison, "you must have paid dearly for it."

Andrew frowned. "There you go, speaking ill of Ian again."

The duke nodded in agreement. "You've no call to do that, lass. Ian was more than fair with us. Aye, more than fair."

"I am sorry, Grandfather. Perhaps I spoke too hastily."

"Indeed you did," said Andrew crossly.

His grace thought it wise to change the subject. "Then let us hear of your day, Duncan. Did you work at your studies?"

Duncan nodded. "I wrote an essay this afternoon after we returned, and Alison thinks it very good, except for the spelling, of course."

"After you returned?" said the duke.

"Aye, from Daingneach Dubh. We went this morning. Allie, Mr. Ferguson, and I. Lord Ravenstoke brought us there in his carriage."

"Ravenstoke?" Andrew frowned. "And he went to Daingneach Dubh? That is akin to sacrilege."

"Don't speak nonsense, Andrew Murray," said Alison.

"And am I to be happy that the grandson of Bloody Wicklow was at Daingneach Dubh? How many Murray ancestors must be turning in their graves?"

"Andrew," cried Duncan, "Lord Ravenstoke is a good man. Mr. Ferguson thinks so. He told me afterward that he was a fine gentleman."

"Ferguson?" Andrew looked incredulously at Duncan. "I knew he was a bore and something of a fool, but at least I took him for a Scotsman."

"Andrew, that is enough." The duke frowned ominously. "You will speak respectfully of Mr. Ferguson. You forget yourself too easily these days, my lad. I see nothing wrong with your sister and brother accompanying Ferguson and Ravenstoke to Daingneach Dubh. Nothing at all."

"Indeed, Andrew, you do mistake Lord Ravenstoke." Alison spoke in what she hoped was a placating tone. "He is not an evil man. Indeed, he is a true gentleman."

Andrew Murray frowned even more at his sister's words. That she always endeavored to defend the Englishman galled him. Even worse was his suspicion that Alison was losing her heart to the man. "That is your opinion, Alison," he said, and then, looking over at the duke and seeing that his grace was eyeing him closely, Andrew said nothing further on the subject. "I have great hopes for this ram," he said, and continued to talk of sheep.

When Mr. Ferguson entered the library at Dornach Castle at his usual morning hour on the following day, he was very much surprised to find young Duncan Murray reading so intently that he did not even look up as the tutor entered the room. Recognizing the book that was so occupying the young man, Mr. Ferguson allowed himself a slight smile.

"Good morning, Master Duncan."

Duncan put the book down with seeming reluctance and rose to his feet. "Good morning, sir."

"Did you complete your essay, young man?"

Duncan nodded. "Aye, sir." He picked up a piece of paper from the table and handed it to Mr. Ferguson.

"Verra good. Now return tae your book, lad, while I read this."

Duncan sat back down and picked up his book. He kept stealing glances at his tutor as the man read the essay. Finally, Ferguson looked over at him. "I cannae believe it. There is hope. This is the best work ye hae ever done, lad."

"Alison did help me with the spelling, sir."

"I can see that, young man." He looked down at the paper again. "Aye, 'tis verra promising. I did nae know ye had it in ye. Now, young sir, we will take up your Latin book. Translate page fifteen."

Duncan suppressed a groan, but obediently took up his Latin book. His brow furrowed in concentration as he tried to make sense of the words and then finally took up his quill pen to begin.

While his pupil was engaged with his translation, Mr. Ferguson took the opportunity to peruse the castle library. His eyes fell on a voluminous tome and he pulled it from the shelf. Lettered on the front was the title, *Debrett's Correct Peerage*.

Ferguson took the book over to the desk and sat down. Thumbing through it, he found the entry for Ravenstoke and stopped to read it carefully. "Fourth Marquess, Arthur George St. James Manville, born 1752," Ferguson read silently. "That would be his father." He then came to the name of Ravenstoke's mother, Anne Wicklow, and frowned. He continued. "Issue, Robert Arthur St. James Manville, Viscount Sheffield. That would be his present lordship."

Ferguson read through the list of Ravenstoke's predecessors. He stopped suddenly, very much excited. "I knew it!"

"What is it, sir? Is something wrong?"

Since he had not realized he had spoken out loud, Ferguson was somewhat embarrassed. "I have found out some interesting information about Lord Ravenstoke."

"Indeed, sir?" Duncan was happy to have an interruption of his Latin assignment.

Ferguson nodded. "I was nae predisposed tae like his lordship, knowing as I did his connection wi' Baron Wicklow, but after making his acquaintance, I found him a most amiable gentleman. There seemed tae me something about him that said he must hae Scottish blood somewhere."

"And does he?"

"Aye, and more than that." Ferguson paused for effect. "His lordship possesses royal Stuart blood."

Duncan's eyes grew wide. "Truly, sir? Och, I must fetch Alison. May I, sir?"

Mr. Ferguson nodded indulgently and Duncan scurried off, returning shortly with a perplexed-looking Alison. "What is it that has got Duncan so excited, Mr. Ferguson? He says I must hear it from you."

Ferguson looked as though he was about to impart a

very great secret. "I hae discovered, Lady Alison, that Lord Ravenstoke hae most illustrious ancestors."

"Surely that is hardly surprising for a man of his high rank."

"Och, but it is more than that, Lady Alison. The blood o' the royal Stuarts flows in his veins."

Alison directed an incredulous look at the tutor. "It cannot be true, sir."

"Indeed it is." He pointed to the entry in the book. "The second marquess, that would be his present lordship's great-great-grandfather, was married tae Charlotte Fitzroy, daughter o' . . ." Ferguson paused again. "King Charles the Second. It is on the distaff side, o' course, but the blood is there."

Alison broke into a broad smile. "Surely Lord Ravenstoke must know this. He might have mentioned it. Really, Mr. Ferguson, is it not quite ironical that his lordship might count among his ancestors the dreadful Baron Wicklow as well as royal Charles? That would mean he would be some sort of cousin to Prince Charles Edward."

Ferguson nodded vigorously. "Indeed so. And, furthermore, the mother o' Lady Charlotte Fitzroy, Anne, Countess o' Dunbarton was a Scotswoman. There are nae many who would know that fact."

"It seems you are well-informed about King Charles' mistresses, Mr. Ferguson," said Alison, trying hard to keep a straight face. "But then you are an authority on the Stuarts."

Ferguson nodded. "Do ye not think this puts a different complexion on the matter, Lady Alison?"

"I do not think I understand you, Mr. Ferguson."

"Well, my lady, there are many who dinnae like his lordship for his ancestry. Surely, they may change their minds when they hear o' the rest o' it."

"Perhaps so," said Alison.

"We must go and see Lord Ravenstoke at once," said Duncan. "To think he has royal blood!"

"Well, young man," said Mr. Ferguson, "dinnae forget the blood o' the old Scottish kings flows in your veins."

"Then I shall tell that to Lord Ravenstoke, too."

"Duncan," said Alison, bursting into laughter, "you shall say no such thing. And I am sure Lord Ravenstoke is well aware of his ancestry. As Mr. Ferguson knows, Charles the Second has many English descendants, and I am sure they are all very proud of the connection."

"But, Alison, could we not go and call at Glenfinnan?"

"At the moment, young man, you are to do your lessons."

"But Allie . . ."

"This afternoon we will see."

Duncan grinned and returned to his Latin.

Alison thanked Mr. Ferguson for his information and then left them. As she walked out into the corridor from the library, Alison smiled again and reflected that she wanted to call upon his lordship just as much as her young brother.

16 Duncan Murray was very much relieved when Bob MacPherson appeared at the door to the library and announced that luncheon was being served. The morning had seemed an eternity. He had struggled with his Latin translation for an hour and then had worked long and hard on a difficult arithmetic exercise.

Although Mr. Ferguson thought Duncan's Latin translation quite abominable, he tempered his criticism in order to encourage the boy. Indeed, the tutor had never seen Duncan work so diligently and did not want to dampen his newfound enthusiasm.

Ferguson was also happy at the prospect of lunch. Food at Dornach Castle was always exceptional, and the tutor considered it an honor to sit at table with the Murrays.

When Duncan and Mr. Ferguson entered the dining room, they found the duke, Alison, and Andrew already seated. The duke greeted them with a grin. "Ah, so there you are! I thought my grandson might have decided to forgo luncheon for his studies."

Duncan regarded his grandfather as if he had lost his senses, and Andrew and Alison laughed. A slight smile appeared on Mr. Ferguson's face. "Indeed, your grace, I daresay even the most serious o' scholars could nae resist one o' Mrs. Thomson's meals."

"Right you are, Ferguson," said the duke, motioning for the tutor to take his place at the table.

Ferguson sat down next to his pupil and watched appreciatively as the servants brought in various plates piled high with cold mutton, tongue, and salmon.

The duke, who was known for his hearty appetite, loaded his plate with the food. He seemed to be in a particularly jovial mood that day and he talked and laughed merrily between mouthfuls of mutton.

Much of the duke's conversation was directed toward Mr. Ferguson, since his grace was quite impressed with the tutor's knowledge of history and current political affairs. Ferguson discoursed at great length on several matters before the British Parliament, and although Alison listened with great interest, Andrew decided his brother's tutor was a terrible bore.

Duncan himself seemed content to concentrate on his meal and took little note of the conversation until his grandfather directed his attention toward him. "So, Duncan," said his grace as he carved a slice of tongue, "how are your studies progressing today?"

"Perhaps you might want to wait until after luncheon to discuss Duncan's studies," said Andrew, winking at his young brother. "You don't want to ruin your appetite, Grandfather."

"Is that so, Duncan?" asked the duke, his good humor quickly fading.

Mr. Ferguson quickly cut in. "Och, nay, your grace. Young Master Duncan hae done quite well today. He wrote a fine essay, and although his Latin and sums need a wee bit o' work, the lad is beginning tae show some real promise."

Although Duncan doubted any amount of work could ever make him understand Latin, he looked gratefully at his tutor.

The duke smiled broadly. "Well, that is good news, Ferguson. A fine essay, eh?"

Alison nodded. "Indeed, sir. I read it and it was very good."

"And what was this essay about?" asked the duke.

Duncan was enjoying the praise, and he eagerly entered the conversation. "It was an essay on Prince Charles Edward Stuart, Grandfather. I have been reading all about him in the book that Mr. Ferguson's grandfather wrote. It is a dashed fine book, sir. Lord Ravenstoke said so, too."

"Well, if Ravenstoke says so, then it must be," said Andrew sarcastically.

The sarcasm was not lost on Alison or the duke. "Do not be impertinent, Andrew," said his grace sternly. "I know you don't like Ravenstoke, but for the life of me I don't know what you have against the man. He seems like a decent fellow to me."

"Aye, the English laird has charmed most of the Murrays, it would seem," said Andrew, directing a meaningful glance at Alison. "I just don't know how you can forget, Grandfather, that the man is a descendant of Bloody Wicklow. I, for one, am not happy to see Scottish land taken over by any Englishman, but it is even more abominable that the Englishman should be the grandson of a vile murderer like Wicklow."

Duncan listened to his brother's speech and could hardly contain his eagerness at disclosing the new information Mr. Ferguson had discovered on the marquess's ancestry. "But, Andrew," said Duncan, "Lord Ravenstoke has Scottish blood, too—"

Andrew cut in abruptly. "Aye, Duncan, he has the Scottish blood of his grandfather's victims still on his hands."

Duncan shook his head. "Och, Andrew, that is not what I mean. Lord Ravenstoke is part Scottish. Mr. Ferguson found out that he is related to Prince Charles Edward!"

Andrew looked incredulously at his brother for a moment and then threw back his head and laughed. "The deuce he is! Duncan, you are a great cabbagehead to believe such fustian! Ravenstoke related to Prince Charlie!"

Mr. Ferguson exchanged a glance with Alison and then eyed Andrew with an expression he usually reserved for his wayward pupils. "Young Master Duncan is right, Lord Culwin. His lordship is, indeed, a distant relation to the prince."

"What the devil do you mean?" asked the duke with a rather bewildered expression. "Ravenstoke? What sort of foolery is this, Ferguson?"

"It is no foolery, Grandfather," said Alison. "Mr. Ferguson looked up Lord Ravenstoke's pedigree in the peerage book and found that he is descended from Charles the Second."

"Aye, your grace," said Ferguson, greatly offended by the duke's question. "His lordship's great-great-grandfather was married tae Charlotte Fitzroy, one of Charles the Second's daughters. As I told Lady Alison, it is on the distaff side, o' course, but the Stuart blood is there all the same."

The Duke of Dornach slapped his hand against the table. "As I live, Ravenstoke descended from that old rascal, Royal Charles."

"Aye, your grace," agreed Ferguson. "When I met his lordship, I thought he showed nae taint o' the Wicklow blood. Indeed, I thought I detected a noble Scottish strain, and now that I think o' it, his lordship hae some o' the Stuart features."

Andrew looked at Ferguson and shook his head. "Good Lord, Ferguson, next you'll be telling us that Ravenstoke is the rightful Stuart heir! Of all the cork-brained things I have ever heard . . ."

"That will be enough, Andrew!" growled the duke.

Andrew frowned but remained silent. His grace gave his grandson one last warning look and then turned back to Ferguson. "And what does Ravenstoke say about all of this? Surely he must know about his illustrious connections to the Stuart kings?"

Ferguson looked a little puzzled. "I cannae say, your grace. It would seem odd that his lordship would nae know, and yet many gentlemen are nae well-versed in their family's history."

"Yes," said Andrew resentfully, "he seemed unaware of his grandfather Wicklow's glorious career as a butcher."

"Really, Andrew," said Alison in exasperation, "must you go on so? Is it not enough that Lord Ravenstoke is a good man?"

"Aye, Andrew," said Duncan. "Allie is right. If you but know him better, you would see that."

Andrew looked around the table and, feeling himself outnumbered, stared down at his plate in stony silence.

The duke had resumed his meal and Duncan looked from Andrew to his grandfather. He thought it was the perfect chance to get his grandfather to agree to go see Ravenstoke. The boy knew he would risk his elder brother's displeasure, but he was too excited at the prospect of visiting Glenfinnan again.

"Grandfather," said Duncan, "don't you think we should find out if Lord Ravenstoke knows about being related to Prince Charles? I daresay one would want to know such a thing as that."

"Indeed, Duncan. I think the subject should be broached with Ravenstoke," agreed the duke.

Duncan smiled over at Alison and then back at the duke. "Well, then, Grandfather, couldn't we go visit Lord Ravenstoke this afternoon? I know he would like to have you see Glenfinnan. And he had asked Mr. Ferguson to explain some of its history to him."

Mr. Ferguson coughed. "Indeed, your grace, his lordship did express a wish that I visit Glenfinnan."

Alison looked hopefully at her grandfather but refrained from saying anything and appearing too eager to see the marquess.

The duke grinned at his grandson. "'Tis a long time since I've been to Glenfinnan. All right, Duncan! We'll go and pay a call on Ravenstoke this afternoon."

Duncan could scarcely contain his excitement but managed to politely thank his grandfather. "And Mr. Ferguson will go along?" asked Duncan.

"Aye. That is, if you care to go, Ferguson."

The tutor nodded vigorously. "Aye, your grace."

"And Allie must go, too . . ." Duncan hesitated and looked at his brother. "And Andrew. Please come with us. You will like Lord Ravenstoke."

Andrew shook his head, annoyed at how his young brother seemed to be idolizing their English neighbor. "No, Duncan, I have other plans. I am to meet Ian and go to the village."

Duncan's face fell. Alison frowned at Andrew and wished again that he was not on such good terms with Ian MacGillivray. She smiled at Duncan. "Well, I shall go along, Duncan. I am most curious to see what Lord Ravenstoke says about his famous Scottish ancestry."

Duncan grinned and took another mouthful of salmon.

Sometime later that afternoon, the Duke of Dornach, Alison, Duncan, and Mr. Ferguson rode in a carriage toward Glenfinnan. The duke's carriage was a large, lumbering vehicle that showed its age as it bumped along the rough road that wound through Dornach lands. Although Mr. Ferguson found himself wishing that the duke's carriage was as comfortable as Ravenstoke's well-sprung, modern vehicle, he gladly suffered the bumps and jolts of the journey for the privilege of accompanying the duke to Glenfinnan.

The duke had retained his high spirits, and as they rode along, he told Duncan and Ferguson about some of the earlier occupants of Glenfinnan. Since the old house had its share of colorful and rather eccentric personages, Duncan and his tutor were kept quite entertained during the short trip.

Alison only half-listened to her grandfather's stories. She thought, instead, of Ravenstoke, and remembered the previous day's visit to Daingneach Dubh. Alison had come very close to declaring her feelings for the marquess there at the romantic ruin by the sea. A wistful smile appeared on Alison's lovely face. There was no denying it. She was in love with Ravenstoke and could only hope that he loved her, too.

Alison's pleasant musings were interrupted when the carriage made an abrupt halt, causing Mr. Ferguson to fall forward into the Duke of Dornach's lap. The duke uttered an oath and Ferguson hastily jumped back to his own side of the carriage, murmuring an embarrassed apology to his grace.

The duke leaned his head out the window. "What the devil is wrong, Robin?"

Before the servant could answer, a horse pulled up alongside the carriage and a smiling Sir Ian MacGillivray peered inside. "Good afternoon, Duke." He tipped his hat at Alison. "Lady Alison, what a pleasure." The baronet acknowledged Duncan with less enthusiasm and snubbed Mr. Ferguson altogether. Sir Ian then turned back to his grace. "It appears that I've come upon a family outing, Duke."

The duke nodded. "Aye, Ian. A family outing but for Andrew. He said you were going into the village together." The duke grinned. "I suspect you two are up to some devilment or another."

Ian laughed and Alison frowned. She wished that her grandfather would not encourage Sir Ian so.

"Are you going far, Duke?" said Ian. "Perhaps I might accompany you a ways."

"I thought Andrew was expecting you," said the duke.

"Aye, but Andrew can wait." Sir Ian grinned. "I must confess, Duke, that I would rather spend my time with your lovely granddaughter here."

The duke laughed. "'Tis a bright lad you are, Ian," he said.

Alison eyed the baronet blackly. "'Tis on the way to Glenfinnan we are, Sir Ian, to visit Lord Ravenstoke." She looked defiantly up at him. "I doubt you would wish to accompany us there."

Sir Ian looked from Alison to the duke. "Is that true? You're on your way to Glenfinnan?"

"Aye, Ian," said the duke. "Come and join us. You and Andrew are being unfair to Ravenstoke. He is a gentleman and a good neighbor to us."

An angry scowl appeared on the baronet's face, but he was not so unwise as to lose his temper in the presence of the Duke of Dornach. "I fear, Duke, our opinions differ on the Englishman." Sir Ian lifted his hat again to Alison and smiled mockingly at her. "I hope you enjoy your visit, Lady Alison." He then kicked his horse harshly and rode off.

The duke shook his head sadly. "It seems Ian bears a grudge against Ravenstoke." He looked thoughtfully at his granddaughter. "Do you know why he hates him so?"

Alison shrugged but avoided her grandfather's gaze. "Och, Grandfather, it is just that Ian cannot forget Lord Ravenstoke's connection with Baron Wicklow."

Mr. Ferguson had viewed the exchange between Ian and Alison with great curiosity. He was well aware of the village gossip that had long ago paired Lady Alison Murray with Sir Ian MacGillivray. Ferguson had thought it a pity that the lovely and charming Lady Alison would marry such a Philistine. He was somewhat heartened to discover that the lady could not abide Sir Ian.

Ferguson had a sudden thought, and a slight, self-satisfied smile appeared on his face. Of course, it was Lord Ravenstoke that Lady Alison preferred! Although a confirmed bachelor, Mr. Ferguson was not without some sentimentality about love and romance. He glanced at Alison and decided that she and the marquess would be perfectly suited.

As the carriage neared Glenfinnan, Alison looked out the window for a view of Loch Craidoch. "Isn't it lovely, Grandfather?" she said.

"Aye, lass," said the duke. " 'Tis a grand sight." The duke looked up ahead. "And there's Glenfinnan. A fine house it is."

Duncan craned his head out of the window. "Och, aye, Grandfather. Lord Ravenstoke says Glenfinnan is his favorite of all his houses."

"Of all his houses?" said the duke. "The fellow must be as rich as they say."

The carriage pulled up in the circular drive in front of the house and a servant rushed out to open the door. Jack Mull had seen the approach of the ducal carriage and also hurried up to greet the visitors.

He assisted Alison down and smiled. "Lady Alison."

"Hello, Mull."

Duncan jumped down from the carriage. "Mull! I've been practicing. Look at this!" Duncan stood in a fighting stance and made a jabbing thrust with one fist.

Mull grinned his approval. "That is very good, Master Duncan."

The duke had witnessed his grandson's pugilistic display and eyed Mull with considerable interest. "You should take that as quite a compliment, Duncan, coming as it does from Jumpin' Jack Mull." His grace smiled at the servant. "I saw you fight in Edinburgh, Mull, and I've never seen anyone do as well as you did that day."

The servant smiled modestly. "Your grace is most kind."

Duncan was eager to show off some other boxing tricks to his grandfather, but Alison hastily intervened. "Is Lord

Ravenstoke at home, Mull? We have some rather exciting news for him."

Mull raised his eyebrows. "Indeed, m'lady? I am sure his lordship will be most happy to see you. Please follow me."

The servant led them through a long hallway, and after announcing them to his lordship, he ushered them into the drawing room.

Ravenstoke was quite delighted at the news of his unexpected company and smiled as he advanced toward them. "What a pleasant surprise!" He shook hands with the duke. "It is an honor to have you here, your grace."

"Thank you, Ravenstoke," said the duke. "I thought it was time that I visited Glenfinnan again. And I also wanted to thank you for your gift. It was dashed fine of you, sir."

"I thought it was fitting that you should have it, your grace," said the marquess.

"Well, I am most indebted to you, Ravenstoke. I must admit that I had long envied Ronald Drummond for possessing such a precious keepsake."

The duke then looked nostalgically around the room. "Aye, I've many fond memories of the place. Sir Ronald was a good neighbor and a good friend." The duke shook his head sadly. "Poor Ronald, how he loved this house. Och, I'm glad he did not live to see the Drummonds lose it!" Realizing that such a remark was not very tactful in the presence of Glenfinnan's new owner, the duke looked slightly embarrassed.

The marquess exchanged a glance with Alison and then turned back to his grace. "I understand how you must feel, Duke. I know this was the Drummonds' home for a good long time, and it must have been very hard for them to give it up. Indeed, although I have been here but a few weeks, Glenfinnan already seems a part of me and I would be most unhappy to leave it."

The duke regarded Ravenstoke closely. "It seems you do care about the place, sir. My granddaughter has told me how you have plans to improve your lands. I would be quite interested in hearing about them."

The marquess smiled. "I should be happy to tell you about them, Duke."

Duncan had listened to this exchange between his grandfather and Ravenstoke a trifle impatiently. "But, Grandfather, don't forget about the news we have for Lord Ravenstoke!"

The marquess lifted an eyebrow quizzically at Duncan and then looked over at Alison. "Indeed, my lord," said Alison, "Mr. Ferguson has discovered some rather interesting information about you."

"About me, Lady Alison?"

Alison almost burst into laughter at the perplexed and somewhat wary expression on the marquess's face.

The tutor stepped forward eagerly. "Aye, my lord. I was—" Mr. Ferguson paused and coughed a bit uncomfortably. "Ye see, I just happened tae be browsing in the peerage book when my eye chanced on the entry for Ravenstoke."

The marquess exchanged an amused glance with Alison. "Please don't tell me, Ferguson, that you have discovered more skeletons in my closet."

"Och, nay, my lord," said Ferguson quickly. "I found ye hae a most illustrious ancestor. Most illustrious, indeed! But surely ye are already aware o' it, my lord."

Ravenstoke knit his brows thoughtfully. "An illustrious ancestor?"

"Aye, Lord Ravenstoke," burst in Duncan. "You are related to Charles the Second! That makes you a cousin of Prince Charles Edward."

The marquess regarded the boy with an incredulous smile. "I fear, Duncan, that this time you are quizzing me."

Duncan grinned. "Och, no, my lord! Tell him, Mr. Ferguson."

The marquess first saw that they were all seated, and then Ferguson proceeded to discuss his lordship's connection to the royal Stuarts at great length. At the end of Ferguson's recitation, Ravenstoke shook his head. "This has been quite a revelation to me. I am most gratified to you, Ferguson, for giving me this information."

"I was most happy tae divulge such news, my lord."

"We knew you would be thrilled, Lord Ravenstoke," said Alison with a mischievous smile.

The marquess returned her smile. "Indeed, I am."

The duke eyed Ravenstoke thoughtfully. "Perhaps there is something in the chin."

"I beg your pardon, your grace?" said Ravenstoke, regarding the duke with a puzzled look.

"Your chin, Ravenstoke! Ferguson said he thought you had some of the Stuart features, and I daresay he is right about your chin."

The marquess eyed the duke with such a ludicrous expression that Alison burst into laughter and then the whole company joined in.

After tea, Ravenstoke took his guests on a tour of the house. Duncan was especially interested in the antique weapons that hung on the wall of one room and wanted to know all about them. Mr. Ferguson patiently answered all the boy's questions and provided some graphic details on medieval warfare. The duke was also quite interested in the tutor's stories and listened raptly to the tales of his warring ancestors.

Alison was not overly enthused by the tutor's vivid battle accounts and she walked over to another wall to study a painting. It was a portrait of one of the early Drummonds, and from the fierce expression on the man's face, Alison had no trouble imagining him wielding a claymore. As she looked up at the portrait, Ravenstoke appeared beside her. "I shouldn't like to meet that fellow in battle."

Alison smiled. "He does appear quite fearsome." She turned to the marquess. "So, my lord, have you recovered?"

"Recovered, ma'am?"

"From learning the startling news of your Scottish ancestry."

Ravenstoke smiled. "It was something of a surprise."

"I find it strange, my lord, that you were unaware of such an interesting connection."

"Indeed, it does seem odd. Of course, knowing my father, I suspect he would wish to hide the fact."

Alison regarded him with some surprise. "Hide the fact of being descended from King Charles the Second? Why would he wish to do that?"

Ravenstoke smiled. "My father was a strict man with some rather puritanical notions. He was probably ashamed of having an illegitimate ancestor in the Manville family tree. That she was the daughter of Royal Charles doubtlessly made little difference to him. And although I should hate to mention it to Mr. Ferguson, my father had a very dim view of the Stuarts and the Jacobite cause." Ravenstoke smiled again at Alison. "But, I assure you, Lady Alison, I am quite proud of my newfound Scottish ancestry."

"I am glad of that, Lord Ravenstoke." Alison smiled again. "Does this mean, sir, that you will wear the Royal Stuart tartan at the next Dornach Ball?"

Ravenstoke laughed. "I do not know if I shall go so far as that, ma'am."

Alison smiled in return and Ravenstoke reflected how wonderful it was to have her there. The marquess suddenly found himself imagining what it would be like to have Alison living with him at Glenfinnan. He had no trouble conjuring up such a picture. Indeed, it seemed quite natural to him that she should be there with him.

Ravenstoke's smile quickly vanished as he remembered that it was Deborah Willoughby, not Lady Alison Murray, who was to be mistress of Glenfinnan. Alison noted the change in Ravenstoke's expression and she looked questioningly at him. "What is it, my lord? Is something wrong?"

"Lady Alison, I have something I must tell you," began the marquess. He looked into Alison's lovely blue eyes and hesitated.

"Yes, Lord Ravenstoke?"

The marquess paused again, wondering what he should say. He must tell her about Deborah and yet he was having great difficulty finding the words.

"Ravenstoke! Alison! You both must come and hear this. Ferguson is telling us the most fascinating tale." The duke's words prevented Ravenstoke from continuing.

Alison regarded his lordship questioningly.

"It was nothing," he said. "Come, let us join the others." Then, offering her his arm, the marquess led Alison toward his other guests.

17 After his visitors had left, Lord Ravenstoke retreated to his sitting room. Looking out the window, he stared glumly out at his property. "Damn," he muttered finally. "Why did I not tell her about Deborah?" Turning away from the window, the marquess went into his bedchamber and opened a drawer of his bureau. He took an object from the drawer and regarded it gloomily. It was a delicately painted miniature, a portrait of his fiancée, Deborah Willoughby.

He frowned and deposited the miniature back in the drawer. Of all the abominable luck, he reflected, to have found Alison Murray after he was engaged to be married to Deborah. A trace of a smile came to his face at the thought of Alison. He was not a romantic or sentimental man, and in the past the idea that he might one day fall in love had seemed utterly ridiculous. Yet here he was totally enamored of the Scottish miss.

The smile faded quickly. No, he was duty-bound to marry Miss Willoughby, and as a gentleman, he could do nothing else. Why had he not admitted to Alison that he was not free? Indeed, he should have mentioned Deborah some time ago. Ravenstoke shook his head. He knew very well that he had intentionally kept silent, not wanting to end the relationship that was developing between them.

"Pardon me, m'lord."

Ravenstoke looked up from his melancholy musings to find Mull standing before him. "What is it, Mull?"

The worthy servant hesitated. Knowing that his master was for some reason blue-deviled, he hated to inform him of a bit of news that was certain to depress him further. "There is a letter from London."

"A letter?"

"Aye, m'lord." Mull extended the silver salver he was holding toward the marquess, and Ravenstoke took up the letter from it. Mull watched his master closely as he broke the seal and unfolded the missive. Knowing that the letter came from Deborah Willoughby, Mull suspected that the marquess would be none too happy to see it.

As expected, Ravenstoke frowned. As he read further, his frown deepened until his dark eyebrows arched in surprise. "By God, I cannot believe it!"

"Is it bad news, m'lord?"

"The worst." Ravenstoke looked up at his servant. "Miss Willoughby is bringing a party from London here to Glenfinnan."

"Here, m'lord? All this way?" Mull was genuinely astonished. He had not thought Deborah Willoughby the sort to undertake such a rigorous journey.

"God in heaven, yes. Of all the ridiculous ideas! Whatever could have got into the girl?" Ravenstoke seemed to be rereading the letter to be sure he had properly understood its contents. "Now, when did she write this? Good God, it is dated some three weeks ago. Are the mails that slow?"

Mull looked slightly uncomfortable. "I fear, m'lord, that the letter arrived some time ago. The servant who took the letter—a mere girl she is, m'lord—did not know who to give it to, you and I both bein' gone. She took it to the kitchen and, there bein' no one else about, put it down. She forgot about it, m'lord, and cook only just found it this mornin'."

"Dear God!" shouted Ravenstoke in a rare burst of temper. "They could be here at any moment! There are no rooms ready, no menus decided upon, and the staff totally unprepared to have guests from London."

"But, m'lord, Miss Willoughby and the other guests cannot expect things to be as polished as in London."

"She can indeed, Mull. Now, you must assist me. Call

the servants together. We shall need each one of them working as hard as possible."

"Aye, m'lord." Mull hurried off, leaving Ravenstoke to once again grimly peruse Deborah's letter.

When Alison came down to breakfast the following morning, she found her brother Andrew sitting alone at the dining-room table. He looked up at her. "Good morning, Alison."

Noting the lack of warmth in her brother's greeting, Alison frowned. They were still not on good terms, and since she was so very fond of Andrew, Alison was distressed that he was still vexed with her. She sat down beside him. "Could we not come to a truce?"

"Truce?" Andrew looked over at her.

"Aye. Come, Andrew, can we not forget our quarreling?"

"I wish to God we could, Alison, but this goes deep. You have formed a fondness for the Englishman, haven't you? And you do not seem to care what I think of it."

Alison looked down and then over at her brother. "I do care what you think, Andrew, but you are not being fair to Lord Ravenstoke. Could you not try to put aside your prejudice for a moment and see the man, not his ancestors?"

"No, I cannot." Andrew regarded her sternly. "And I shall warn you, Alison. If you have any thoughts of wedding this Englishman, you should reconsider them carefully. Even if Grandfather would agree to the match, I never shall do so. If you ally yourself with Ravenstoke, I shall never speak to you again."

Before she could reply, they were interrupted by the appearance of Duncan. He seemed in great spirits and rushed in to join them. "Andrew, Allie, good morning!"

"Must you be so cheerful, Duncan?" scowled Andrew.

Duncan looked over at Alison, who shrugged. "You are in an ill temper, Andrew," said the younger brother, sitting down across from them.

Alison changed the subject. "Did you see Grandfather?"

"Aye," replied Duncan. "He will be down after a time. He seemed to be feeling quite well."

"Good," said Alison. "I do worry about him some-times."

"You might do better worrying about yourself, Alison Murray."

Duncan regarded his brother with a puzzled look. "What do you mean, Andrew?"

"Oh, your brother is in a terrible humor, Duncan. We must ignore him."

Duncan eyed Andrew for a moment and then grinned at Alison. "I have it, Allie, let us all go riding! The day is perfect."

"That is a good idea," said Alison cheerfully, but Andrew only continued to frown.

"Couldn't we call upon Lord Ravenstoke at Glenfinnan today?" said Duncan. "I could see Mull and he could teach me some more about boxing."

"Duncan Murray, I forbid you ever to go to Glenfinnan while that Englishman is there!"

Duncan was startled by the vehemence of Andrew's words. He looked hurt and Alison grew indignant. "Andrew Murray! You have no right forbidding us to do anything. Grandfather is laird of Dornach, not you!"

Andrew rose angrily from the table. "You may go to your damned Englishman, then, the both of you!"

Alison was too surprised by her brother's words to make any reply and Andrew said nothing more but stalked off.

Duncan watched his brother leave the room with a concerned look. "What is wrong with Andrew, Allie?"

"Oh, I don't know, Duncan. He does not like us seeing Lord Ravenstoke and he has such a temper."

Duncan nodded solemnly. "Aye, that he does." He looked over at Alison. "Does that mean we cannot go to Glenfinnan?"

"It does not. Indeed, later we shall take a ride and visit Lord Ravenstoke."

"Good," said Duncan with a grin. He continued to smile as Annie Thomson appeared with breakfast.

It was not until early afternoon that Alison and Duncan were able to set out on their ride. It crossed Alison's mind, as she and her brother made their way toward

Glenfinnan, that it was perhaps a trifle forward of her to call upon the marquess so soon. After all, she had just seen him the previous day. Indeed, considered Alison, it would have been more suitable to allow his lordship to make the next visit.

Alison smiled. She did not really care. She wished to see Ravenstoke and it was silly to stand on convention. Besides that, she could not allow Andrew to think he could order her about. One day he would be Duke of Dornach, but while her grandfather lived, he had no authority over her and she wanted him to know it.

It did not seem long before they arrived at the great house of Glenfinnan. A harried-looking servant came out to take their horses and they were admitted by a red-faced woman whose cap was askew and whose gray hair spilled out untidily beneath it. "Lady Alison Murray?" said the woman. "Och!"

"Whatever is the matter?" said Alison. Peering into the entry hall, she saw several servants scurrying about, looking as if some calamity had struck.

"Och, your ladyship," replied the servant at the door. "His lordship is having company frae London and there is sae much tae do."

"Then we have come at a bad time," said Alison. "I would not want to disturb Lord Ravenstoke. Do tell him we called."

Duncan looked disappointed. "But is Mull busy?"

The servant grinned down at him. "Aye, young master, Mull is the busiest o' all."

"Come along, Duncan, you will see Mull another time." She put her arm around the boy's shoulders and started for the door.

"Lady Alison!"

Alison stopped, turned, and found that Ravenstoke had just entered the entry hall. "Oh, Lord Ravenstoke, we have called upon you at a most inopportune time. Do excuse us."

"No, please stay, and I hope you will forgive the confusion. My guests were quite unexpected and there is so much work for the servants in preparation. Do come to the drawing room."

"If you are sure, my lord. I do not wish to interrupt you."

"No, please stay. I wanted to talk with you about something."

Their eyes met briefly and the marquess seemed suddenly embarrassed. He led Alison and Duncan into the drawing room, and once inside, Duncan looked around. "Would Mull be about, Lord Ravenstoke?"

"Mull?" The marquess smiled. "So you have come to see my servant? I should have known it was not me who you wished to see."

"Oh, I wish to see you, too, sir," replied Duncan hastily.

Ravenstoke laughed. "You will find him in the kitchen. Any of the servants can show you the way."

"Thank you, sir," said Duncan. He looked at Alison, who nodded, and then the boy hurried off.

"I seem to pale beside the great Mull," said Ravenstoke, "but he is an exciting fellow."

"That he is," said Alison with a smile. "But I shall not desert you."

To Alison's surprise Ravenstoke did not smile at this remark. Instead, his face took on a very serious expression. "I am glad you came, Lady Alison. There is something I must tell you. It is of some importance."

Alison looked questioningly into his gray eyes. "What is it?"

The marquess turned away for a moment and then looked back at her. "I did not tell you before, although I should have done so. It is about the visitors arriving here. You see, one of them is—"

His words were cut short by the appearance of the gray-haired woman who had admitted Alison and Duncan. "They're here, m'lord!" she cried, wringing her hands in consternation. "The guests are here!"

"Here already! Good God!"

"Robert!" A feminine voice called out, and a moment later a diminutive young woman appeared in the drawing room. She was followed by a stout older woman and two young gentlemen. "There you are, Robert! You will forgive me for not waiting for you, but really, your household here is most ramshackle. Everyone running about like silly hens. We did not wish to wait in the entry hall for fear we would be knocked down."

Alison stared at the stranger with great interest. She had never before seen anyone dressed so elegantly and knew that before her was a lady of fashion accustomed to the best and most expensive clothes London and Paris might offer. Alison felt suddenly dowdy in her riding habit and carefully studied the carriage dress worn by the young woman. It was fashioned of blue-gray bombazine trimmed with black satin and over it she wore a Russian wrapping cloak trimmed with black fur.

Alison studied the young lady's lovely face, finding it marred only by her somewhat petulant expression. Pale-gold curls peeked out from beneath her matching blue-gray Parisian bonnet trimmed with black satin roses.

"Well, Robert, I must say your greeting is most unenthusiastic."

Ravenstoke frowned and then approached the young lady and placed a kiss on her cheek. "Welcome to Glenfinnan, Deborah." He looked at the older woman and bowed slightly. "Lady Willoughby." The marquess nodded to the two gentlemen. "Willoughby, Ensdale."

"How do, Ravenstoke?" said the taller of the two young gentlemen. "If you but knew how glad we are to finally arrive here. By my faith, our journey was not easy."

"I am sorry to hear that, Ensdale."

Alison studied the young gentleman named Ensdale curiously. She had never seen a real London dandy, but knew that that is what this young gentleman could be called. He spoke in a languid drawl and looked about the room with a bored expression. Despite the trials of his long journey, Ensdale was dressed with infinite care. He wore buff-colored nankeen pantaloons and a tight-fitting striped coat. The snowy linen neckcloth about his throat was intricately tied and his shirt points were so high that Alison wondered how he could possibly stand to have his neck so constricted. He was a handsome young man, conceded Alison, but she also noted that he seemed well aware of it.

His companion, Willoughby, was also dressed elegantly, but since he had the misfortune to be somewhat plump, his perfectly cut coat and tight pantaloons did not suit him nearly so well. Willoughby, it appeared to Alison, was taking great pains to ape his friend, but the effect was a trifle off the mark.

The fourth member of the party, an older woman, was also dressed at the height of fashion. Although quite stout, she carried herself regally and seemed to be a lady of great consequence. The carriage dress she was wearing was as splendid as that worn by the younger lady. It was a high-collared garment fashioned of rose-colored twilled silk and festooned with cream-colored satin ribbons. Perched atop her head was an elaborate wide-brimmed bonnet tied under her chin with rose-colored satin ribbons.

The older lady was eyeing Ravenstoke sternly, and when she looked from him to Alison, her gaze was decidedly unfriendly. Alison regarded Ravenstoke curiously, wondering what relationship these rather unpleasant visitors could have to him. Seeming to read her thoughts, the marquess started to make introductions.

"Lady Alison Murray, may I present Lady Willoughby?" The older woman in the rose dress nodded grimly at Alison. "And her daughter, Miss Deborah Willoughby?"

"Lady Alison," replied Deborah, nodding toward her like a reigning queen acknowledging a subject.

"And this is Lord Ensdale and Mr. Fenton Willoughby, Deborah's cousin."

"Charmed, Lady Alison," said Ensdale, taking Alison's hand and bowing over it.

"Indeed," said Willoughby, who, not wanting to be outdone by his friend, took Alison's hand and bowed even more deeply.

"How do you do?" said Alison, still wondering who these new arrivals were. She suspected they were relatives of some kind, for they certainly did not seem to be the sort of friends she would expect Ravenstoke to have.

The marquess looked over at Alison. "Miss Willoughby," he said, pausing for a moment, "is my fiancée."

Alison's large blue eyes grew even wider in surprise and she felt a sudden pang of disappointment and incredulity. So Ravenstoke was engaged and this lady of fashion was his betrothed! Alison somehow managed to recover her composure. She looked at Deborah. "How good it is that you could come to Scotland. I do hope you enjoy your visit."

"I shall attempt to do so, Lady Alison," said Deborah, directing a shrewd gaze at the other young woman.

"And I assume you are one of Ravenstoke's neighbors, Lady Alison," said Lord Ensdale.

"Yes, my grandfather's estate is nearby."

"How convenient," said Lady Willoughby, frowning at Ravenstoke.

There was then an awkward silence, but it was cut mercifully short by the appearance of Duncan. He rushed into the room and jumped into his fighting stance. "You must see what I have learned," he cried, and then, seeing the London company, he reddened with embarrassment. "Oh, I am sorry."

"That is all right, Duncan," said the marquess. "Come in, my boy. This young gentleman is Master Duncan Murray, Lady Alison's brother."

Lady Willoughby's face clearly expressed her opinion of children, especially noisy ones. She frowned disapprovingly at Duncan and looked over at Alison reproachfully.

"Duncan and I were just going," said Alison. She wanted very much to get away from Ravenstoke and his horrid guests. "It was very nice to meet you and do have a pleasant stay."

"I shall show you out, then," said Ravenstoke.

"That won't be necessary," replied Alison coldly.

"No, I insist. Do excuse me." Ravenstoke took Alison's arm and, abandoning his guests, escorted her and Duncan from the drawing room. As they neared the entry hall, he spoke. "I am sorry. I tried to tell you."

"So this is what you wanted to tell me."

The marquess nodded. "I must explain . . ."

"There is no need of explanation, my lord. I understand perfectly well."

"Alison, wait. I don't think you do understand."

Directing an icy look at the marquess, Alison took Duncan's hand and, without another word, left him. Once outside, Duncan was full of questions. "Allie, who were those people and why are you vexed with Lord Ravenstoke?"

"Those people are his guests. And I am not vexed with Lord Ravenstoke."

"But the way you looked at him . . ."

"Please, Duncan, I beg of you. Say nothing more."

Duncan regarded his sister strangely, but made no reply as one of the Glenfinnan servants brought their horses around and they mounted and started for home.

The marquess returned to his guests and found the ladies and gentlemen seated comfortably. Deborah was removing her bonnet as Ravenstoke entered. "Did you see Lady Alison and her brother off, then, Robert?"

"They are on their way now."

"Pity they could not stay," said Fenton Willoughby. "She was a dashed pretty girl, don't you think, Cyril?"

Lord Ensdale seemed to reflect on this carefully, and then, pulling a gold snuff box from his pocket, he delicately took a pinch between his fingers. "I don't know, Fenton, I daresay some would find her attractive, but I found her too . . . How shall I say it? Unpolished for my tastes. One might expect Scottish women to be that way, coming from such a godforsaken place as this." He smiled over at Deborah and then turned once again to Fenton. "I prefer our own English beauties such as your lovely cousin."

Deborah smiled back and Ravenstoke found himself becoming increasingly irritated. His parting from Alison had not put him in a favorable frame of mind and he controlled himself with some difficulty.

"Do stop your flummery, Ensdale," said Miss Willoughby, who, despite her words, seemed very pleased at the gentleman's remark. "I must say in poor Lady Alison's defense that she was quite above the ordinary for these parts. Poor thing. Did you see that riding habit she was wearing? I have not seen one like that in ages."

Lady Willoughby nodded. "Though she may be a titled young lady, it is obvious she is either too poor to dress properly or indifferent to fashion. I daresay I do not know which is worse."

"Lady Alison's grandfather is the Duke of Dornach,"

said Ravenstoke, trying to mask his indignation. "The Murrays are a most distinguished family in Scotland."

"My dear Ravenstoke," drawled Ensdale, "what does it signify if a family is distinguished in Scotland? It is still Scotland, after all."

Deborah and her cousin Fenton smiled at this remark and Lady Willoughby nodded solemnly. "I do not like Scotland overmuch, Ravenstoke," she said. "It is the most dreary country. And so barbarous. Oh, the inns in which we were forced to stay! You cannot know how much we have all suffered."

Fenton Willoughby nodded. "Indeed, Aunt. And the food, Ravenstoke. I have not had a decent meal since crossing the border. I do hope you have an English cook."

"My cook is Scottish, Willoughby," said the marquess. "I hope you can endure your stay."

Fenton Willoughby looked uncertain as to whether he would be able to do so, and Lord Ensdale laughed. "My dear Fenton, it will be good for you." He looked over at the marquess. "I certainly admire your spirit of adventure, Ravenstoke, coming up here amid the barbarians."

"And I admire your spirit of adventure, Ensdale. I would not have expected you, nor indeed any of you, to come. I imagine the weather in London is much better."

"Indeed it is," said Deborah. "But I must admit, Robert, I was terribly curious as to why you were so eager to leave London and come here. It seemed very odd to everyone, you hurrying off like you did. Indeed, everyone was talking about it. I knew I had to find out what the attraction was." She smiled sweetly. "Have I discovered it already?"

"Deborah." Lady Willoughby directed a warning look at her daughter.

"Well, Robert," said Deborah, "perhaps you will have someone show my mother and me to our rooms. We are so very tired. It has been an arduous journey."

"Yes, of course." Ravenstoke rang for a servant and the bell was answered by one of the maids. Ensdale and Fenton Willoughby also expressed their desire to retire to their rooms and so, soon, the marquess was left alone. He sat down in a chair and frowned. Now, seeing Deborah once again, Ravenstoke wondered that he had ever agreed to marry her. And how he detested her mother and cousin, not to mention the loathing he felt for Cyril Feversham, Baron Ensdale.

Ravenstoke's frown grew deeper as he remembered Alison's expression when he had told her Deborah was his fiancée. Whatever feelings she had had for him were certainly gone forever. Indeed, he had acted badly and could never expect to make amends. After all, he was to marry Deborah and must give up all thoughts of the lovely Alison. The marquess rose and paced across the room, well aware that forgetting Alison Murray would not be easy.

18   The following morning Ravenstoke joined his guests for breakfast. He reflected as he did so that he had never been more miserable. The previous night's dinner had been disastrous and the visitors had made it very clear that the food was not to their liking. The conversation was definitely not to his lordship's liking, for Ensdale had dominated it, discoursing on the trials and tribulations of overland travel in Scotland.

In London circles Ensdale was accorded a wit, but Ravenstoke found nothing amusing about his insulting remarks. Unlike the marquess, the other guests thought young Lord Ensdale terribly funny and Deborah laughed merrily at everything he said. It was a great relief to Ravenstoke that they all retired early, claiming weariness from the long day's journey.

This allowed the marquess more time by himself for melancholy pondering and he got little sleep that night. Unlike Ravenstoke, the guests seemed well-rested when his lordship joined them in the dining room. He nodded to them all and sat down beside Deborah, who was carefully attired in a pale-blue morning dress of jaconet muslin that featured tiny puff sleeves trimmed with narrow French lace. Miss Willoughby's stylish appearance was lost on Ravenstoke, who barely noted what she was wearing.

"Good morning, Robert."

"Good morning, Deborah. I trust you slept well."

"Indeed I did, Robert, but then I was completely exhausted from our ordeal."

Fenton Willoughby nodded. "It was that. What a relief it was to awaken this morning and know I did not have to sit all day in a coach traveling over dreadful roads."

"How true, Fenton," said Lady Willoughby. "And I am pleased to say that my room was quite comfortable. A very pleasant change from those inns."

Realizing that the conversation was once again focusing upon the horrors of Scottish travel, Ravenstoke changed the subject as the servants began to serve breakfast. "The salmon is from the river here at Glenfinnan."

"How wonderful," said Ensdale. "And are you a fisherman, Ravenstoke? I did not take you for one."

"This land is well-suited to it," replied the marquess glumly.

"Well, I never thought there was much sport in fishing," said Fenton Willoughby, eyeing the salmon hungrily. "Not like hunting, what?"

"But then, one must take what sport one can, is that not so, Ravenstoke?" commented Ensdale with a sardonic smile. "I daresay there is little to do here but fish."

"But there is some society, surely," said Lady Willoughby.

"Oh, Mama, what sort of society could one expect in such a place?" said Deborah. She looked over at Ravenstoke. "Have you attended many local functions?"

"The Dornach Ball has been the only event."

"The Dornach Ball?" said Deborah. "Given by the family of Lady Alison, whom we met yesterday?"

"Yes."

"I suspect it was a grand occasion," said Deborah with a trace of sarcasm. "I should have liked to have been there."

"And did the gentlemen wear kilts?" asked Fenton Willoughby, suddenly interested.

"Yes, most of them did."

"Now, I should especially like to have seen that," said Deborah, smiling over at Ensdale.

"I wonder how I would look in Highland dress," mused Fenton. "What do you think, Cyril?"

"My dear Fenton, do not force me to conjure up such a picture," exclaimed Ensdale in mock horror.

They all laughed, save Ravenstoke. "And did you dress like a Highland chieftain, Robert?" said Deborah.

"Don't be absurd."

"Well, it would not have surprised me, Robert. This place has exerted a very strange influence upon you, and I shall be very glad when you return to England."

"I have no intention of doing so soon."

Deborah regarded him with disapproval. "There is a small social occasion planned in London that you are expected to attend, and I do hope you will return in time for it. Our wedding, if you have not forgotten."

"I have not forgotten, madam," replied Ravenstoke testily, and Lady Willoughby hastened to turn the conversation to more neutral subjects.

"The weather looks as if it will be quite good today."

"It does indeed, Aunt." Fenton looked over at Ravenstoke. "I should like to go riding, if I may."

"You may choose any of the horses. You will find my stables more than adequate."

"I wish I enjoyed riding," said Lady Willoughby. "I daresay it appears there is little else to do here. If there is no society . . ."

"Really, Mama, there is society. Robert has said he attended a splendid ball. Surely, we will have many interesting visitors."

"Do not expect any calls, Deborah."

"And why is that?"

Ravenstoke frowned. "I have not been welcomed here. As an Englishman taking Scottish lands, my position is awkward. And then, when it was discovered that my grandfather was the Baron Wicklow, who fought at Culloden, most of my neighbors completely ostracized me."

"Good God!" said Ensdale. "You mean to say that no one will speak to you and yet you stay on in this place?"

"Robert never did care for society," said Deborah. "I fancy he is content to be ostracized. But, Robert, you did have some callers yesterday, Lady Alison and her charming brother."

"Charming?" said Lady Willoughby. "The boy had the manners of a stableboy."

"Lady Willoughby," said Ravenstoke severely. "Duncan Murray is guilty only of a certain youthful exuberance. He is as well-mannered as any boy of his age in town."

"Do you think so, Ravenstoke?" returned Lady Willoughby. "I cannot agree. If you had but seen my nephew Fenton when he was a boy, you would know this Duncan Murray cannot compare. Fenton's manners were . . ." She paused and looked fondly at her nephew. "And are still quite perfect."

"Oh, Aunt Harriet, you embarrass me." Fenton's round face flushed slightly and he looked down at his plate and took up a forkful of salmon.

Not trusting himself to make a reply, Ravenstoke kept silent.

"I shall be so awfully bored if there is no society at all," said Deborah.

"Indeed." Lady Willoughby nodded. "But if you are on good terms with this Lady Alison and her family and her grandfather is a duke, it seems there is the prospect of some society."

"Yes, of course," said Deborah. "We must have them over for a dinner party."

"What a remarkably good idea, Miss Willoughby," exclaimed Ensdale. "I say, Ravenstoke, you must make haste to invite them. Indeed, if there is anyone else you could invite, you must do so. Oh, I think it will be so amusing to meet Ravenstoke's Scottish neighbors. I suspect they will make a change from London society."

Ravenstoke frowned and paused before replying. "I really don't think—"

Deborah cut him off. "Oh, Robert, you cannot refuse. And I shall attend to everything. It would be such fun, wouldn't it, Mama?"

Lady Willoughby nodded. "It would present a diversion, in any case, Ravenstoke. Yes, directly after breakfast you will tell us whom we should send invitations."

Having the matter thus decided, the marquess could only frown and direct his attention to his breakfast.

Although not in the least hungry, he took up his fork and began eating.

Alison was seated on the sofa in the library trying to read. A cold rain was falling and the sky was dark, making it necessary to use an oil lamp despite it being midday. A sigh escaped Alison and she put the book down on her lap. It was no use, she told herself. She was far too miserable to read.

Rising from the chair and depositing the book on a table, Alison walked to the window and gazed out at the rain. It had been two days since she had last seen Ravenstoke, two days since she had learned that he was engaged to be married, and the hurt and disappointment had not lessened at all. If only she had known about Deborah Willoughby, she could have guarded her heart and prevented herself from falling in love with him.

A slight smile came to Alison's face. What a goose I have been, she thought, and wondered how she could have so misjudged him. She had not taken Ravenstoke for the sort of man who would trifle with a lady's affections. He seemed an unlikely gallant, and indeed, when she had first met him, she had thought him decidedly unlikable.

Alison's thoughts turned to Deborah Willoughby, and she frowned. Miss Willoughby was certainly beautiful and her stunning clothes made her even more so. A man could not be faulted for finding her very attractive. Alison knitted her brows in concentration. Still, she reflected, she would not have thought Deborah the sort of woman Ravenstoke would choose for his wife.

Her thoughts were interrupted by the appearance of her brother Andrew and the duke. "There you are, lass," said her grandfather. The elderly man leaned heavily on his cane as he entered the library, and Alison hurried over to him.

"Are you all right, Grandfather?"

The duke nodded. "This accursed gout always pains me in such weather as this, but it is not so bad. Quit fussing about me, Alison. I am no invalid."

"Of course not, Grandfather." Alison looked over at her brother, prepared to exchange a knowing look with him, but Andrew only stared past her and then assisted the duke to sit down in his favorite chair. Alison eyed Andrew, reflecting that her brother had not got over his irritation with her. Of all the Murrays, it was Andrew who would hold a grudge the longest.

"And how is Claymore faring, my girl?" asked the duke.

"Claymore?" Alison smiled. "I suspect he is quite unhappy about this rain preventing him from his usual run."

"Aye, he is a fine horse, Claymore," said his grace. "I shall be most interested to see him race at the fair." The duke looked over at Andrew. "You had best be exercising Claymore, Andrew. 'Tis you who will be racing him."

"Aye," muttered Andrew, "but Alison hardly ever lets me get near him."

"Andrew Murray, you know very well that you may take Claymore out whenever you please. If you were not always with Ian MacGillivray, you might have time to do so."

Andrew scowled at his sister and the duke hastened to stop their quarreling. "That is enough, both of you. I want you to give thought to the race, for it is important Claymore do well."

"He will, Grandfather," said Alison.

Andrew nodded. "You need not worry about Claymore. I shall ride him every day until the race."

"Good. And where is young Duncan?"

"He is with Mr. Ferguson, Grandfather." Alison smiled. "The poor man has agreed to try once more and Duncan has promised to try harder to master his studies."

"I am glad of it," said the duke. "And the young rascal had best attend Mr. Ferguson or he will answer to me."

Bob MacPherson entered the room at that moment and cleared his throat. "Your pardon, your grace, but a messenger arrived frae Glenfinnan wi' a letter for ye."

"A letter from Ravenstoke?"

The servant nodded and gave the duke the letter. Alison tried to show no emotion as her grandfather broke the letter's seal and then read it. He looked up at her. "We are invited to dinner at Glenfinnan."

"Oh." Alison appeared uninterested, a fact Andrew did not fail to note.

"What is wrong, Alison?" he said. "You cannot mean you are not eager to go?"

"I am not eager to go. Indeed, I should prefer declining the invitation."

The duke regarded his granddaughter in some surprise. "What is the matter, Alison? I know very well your brother bears no love for the Englishman, but I thought you liked him well enough."

"Lord Ravenstoke has guests from London. Duncan and I met them when we called at Glenfinnan the day before yesterday."

"What sort of guests were these, coming all the way from London?" Andrew asked.

Hoping to appear indifferent, Alison replied offhandedly. "There were two ladies and two gentlemen. A Miss Willoughby and her mother as well as her cousin and a friend, a Lord Ensdale. They were all quite grand. Lord Ravenstoke is engaged to be married to Miss Willoughby."

"So that explains them coming so far," said the duke.

"He is engaged to be married?" Andrew looked over at his sister, who nodded.

"Miss Willoughby is very pretty and wore such a lovely dress."

Andrew found himself overjoyed at the news, but irritated with Ravenstoke for his attentions to his sister. So the man was betrothed and still played up to Alison! Perhaps now his sister would heed his warnings. Andrew tried not to appear smug. Not completely insensitive, he knew that Alison was doubtlessly very much upset. "I would be very much surprised if this Miss Willoughby can hold a candle to you, Allie."

She smiled at him, grateful to Andrew for not commenting further. "Well, she is very much the lady of fashion."

The duke did not seem to be attending. He was rereading the invitation. "It would not be polite to refuse this invitation."

Andrew looked over at his grandfather in astonishment. "You cannot mean, sir, that you will accept it?"

"And why not? Indeed, Ravenstoke has been decent to me. He did rescue Alison from the crevasse and his man saved your brother from drowning. And do not forget that he so generously gave me Glenfinnan's most cherished relic. To refuse this invitation would be ungentlemanly."

"Really, Grandfather," cried Andrew. "You cannot expect me to sit down with such a man. Och, you know how I feel about him, and now he has treated my sister so shabbily."

"Treated your sister so shabbily? What do you mean? Alison, what is your brother talking about?"

"Oh, Grandfather, Andrew is speaking nonsense. Lord Ravenstoke has always treated me with consideration."

Andrew looked at his sister in surprise. "You still defend him? Och, Alison Murray, you are the greatest goosecap!"

"Andrew!" The duke directed an imperious look at his grandson. "You are not to speak to your sister in such a way. I have heard enough from you, young man. I am the Murray of Dornach, am I not?"

"Aye," muttered Andrew.

"And you owe me obedience. You'll say not one more word about Ravenstoke and you will accompany me and your sister to Glenfinnan for dinner. Do you understand?"

Andrew hesitated and looked over at Alison. "Aye, sir," he said finally.

"And that settles it." The duke seemed glad that his authority was no longer in question and once again turned the topic to Claymore's racing prospects.

19 Since he had been in Scotland, Ravenstoke
had got into the habit of rising early. Therefore, the marquess was up long before his guests, who
were still accustomed to keeping town hours. Leaving the
house in the early morning, his lordship felt a sense of
relief at being alone. He knew very well he was not a
sociable person, but he suspected his unwelcome house-
guests would try even the most gregarious of hosts.

It had rained for the past two days and Ravenstoke was
glad to see that the sky had finally cleared. The weather
was too chill to be pleasant, but at least it was dry. One of
the grooms brought him his horse and the marquess
mounted the bay gelding and started off. He headed in the
direction of Dornach Castle, although he had no intention
of calling there.

However, the prospect of happening upon Alison Murray explained his choice of direction. Knowing that she
rode Claymore each day, his lordship thought there was a
chance he might meet her. Ravenstoke felt a compelling
need to see Alison again. She was seldom out of his
thoughts and the idea that she was angry with him was
intolerable. If he were fortunate enough to see her, he
would attempt to explain.

Ravenstoke frowned. Explain what? That he was to
marry Deborah Willoughby even though he was in love
with Alison? The marquess eased his horse from a trot
into a canter and continued his reflections. Could he not

break his engagement to Deborah? The idea had been with him since before her arrival, and now it dominated his thoughts. If only he could consult his solicitor, he thought, and then reproved himself.

If he were any sort of man, he reflected, he would inform Deborah he would not marry her and the consequences be damned. What did it signify that the marriage contract was already signed? Did it really matter so much? Ravenstoke frowned. He had always been a man who set great store by propriety. Surely it was his duty to carry out his obligations. Indeed, he was allowing his infatuation for Alison to cloud his judgment so much that he would consider going back on his word as a gentleman.

Ravenstoke was so deep in concentration that he barely realized it when he reached the boundary of his property and entered the duke's lands. He continued on and then, seeing Alison riding toward him, he pulled his gelding abruptly to a stop.

Alison recognized Ravenstoke immediately and debated with herself if she should turn Claymore around and return home. Although she was unsure whether she wanted to talk to the marquess, Alison continued on, coming to a stop beside him. "Good morning, Lord Ravenstoke."

"Lady Alison."

"You are about early, sir." Alison tried to sound cheerful, deciding that it would be best to act as if nothing were wrong.

"Yes," said Ravenstoke.

"It is good to see the rain has stopped."

"It is," replied the marquess, looking down at his horse and then back at Alison. "I am glad you and your family are coming to dinner Thursday."

"We look forward to it," replied Alison lamely.

Neither said anything for a moment and then Ravenstoke broke the silence. "Damn it, Alison, I did mean to tell you about Miss Willoughby. I did not mean to hurt you."

"Lord Ravenstoke, I beg you say nothing more about it. I assure you I wish you all the happiness in the world."

"But I know it was most upsetting to find out about Deborah in such a way."

"My lord, do not mistake my surprise for something else," said Alison, managing to smile, but inwardly resenting the marquess. So he thought she was dying of a broken heart? Well, she would show him that he was presuming far too much. "Forgive me, Lord Ravenstoke, but Claymore grows restless and we have a long way to go. Do excuse me. I shall see you and your guests Thursday evening. Good day."

With these words, Alison turned her horse and, touching Claymore lightly with her riding crop, galloped off.

Ravenstoke watched her ride away and then solemnly turned his own mount and started back to Glenfinnan.

Lady Alison Murray stared critically into the mirror of her dressing table and studied her auburn hair. "Thank you, Jean, I think that shall do very nicely." Her maid nodded and regarded her mistress with some satisfaction. Alison's auburn tresses had been stylishly dressed in the French mode with a profusion of curls at the sides of her face. Her back hair had been pinned at the crown of her head and was partly concealed by a garland of ivory silk roses.

"Ye look just like the picture, m'lady, but more beautiful," said the maid proudly. Jean had attempted arranging her mistress's hair according to an illustration in a London fashion magazine that was sitting open on the dressing table. She had succeeded admirably, and glancing down at the illustration and then once again into the mirror, Alison nodded.

"It appears that I am ready to go."

"Aye, m'lady."

Alison rose from the dressing table and cast one last look in the mirror. Her dress, although certainly not new, looked very lovely. It was a simple gown of ivory satin, and the bottom of the skirt was embroidered with roses. It was comforting to know that she looked her best. It made it easier to face dinner at Glenfinnan with Miss Deborah Willoughby, who would doubtlessly be garbed in the height of London fashion.

A frown crossed Alison's fair countenance. If only she did not have to attend this dinner, she thought. She knew how horrible it would be, sitting there attempting to be civil and all the time thinking of Ravenstoke and being miserable.

"Alison, are you ready?" Andrew Murray called to her from the hallway.

"Aye," she said, joining her brother. "You look very handsome, Lord Culwin."

Andrew smiled. He had reconciled himself to going to dinner at Glenfinnan and seemed to be in a good humor. Indeed, Alison reflected that she was probably more reluctant to go than her brother. The young man did look splendid in his Highland dress. He wore a black velvet jacket and the Murray of Dornach tartan kilt. "And you look absolutely beautiful, Lady Alison Murray."

Alison smiled in return. It was good being on friendly terms with her brother once again. She took his arm and they went downstairs to join the duke, who was waiting for them. His grace was dressed like his grandson, and Alison thought that her grandfather looked every inch a duke and clan chieftain. The duke eyed his grandchildren with approval and then the three of them set off for Glenfinnan.

Lord Ravenstoke was not looking forward to his dinner party, knowing that the occasion was doomed to disaster from the first. The prospect of seeing Alison Murray under these circumstances seemed almost unbearable, and he dreaded the impersonal civility he knew would now mark their relationship.

The marquess frowned as Mull helped him into his evening coat. "Will there be anything else, m'lord?"

"No, Mull, that is all. You go along."

Mull made a quick bow and left his master, thoughtfully regarding his reflection in the mirror. Ravenstoke turned away from the mirror and went over to the window to stare out into the blackness. It would not be a large party dining at Glenfinnan. Not wanting the Murrays to be the only additional guests, Ravenstoke had thought hard about whom else to invite. Mull had suggested the Reverend Mr. Farquhar and his family, and to his lordship's relief, that gentleman had accepted his invitation.

The marquess was only slightly acquainted with the Reverend Mr. Farquhar, who had called upon him once at Glenfinnan and had made it clear that he held neither Ravenstoke's unfortunate family connections nor his membership in the Church of England against him. A devout and learned Presbyterian, the Reverend Mr. Farquhar was an amiable gentleman of good family. He had lived in London and Paris and was, therefore, much more cosmopolitan and tolerant than many of his neighbors.

In addition to the Reverend Mr. Farquhar, there would be his wife and his mother-in-law, Lady Sarah Sinclair, and his unmarried daughter. This meant there would be twelve at table, and though a small group, it was of respectable size.

Ravenstoke looked over at the mantel clock and, noting the time, decided that he could no longer wait. The guests would be arriving soon and Deborah was probably wondering why he was taking so long. Another frown came to the marquess as he thought of his future bride. She had taken great interest in this dinner party, spending what seemed to him an excessively long time discussing the seating arrangements and menu. Deborah had taken a keen dislike to his cook and, thinking her highly incompetent, personally supervised the dinner preparation, insisting to Ravenstoke that she wanted this, "their" first dinner party, to be perfect.

His lordship had to admit that Miss Willoughby was most adept at planning such affairs. He also noticed that she had an imperious way with servants, and although a trifle harsh, she had the Glenfinnan staff working as they had never worked before. Certainly, Ravenstoke told himself, Deborah Willoughby had many qualities that would make her an effective marchioness. Such thoughts did little to console his lordship, who, despite his resolve to force Alison Murray from his mind, continued to find her the object of his reflections.

Going downstairs and entering the drawing room, Ravenstoke found his London guests in good humor. They were all laughing, save Ensdale, who looked rather smug and was obviously the cause of the merriment.

"Oh, Robert," said Deborah. "It is a pity you did not hear what Lord Ensdale just said. It was too droll."

"Sorry, Ravenstoke," said Ensdale. "I never repeat my stories. I find it so dull for those who have heard them."

"You are a hard man, Ensdale," said the marquess ironically. He then turned toward his fiancée and realized that she looked marvelous. He noted her charming dress of pale-blue lace-trimmed satin and the deft arrangement of her blond hair. Surely there was not a woman in London who could compare with her. Ravenstoke looked thoughtful and wondered at the fact that Deborah's beauty did not excite him.

"Robert, is something the matter?"

"What?" Ravenstoke regarded Miss Willoughby with a faintly puzzled look. "Oh, nothing is the matter."

He was spared the necessity of saying anything further, for his butler arrived to announce the arrival of the Farquhar party. Ravenstoke had thought that the Reverend Mr. Farquhar was an engaging man, but he and his family seemed sadly out of place alongside Lord Ensdale and the Willoughbys.

Mrs. Farquhar was a large woman with piercing blue eyes and a strong personality. She did not seem at all intimidated by the obvious wealth and rank of Ravenstoke's guests and cast disapproving looks at Lord Ensdale and Fenton Willoughby. Her mother, Lady Sarah Sinclair, also appeared to be a woman of strong character. Extremely talkative, she spoke in broad Scots dialect, much to the amusement of Lord Ensdale. Miss Farquhar was a pretty girl of eighteen who was dressed in an unflattering yellow frock. She seemed too awed by her surroundings and the London company to say anything, and standing there beside her mother, Miss Farquhar reminded the marquess of a fledgling that had fallen from its nest.

After what seemed to Ravenstoke a very long time, the butler announced his grace, the Duke of Dornach, Lord Culwin, and Lady Alison Murray. Ravenstoke turned and stared as Alison entered the room. She glanced over at him, meeting his gaze for a brief moment and then looking quickly away.

Somehow Ravenstoke managed to retain his composure and he calmly went about introducing his guests. His grace's exotic dress and regal demeanor caused Lord Ensdale to raise an eyebrow. The marquess watched

Ensdale exchange an amused look with Deborah, and he frowned.

Although he had known that it would scarcely be an enjoyable evening, Lord Ravenstoke had not realized how difficult the dinner party was to prove for him. He was glad when they departed the drawing room and took their places at the table. The food provided some diversion and displaced the need for conversation. Most of the guests, even Lord Ensdale, seemed well-satisfied as the courses were brought out to them.

Conversation at Ravenstoke's end of the table was desultory at best. Lady Willoughby directed a few polite comments to the marquess and then fell silent. The duke, who was seated at Lady Willoughby's right, was kept occupied by Lady Sarah Sinclair, who talked loudly in her Highland burr about horses and myriad other subjects. Lady Willoughby kept looking down the table at Lady Sarah, eyeing both her and the duke with a stern humorless gaze.

Deborah Willoughby was seated at Ravenstoke's left, and next to her sat Lord Ensdale. That gentleman seemed to take great interest in what Lady Sarah and the duke were saying across table, and every so often Ensdale would lean toward Deborah and whisper something to her. Miss Willoughby would place one delicate hand up to her lips as if to surpress her laughter and then comment back to Ensdale in a low voice. The marquess would have been quite annoyed with his fiancée if his attention had not been fixed completely upon Alison.

She was seated three chairs down from him and seemed to be taking great care not to look in his direction. On one side of Alison was Lord Ensdale and on the other was the Reverend Mr. Farquhar. She was dividing her attention between them and Ravenstoke noted a bit unhappily that Alison appeared to be enjoying herself.

He watched her nod to Lord Ensdale and was irked to see her smile at one of that gentleman's remarks. He had thought she had better judgment than to find Ensdale amusing. Then, when the Reverend Mr. Farquhar directed a remark to her, causing Alison to burst into delighted laughter, Ravenstoke frowned. It appeared the young lady was well over him, thought Ravenstoke. Or perhaps, he mused cynically, she had never possessed any feeling for him at all.

Even Andrew Murray seemed to be having a good time, seated between Miss Farquhar and that young lady's mother. Andrew was well-acquainted with these two ladies and had no trouble discoursing with them on a variety of subjects.

Ravenstoke grew gloomier by the minute as he noted the comparative happiness of his guests. Indeed, the only other person looking displeased with the company was Lady Willoughby, and his lordship knew very well that that was her ladyship's usual state.

It would have surprised Alison to learn that Ravenstoke had mistakenly assumed she was taking pleasure in the company. In truth, she found Lord Ensdale quite insufferable, although she took care to appear civil to him. Knowing the Reverend Mr. Farquhar very well and being sincerely fond of him, Alison did enjoy conversing with him. However, she was all too aware of Ensdale's amusement over Lady Sarah and her grandfather. She saw clearly the baron's arched brows and amused glances and how he whispered comments to Deborah Willoughby.

Alison had to rein in her Murray temper as she noticed Lady Willoughby's haughty looks of disapproval directed primarily at Lady Sarah, but also at her grandfather. It was clear that Lady Willoughby, her daughter, and the dreadful Lord Ensdale thought of them as ludicrous bumpkins and she was certain that he would regale his London friends with tales of his experiences with the uncivilized Highlanders.

"Perhaps you might be able to help me, Lady Alison." Ensdale was addressing her and smiling his usual bland smile.

She looked over at him. "Help you, Lord Ensdale?"

"Why, yes, I am so impressed by how dashing his grace and your brother look this evening that I should like to have such a costume."

"I doubt that you would have much opportunity to wear it in London."

"My dear girl, I do as I please in town, and should I

appear in Highland dress, I daresay a good many others would soon do so. I do not wish to appear immodest, but I do exert some small influence upon the sartorial tastes of my fellows." He glanced over at the duke and then back at Alison. "And I am mad for that tartan! It would suit my coloring to perfection. It is, I assume, the badge of your Murray clan."

Alison directed a discerning look at the baron and decided that he was mocking her. There was a slight smile on his pale face and a glimmer of laughter in his close-set hazel eyes. "There are many good shops in the village that would be only too happy to serve you. But I caution you, Lord Ensdale, do not attempt to wear the tartan of Murray of Dornach." Alison tried hard to appear serious. "There is a saying in our clan."

Alison spoke some Gaelic words and Ensdale looked bewildered. "Whatever does that mean, Lady Alison?"

"It may be translated as 'Death to him who dares wear the Murray colors and is not of our blood.'"

The baron laughed. "Surely you jest, Lady Alison."

Shaking her head solemnly, Alison replied, "Indeed not, sir. Oh, of course, I do not wish to alarm you, but here in the Highlands, the people cling to the old ways and it would be considered a grievous insult should an Englishman be seen wearing the tartan of Murray of Dornach."

"You cannot mean I might come to harm should I do so?"

"Perhaps not." Alison paused. "But then, one could not be certain. My grandfather's Highlanders are not known to be moderate men and they are so devoted to the old traditions. Indeed, if you but knew of the story of my kinsman, Ranald Murray, called the Mad Murray, but no, it is hardly an appropriate topic for dinner. Suffice it to say that he dealt very harshly with an Englishman who dared wear a brooch with a bit of Murray of Dornach tartan clinging to it."

Ensdale's incredulous and rather nervous expression caused Alison to almost burst into laughter. He looked at her, suspecting that she was quizzing him, but not entirely sure. A fainthearted man, the baron did not enjoy the thought of wild vengeful Highlanders swinging broad swords and decided that if Lady Alison were indeed making a joke, he did not appreciate her sense of humor. "Perhaps I shall give up the idea of Highland dress, after all," he said.

Alison nodded and then turned her attention to the Reverend Mr. Farquhar. Ensdale seemed glad of this and returned to Deborah.

It seemed to Lord Ravenstoke that dinner was interminable. When the meal was finally over, the ladies were excused, leaving the gentlemen free to indulge in serious drinking. A moderate man himself, the marquess hoped the presence of the Reverend Mr. Farquhar would exert a temperate influence. However, it was soon apparent that the duke and Andrew Murray did not allow the fact of having a clergyman among them impede them in the least. Likewise, Fenton Willoughby and Ensdale began downing glasses of port with gusto, and then, when in deference to Scottish customs the marquess supplied the gentlemen with whiskey, they seemed overjoyed and cheerfully indulged themselves.

Ravenstoke sat at the head of the table and frowned slightly. He wondered how the ladies were doing and whether Alison was talking to Deborah. He frowned again and sipped his glass of port.

Once the ladies had gathered in the drawing room, Alison wished desperately that the evening were over. She did not feel very sociable and was finding it a strain to appear civil for such a lengthy period of time. The fact that she had successfully hoaxed Lord Ensdale into abandoning the idea of obtaining his own Highland costume was small consolation for having to endure such a night as this.

"Alison, what do you think of Miss Willoughby? She is very grand, is she not?" Miss Farquhar stood beside Alison at the far end of the room. They were a good distance away from Deborah and her mother, who were making conversation with Mrs. Farquhar and Lady Sarah.

Lady Sarah's stentorian voice could be heard. "That may be the custom where ye come frae, Miss Willoughby, but here we do things verra different."

Alison heard Deborah reply ironically, "That is certainly true, Lady Sarah."

Alison frowned. "She is grand, Mary, far too grand for my liking."

Miss Farquhar nodded. "Aye. I was so glad I was not seated near her. I should have died of fright. And Lord Ensdale! I have never seen anyone so splendid. Don't you think he is so very handsome?"

"Ensdale handsome? Indeed not. He is too much the fop for my taste. Did you not think his neckcloth ridiculous?"

Mary Farquhar thought the matter over and then shrugged uncertainly. "Perhaps you are right, but he does seem such an elegant gentleman. Mr. Willoughby was quite civil to me. He is less grand than Lord Ensdale, of course, but very pleasant. I do fancy that English gentlemen seem better able to talk to ladies, don't you think?" When Alison did not express an opinion on this matter, Miss Farquhar continued. "Of course, Lord Ravenstoke did not seem very friendly. I found him rather fearsome-looking." Mary Farquhar hesitated. "Perhaps I should not mention it, but he seemed very interested in you."

"In me?"

"Aye. I would steal a glance at him now and then, and every time I did so, I found he was looking at you! But then, you are so beautiful, Alison. You put even the grand Miss Willoughby to shame."

"Nonsense, Mary." Alison hoped she was not blushing and quickly changed the subject. They stood talking for some time and Alison was surprised when Deborah Willoughby made her way over to them.

"May I join you?"

"Of course," said Miss Farquhar, smiling pleasantly but somewhat intimidated by Deborah's regal manner.

"I have had no opportunity to talk with either of you," said Miss Willoughby. She spoke as if the fact distressed her and fixed a disingenuous smile on Alison. "I am so enjoying this evening. It is so wonderful having the opportunity to meet Lord Ravenstoke's Scottish acquaintances. You are all so very charming. And how I admire your mother and grandmother, Miss Farquhar. They are such original women."

Miss Farquhar did not detect the sarcasm in Deborah's voice and smiled. "Thank you, Miss Willoughby."

"Perhaps you might wish to join them, Miss Farquhar."

Mary started to reply in the negative, but then, sensing that Miss Willoughby expected her to leave them, she nodded and went off. "Poor girl," murmured Deborah. "She is so unexceptional, and that dress! It was kind of Ravenstoke to invite her and her family, was it not? But then, he sometimes has the most democratic tendencies."

Miss Willoughby's words and the haughty manner in which they were spoken aggravated Alison, but she ignored the remarks and made no reply.

Miss Willoughby watched Mary join her mother and Lady Sarah and then turned to Alison. "How trying it must be for you to associate with a woman like Lady Sarah. Is it not too funny how the woman prattles on and in that dreadful dialect? It is so hard to understand. And knowing how well you speak, Lady Alison, it is quite surprising."

Alison directed a warning look at Deborah. "I am very fond of Lady Sarah."

"Oh, I do not mean to criticize the poor woman. She is so very quaint and amusing. One might say she has a certain picturesque charm, I suppose. I do not doubt Robert thinks her quite delightful, but then, he has such a passion for things Scottish." Deborah smiled knowingly at Alison. "Perhaps I should be glad of it. Indeed, I had not thought Robert the sort of man who had a passion for anything."

Alison felt her cheeks reddening and she restrained her urge to give Miss Willoughby a propepr set-down. She said nothing and Deobrah continued. "Have you never been to London, Lady Alison?"

Alison shook her head and Deborah regarded her pityingly. "How sad. I imagine you often dream of going there to be part of true society."

"I have no desire to go there," replied Alison quickly. "I find the society here quite sufficient for me."

Deborah looked amused and smiled patronizingly. "How lucky for you. I know I would go mad if I had to stay here very long. My dear, I admire your courage for enduring such dreariness."

"The only thing I am enduring is your foolish blather, Miss Willoughby." Alison was no longer able to restrain her temper, and her blue eyes flashed angrily. "Why don't you go back to London if you are so miserable?"

Deborah looked shocked. "Why, I never expected—"

Alison cut her off. "Do you think I shall allow you to go on making sport of us, speaking about us like we are some sort of barbarians? I am sick to death of you and I'll not listen to another word!"

Alison's outburst caused the Farquhars to turn and stare at her in some astonishment. Not wanting to stay a moment longer with the obnoxious Miss Willoughby, Alison rushed from the room. Angry tears welled up in her eyes as she came out into the hallway and hurried on toward the entry hall. She was so upset that she barely knew where she was going and, quickly turning the corner, found herself bumping directly into Lord Ravenstoke.

"Lady Alison!" Ravenstoke caught her in his arms. "Whatever is the matter?"

"Nothing!" cried Alison, pulling away from him. She saw that the other gentlemen were behind him, evidently on their way to joining the ladies, and she tried desperately to compose herself. She looked at the duke. "I am sorry, Grandfather, but I wish to go home."

"Are you unwell, Alison?" asked the duke.

Andrew hurried to his sister. "What is wrong?"

"Oh, nothing. I pray you do not worry." Alison looked beseechingly at her brother. "I wish to go home, Andrew."

"Very well," said Andrew gallantly. "I shall take you. Is that not all right, Grandfather?"

"Of course," replied the duke. "It is time I made my farewells. An old man should go to his bed at an early hour, and it grows late."

Ravenstoke looked at Alison, but she ignored him and took her brother's arm. "I am sorry if you are ill, Lady Alison," he said.

"I am sure my sister is only tired, sir," said Andrew.

The duke nodded. "Good night to you gentlemen and give our farewells to the ladies."

Ravenstoke nodded and shook the duke's hand. He then watched them go with a worried and unhappy expression.

"I demand to know what you said to Lady Alison."

Deborah Willoughby looked up at Ravenstoke, an expression of disbelief on her pretty face. She had never seen him angry, and it surprised her. The marquess stood there in the drawing room, his arms crossed on his chest. Miss Willoughby sat on the sofa, her mother beside her.

Lord Ensdale stood behind Deborah, and Fenton sat some distance away asleep in an armchair. "Why do you think I upset her?" Deborah pursed her lips in a pout.

"I know very well that you did. I will not have my guests insulted!"

"Your guests?" Lady Willoughby frowned. "Why should you care about such persons? They were all simply horrid, every one of them."

Ravenstoke cast a warning look at his future mother-in-law and she fell immediately silent. "I will not have it," repeated the marquess. "Anyone whom I choose to invite into my home is entitled to respect."

"Now, come, Ravenstoke," said Ensdale soothingly. "Do not be so upset. I am sure this is no serious matter. You know how some silly little thing can upset a young lady. And doubtlessly Lady Alison felt unwell."

"I swear to you, Robert, I said nothing to offend her," continued Deborah. "But I must say that she is a most volatile and unstable person, flying up into the boughs at the least provocation."

Ravenstoke directed a scathing look at Deborah and Ensdale and, not trusting himself to say anything further, abruptly turned and left the room.

"My poor Miss Willoughby!" Lord Ensdale hurried to sit beside her. "How ever could he treat you in such a manner?"

"I do not know." Deborah brushed a tear from her eye.

Lady Willoughby cast a disapproving glance at Ensdale. "My dear Lord Ensdale, I would be obliged to you if you would see to my nephew. I shall sit with Deborah for a time."

"Very well." Ensdale rose somewhat reluctantly and, taking Fenton by the arm, helped that young gentleman to his feet. He then led a very groggy Fenton Willoughby from the room.

"Deborah," said Lady Willoughby, "I think you had best be careful. Ravenstoke was sorely vexed with you."

"Oh, why should I care? It is I who should be vexed with him. He is making a fool of himself over this Scottish minx, and I find it disgusting. Can he not wait until after we are married to take his mistresses?"

"Deborah!"

"Oh, really, Mama, you are growing tiresome."

Lady Willoughby shook a disapproving finger at her daughter. "I warn you, my girl. You do not have Ravenstoke yet, and unless you want him to slip away, you had best take care."

"I don't know why I am marrying him in the first place!"

"You always were a willful child," said Lady Willoughby with a frown. "But I did not think you so addlepated to forget that you are marrying one of the richest men in England." She looked shrewdly at her daughter. "Ensdale's fortune is nothing in comparison."

"Mama!"

"Do not look the innocent. I see how you look at him. When you marry Ravenstoke, you will gain wealth and an illustrious title. You will have great houses and everything you could wish."

Deborah nodded glumly. "I will also have Ravenstoke," she said. "Oh, don't worry, Mama, I shall not provoke him any further."

Somewhat mollified, Lady Willoughby patted her daughter's hand and then the two women rose from the sofa and left the room.

20 After returning home from Glenfinnan, Alison went directly to bed. She slept restlessly, waking many times throughout the night, and was relieved to see the first morning light make its appearance in her bedchamber. Rising from her bed, Alison went to her window and stared out onto the castle grounds, noting that the early-spring flowers looked lovely.

Alison sighed and turned away from her window. She doubted that she would ever appreciate such things again. She had never been so depressed and disheartened as she was at that moment.

Trying to suppress thoughts of Ravenstoke and the dinner at Glenfinnan, Alison dressed quickly, putting on her green riding habit and hat. She wanted only to be alone and hoped as she started downstairs that none of the family would be about at this early hour.

Alison made her way to the stables and surprised a still-sleepy groom, who had not expected any of the Murrays to rise so early. Alison waited impatiently as the servant saddled her horse. She was eager to get out onto the moors and hopeful that a spirited gallop atop her dear Claymore would help her forget the marquess and Miss Deborah Willoughby.

"Alison?"

"Andrew!" Alison regarded her brother in astonishment. "What ever are you doing up at this hour?"

"You are up, aren't you?"

"But I had none of Lord Ravenstoke's whiskey."

A grin appeared on Andrew's handsome face. "I admit that I might have liked to stay in bed a bit longer, but I wanted to talk to you. We didn't have much chance last night."

Alison looked down. "I know, and I do appreciate you and Grandfather not pressing me."

"Look, Allie, I know that we have quarreled lately. Indeed, we have never really made amends, not to my satisfaction anyway. But I am sorry about everything. I'll try to hold my temper and be more reasonable in the future. It was just the idea of you and that Englishman. Oh, do not look at me like that, Allie. I know how fond you were of Ravenstoke and how upset you must have been to find that he is to marry another! Well, I did always think him a blackguard—"

"I pray you, Andrew, do not say you hope I learned my lesson."

"I was not going to say that at all. Truly, Allie, I am sorry that you were hurt. It will be better in time."

Alison fought back her tears. "Thank you, Andrew," she managed to say.

"Would you like me to go riding with you? We haven't done so for a long time."

Alison kissed her brother on the cheek. "If you wouldn't mind, Andrew, I really wish to be alone."

Andrew nodded. "Very well. I do understand." He glanced over at Claymore. "It seems he's ready. I'll lift you up."

Once Alison was atop Claymore, she positioned her leg around the horn of the sidesaddle and then adjusted the skirt of her riding habit. "Don't worry about me, Andrew Murray." Alison smiled. "And you go back to bed."

Andrew grinned and slapped Claymore on the flank. The big stallion snorted and horse and rider were quickly off.

As soon as she was away from the castle and on the village road, Alison began to feel much better. Claymore was eager to run and Alison gave him his head. As usual, once the stallion was in full gallop, Alison was aware only of the speed of the big chestnut and the almost mystical feeling that horse and rider were one. All thoughts of Ravenstoke were gone, replaced by a sense of happiness in being alive, of being part of Claymore with his mighty strides and steady even breathing. The noble horse lived to run, and his joy in being free to do so was communicated to Alison, who urged him on faster and faster.

They covered more than a mile and Claymore showed no signs of tiring. Knowing that the stallion would run until he dropped, Alison slowed him down. "There, there, my friend, we have run enough for now." She patted his neck affectionately. "You must save some of your strength for the fair, and that is not so very far away. You must run for Andrew the way you do for me."

Alison patted her horse once again and hoped that Andrew would ride Claymore to victory in the important race next week. She had little doubt that he would do so, for after all, she told herself with a smile, Andrew was an excellent horseman, nearly as good as she.

Now in a much happier frame of mind, Alison continued on down the road, turning at the fork and going quite some distance before swinging back toward Dornach Castle. She passed through the village at midmorning. It was astir with activity, villagers and farmers going about their business in the bright sunshine. They were all known to Alison and she greeted one and all with the courtesy and easy grace that so endeared her to her neighbors.

Alison had not got far past the village when she espied the familiar figure of Ian MacGillivray mounted on his stallion Gaisgeach. He was talking to a man in a rude cart pulled by a decrepit pony. MacGillivray was speaking Gaelic and talking so loudly that Alison could hear him at some distance.

"I care not for your excuses, MacDowell. Pay me you will, or off my land!"

The other man was a sad-looking fellow of middle years who wore a ragged tartan kilt and shapeless coat. He was clutching his cap to his chest and eyeing Sir Ian fearfully. "But, sir, 'tis my wife. So ill is she, sir. A little more time is all I ask."

MacGillivray shouted a Gaelic epithet at the man that made Alison blush. "Sir Ian!" she cried.

The big man spun around in his saddle and, seeing Alison for the first time, grinned. "Alison, I did not think I would see you this morning. And there is noble Claymore." He turned back to the man in the cart and growled in English, "Be off with you, then, MacDowell, and remember what I told you."

MacDowell nodded and then bowed slightly toward Alison before driving off toward the village. Alison watched him go and then turned to Sir Ian. "And what was that about, Ian MacGillivray? The poor man looked frightened to death."

"Och, the poor man! Were he your tenant, Alison Murray, you would think differently. The man's a fool and a drunkard. You know the MacDowells, and 'tis a bad lot they are."

"But his poor wife and all the wee children!"

"He might think of them before he fritters his rent money on drink."

"But, Ian—"

"No, lass, I'll not discuss it anymore, although I am glad to hear you call me Ian. Let us not quarrel about such a one as MacDowell." The baronet grinned. "There are far better ways we might spend our time together."

"Any time spent with you, Ian MacGillivray, is illspent."

MacGillivray laughed, but before he could make a reply, they heard the sound of approaching riders. Turning toward them, Alison was filled with dismay. There was Ravenstoke accompanied by Lord Ensdale, Fenton Willoughby, and Deborah.

Alison frowned and MacGillivray did not fail to note her response. "It is the Englishman," he said. "And who are the others? I was told he had guests from London."

Alison nodded. "Aye, the lady is Lord Ravenstoke's fiancée."

MacGillivray was surprised at this and wondered if Alison's seeming indifference was genuine. "His fiancée?"

Alison nodded again. "The gentleman on her right is her cousin, Mr. Fenton Willoughby, and the other gentleman is Lord Ensdale."

MacGillivray eyed the oncoming riders with undisguised scorn. "A couple of fops they appear to me. The lass is not so bad-looking for them that like that type." He smiled over at Alison. "I prefer a different sort myself."

Alison frowned at him but made no comment.

Ravenstoke and his party were upon them within moments, and the four riders pulled up their horses. The marquess and the other English gentlemen raised their hats to Alison and Sir Ian did likewise, although a trace reluctantly.

Because of the previous night's events, Alison found the meeting most awkward. She regarded Deborah Willoughby coolly and made no remark.

Deborah glanced over at Ravenstoke who directed a warning look at her. "Lady Alison," she said. "I trust you are feeling better. We were all so worried about you, weren't we, Robert?"

Ravenstoke frowned. "Yes, we were."

Sir Ian looked questioningly at Alison. "Worried? Why would they be worried about you?"

"It is only that I developed a headache at Glenfinnan last night."

"Glenfinnan?" said Ian. "You were at Glenfinnan?"

"Yes," said Deborah Willoughby, entering the conversation. "We had the pleasure of having Lady Alison and her charming brother as well as the duke to dinner." She directed a sweet smile at Alison and then looked at Ian. "I don't believe we have met this gentleman."

MacGillivray grinned. "I have had the honor of meeting Ravenstoke," he said ironically, "but I much prefer meeting a lovely lady like you."

Alison and Ravenstoke exchanged a glance, and Alison made the introductions. "Miss Willoughby, may I present Sir Ian MacGillivray?"

"I am so very charmed," said Deborah.

"And these gentlemen are Lord Ensdale and Mr. Willoughby."

Lord Ensdale nodded serenely toward Sir Ian. "How do you do, sir?"

"Well enough," said MacGillivray, eyeing the baron with disfavor.

"I say, that is a dashed fine-looking horse you are

riding, sir," said Fenton Willoughby, regarding Gaisgeach with approval.

Sir Ian, despite his natural aversion to Englishmen, was willing to accept the compliment. "Aye, there is no finer horse than Gaisgeach in this county, save for Lady Alison's Claymore."

"Oh, yes," replied Fenton. "That is a fine one, too." He looked over at Ensdale. "You see, Cyril, there are some things of note in Scotland. These two horses prove it."

The tactlessness of this remark was not lost on MacGillivray, who frowned.

"Yes, Fenton, these are very nice horses. Indeed, Sir Ian and Lady Alison, you are well-mounted. I expect neither would disgrace one so very badly in a race."

Sir Ian scowled. "There is not a horse in Scotland who could beat Gaisgeach, except perhaps Claymore."

Ensdale looked slightly bored. "Perhaps so. Your horse has a rather curious name, doesn't he?"

Noting that MacGillivray was directing a black look at Lord Ensdale, Alison replied, "It is Gaelic. It means warrior."

"How very appropriate, I'm sure," said Ensdale, taking his snuffbox from his pocket.

Deborah smiled disingenuously at Ian and then turned to the marquess. "But surely, Robert, your horse would win against them."

"I really don't know—" Ravenstoke was cut off by Fenton Willoughby.

"Indeed, Ravenstoke, your Jupiter is of Eclipse's blood."

Ensdale nodded. "I expect that even in Scotland one has heard of Eclipse. He was the finest horse that ever breathed."

"Aye," muttered MacGillivray. "We have heard of Eclipse, but whatever the blood, that animal of Ravenstoke's is no match for either Gaisgeach or Claymore! And were he entered in the race at the fair next week you would find that out."

"Robert!" cried Deborah. "That sounds like a challenge. You must race Jupiter next week. Oh, it would be so amusing!"

Ravenstoke frowned. "I do not think that would be wise. Jupiter has never raced before and I know very well that Lady Alison's horse is faster."

"Oh, Robert!" Deborah regarded him in mock dismay. "Where is your sporting blood?"

"My dear Miss Willoughby," said Ensdale, "Ravenstoke has no sporting blood, which is why he shall make such an admirable husband."

Fenton and Deborah laughed at the remark and Ravenstoke frowned. "Come, Ravenstoke," said Sir Ian, "you should not disappoint your future bride. The lady wishes you to race. But then, I can understand if you are reluctant to try an English horse against our Scottish ones."

"Now, Ravenstoke," said Ensdale. "Our national honor is at stake! You cannot refuse now!"

"No, you cannot," cried Deborah, smiling over at Ensdale. "Do say you will."

"Oh, very well," muttered Ravenstoke. "As you wish."

"Good!" said Fenton. "It will give us all something to look forward to. It will make our stay here far less dreary!"

Ravenstoke looked at Alison and once again their eyes met briefly. Deborah, who was watching her fiancé closely, spoke again. "Should we not be going, Robert? I do not wish to delay Lady Alison and Sir Ian any further. They must have some distance to go."

"Aye, I am accompanying Lady Alison to Dornach Castle," said MacGillivray.

Alison directed a surprised look at Ian, but caught herself before making a tart reply. Deciding it would be better to allow the baronet to ride with her than to make a scene, she nodded.

"Dornach Castle," repeated Deborah. "It sounds so romantic. Do allow us to call upon you there, Lady Alison."

"If you like," Alison said coolly. "Good day to you all." She did not glance in Ravenstoke's direction, but started off and MacGillivray followed, happy to be accompanying her.

The others hesitated before continuing on into the

village. "A rough fellow, MacGillivray," commented Ensdale as he watched Alison and Sir Ian ride away.

"He certainly is." Deborah turned to Ravenstoke. "Did you note the dreadful coat he was wearing? And that hat! Why, our gardener in town wears better. And the way he looked at me! I daresay he thought I would be swept off my feet! The fellow's conceit was quite laughable. I must say I pity Lady Alison marrying a man like that."

Ravenstoke looked over at her. "Marrying MacGillivray? Don't be absurd."

"Then she is not marrying him?" Deborah's eyes grew wide, feigning astonishment.

"Why ever would you think so?"

"Why, one would just assume," said Deborah. She turned to Ensdale and then looked back at the marquess. "My dear Robert, one does not expect a young lady to be out riding alone with a gentleman unless she is engaged to him. Of course, perhaps standards of behavior for Highland ladies are not so rigid as those to which we must adhere."

"Indeed, yes," said Ensdale. "Conduct considered totally unsuitable to us is, in places like this, considered quite proper. We must not judge persons from this godforsaken place by our rules."

Although very much irritated by these comments, Ravenstoke chose to ignore them. "I think we had best go," he said, and not waiting for a reply, he kicked his horse and continued on. Deborah and Ensdale exchanged a glance and then followed.

21 The annual Dornach Fair was an event eagerly awaited by everyone living in the area surrounding Dornach Castle. It was a dearly beloved rite of spring and without a doubt the most welcomed occurrence of the year. The fair attracted people from miles around, and for a few short days the village seemed a bustling, exciting place.

Alison Murray tried to appear enthused as she accompanied her brother Duncan to the fair. She had hoped that she would have stopped thinking about Lord Ravenstoke by now. A week had passed since she had last seen him, but it was quite clear to Alison that it would take considerably longer for her to get over him. The marquess was still seldom out of her thoughts, a fact that caused her much pain, and as she walked with Duncan, Alison tried hard to concentrate on other matters.

"Oh, look, Allie! Jugglers!" The boy took his sister's hand and propelled her toward a crowd of people. They stood and watched the jugglers for a time. "They are good," said Duncan appreciatively, but after a short time, the boy grew restless. Taking Alison's hand once again, he led her away. "Annie said there was a dancing bear. I should like to see that. And I am getting hungry. Could we get something to eat?"

Alison smiled indulgently. "Of course, anything you want."

Duncan grinned and they started off in search of the

dancing bear. They found the creature in the midst of a large and noisily enthusiastic audience. It wore a felt hat and stood on its hind legs, its tongue hanging out and its giant paws flailing about. Around the bear's neck was a heavy chain, the end of which was held by its keeper, a small dark man who whistled and every so often nudged the bear with the end of a formidable-looking bullwhip.

The sight depressed Alison, who was glad when Duncan lost interest and led her away in search of food. "Allie! There is Mull! Do you see him?"

Alison espied Mull standing some distance away. He was alone and looking in their direction. Duncan waved and Mull returned the gesture and then started toward them. In spite of her desire to put all thoughts of Ravenstoke from her, Alison found herself happy to see Mull's unfortunate-looking countenance.

The servant grinned at them as he approached, and once beside them, he pulled his hat from his head and made a slight bow. "M'lady and Master Duncan, 'tis an honor to see you."

"Mull, have you seen the bear? It is not very fierce and I suspect it is missing some teeth, but it is a bear, and a large one."

"Aye, young master, I have seen the bear."

"I should fancy having a bear," said Duncan. "It would be such fun."

"Indeed it would, young sir." Mull nodded and then grinned at Alison. "Perhaps the fellow might wish to sell his bear."

"Mull!" Alison regarded the servant with mock horror. "Do not give him ideas! Bears, indeed! Could you imagine a bear running about Dornach Castle?"

Duncan looked as if he could very well imagine it and thought the idea worth considering. "Perhaps a small bear, Allie," he said.

Alison laughed. "You would do well to forget all about bears, young man." She turned to Mull. "And are you enjoying the fair, Mull?"

"Aye, m'lady. 'Tis a fine fair, and fine weather for it. I have been to many a fair in my day and I can truthfully say this be as fine as any."

Duncan seemed well-pleased by this remark. "As fine a fair as those in England?"

"Finer, lad. Why, there are so many things to see. Have you been to the puppet show, Master Duncan? 'Tis well worth a look."

"Puppet show? Aye, I should like to see it. Could we go, Allie?"

"Aye, I daresay I should like that better than the dancing bear."

"Better than that, m'lady?" said Mull. "Your expectations must be very high indeed."

Alison smiled. "They certainly are. Would you care to escort us to the puppet show, Mull?"

"It would be my pleasure, m'lady." Mull grinned once again and led Duncan and Alison away.

It would have surprised and very much disconcerted Alison to realize that while she and Duncan were talking with Mull, they were the objects of intense scrutiny. Miss Deborah Willoughby had spotted Alison and Duncan when the boy had waved to Mull, and she did not hesitate to point them out to Ravenstoke and the others who accompanied them. "Robert, it is Lady Alison and her dear little brother, and they are talking to your man Mull."

Ravenstoke looked over and tried to mask the feelings the sight of Alison engendered within him. "Yes, it is," he said with seeming disinterest.

They were accompanied by Lady Willoughby, Lord Ensdale, and Fenton Willoughby, and all seemed quite interested. "She is speaking with your servant, Ravenstoke," said Lady Willoughby with some annoyance. "I daresay I do not think it quite the thing for a lady to hold a conversation with a servant."

"Especially one who looks like Mull," drawled Ensdale. "Do forgive me, Ravenstoke, but your man is the most hideous creature I have ever seen."

Deborah laughed. "Is he not? The sight of him would give one nightmares. I do not know what Robert sees in him, for he is in my mind nothing but a ruffian."

"I must say, Ravenstoke, you have a dashed odd taste

in servants." Ensdale smiled over at Deborah, and Ravenstoke had a decided urge to strike him in the face.

Deborah sensed her fiancé's irritation and smiled. "I do think Lady Alison is charmed by Mull. See how she laughs at his words."

"I think it unseemly," muttered Lady Willoughby.

"Oh, Mama, it is just that Lady Alison is so very democratic. Is that not so, Robert?"

Not trusting himself to answer, the marquess remained stonily silent.

Deborah continued. "I myself would not stand in public conversing with someone's servant, especially an unsightly one like Mull. Really, Robert, I must insist that once we are married, you dismiss Mull. You cannot expect me to endure having such a man about me."

"You had better accustom yourself to him, madam," said Ravenstoke icily. "I have no intention of dismissing Mull to suit you or anyone else, and I will not tolerate any further comments about him. Now do excuse me. I must make ready for the race." The marquess directed an angry look at Deborah and left them.

"I say," said Fenton Willoughby, watching Ravenstoke's retreating form, "what has got into the man? Can he be so fond of that Mull fellow?"

"My dear Fenton, one can never know with Ravenstoke." Ensdale took his snuffbox from his pocket and took a pinch, inhaling it noisily. "The man is an enigma to me. I find him deuced odd, and so ill-tempered most of the time. Forgive me, Miss Willoughby, but I cannot help thinking such a man does not deserve you."

Deborah directed a fond look at Ensdale, and Lady Willoughby frowned. She did not allow her daughter to reply, but took her arm and began to talk loudly about an entirely different subject.

The puppet show was a great success and Duncan enjoyed it immensely. When it ended, Alison, Duncan, and Mull made their way toward the racetrack. Duncan hurried on ahead to find his brother Andrew, leaving Alison and the servant far behind.

"Master Duncan is eager for the race," commented Mull.

Alison nodded. "We have prepared for it for a long time. My brother Andrew will ride Claymore. I do hope he wins."

"And though I be no true judge of horses, I can recognize a champion in that one. I am not a bettin' man, m'lady, but I reckon I shall place a wager on your Claymore."

"And will you wager against Lord Ravenstoke's horse? What would your master think of that?"

"He would think me wise, m'lady."

Alison laughed. "Does Lord Ravenstoke have no confidence in his own horse?"

"His lordship is a practical man. He knows very well that his horse is no match for your Claymore or indeed Sir Ian MacGillivray's stallion."

"But he still persists in entering the race?"

Mull nodded. "He has no fondness for racing, and yet, having said he would do so, he cannot withdraw. Indeed, m'lady, it is not the only time his lordship has wished he might retreat from a course he has set." The servant cast a knowing look at Alison. "Once a gentleman gives his word that he will do something, he must do it, no matter how much he wishes it could be otherwise."

Alison made no reply, but pondered these remarks thoughtfully.

"There is your Claymore, m'lady," said Mull. "What a handsome fellow he is."

"Aye," said Alison absently.

"Would you excuse me, then, m'lady? I must find Lord Ravenstoke."

"Of course. Thank you, Mull." The servant went off and Alison walked over to the area where the horses and riders had gathered. Duncan was already beside Andrew and the duke. "Andrew! Grandfather!" called Alison.

"There you are, lass," said the duke. "This is the day your Claymore will prove himself, a great day for the Murrays."

Alison patted the big horse's neck. "Well, my friend, you do your best for Andrew and for all of us." She turned to her brother, smiled, and then kissed him on the cheek. "That is for luck, Andrew."

Andrew grinned. "Thank you, Allie."

"And would you wish me luck, too, Alison Murray?" Ian MacGillivray's booming voice startled Alison, and she spun around to face the massive baron.

"Why would I wish you luck, Ian MacGillivray? 'Tis my horse I want to win."

"That I know well, lass, and you must not be disappointed if Gaisgeach and I leave your poor brother far behind."

"Disappointed? I should be astonished."

Sir Ian laughed. "We shall see, Alison." He then turned to the duke. "Well, then, Dornach, 'tis finally the day of reckoning."

"Aye," said the duke. "This race is between you and Andrew, though there are ten others in the field. There is not another horse that can touch those two, except perhaps that English horse of Ravenstoke's. Good-looking bit of blood and bone, that one." His grace nodded in the direction of Ravenstoke's horse, and Alison looked over to see the marquess talking with Mull. He was mounted on the bay gelding and the high-spirited animal seemed eager to run.

"I'm not worried about him," said Sir Ian contemptuously. "The horse may be good, but Ravenstoke has not the heart for racing. No, it will be Claymore and Gaisgeach."

"You had best both be mounted," said Alison, unimpressed with MacGillivray's boasting and tired of his company.

"Alison is right," said Andrew, climbing atop Claymore. "Go on with you, Ian. The race is about to start." Andrew leaned down to shake the duke's hand and then Duncan's. He smiled at his sister and then turned Claymore and headed toward the starting place.

Ian grinned at Alison and then turned to go to his own horse.

"Ian won't win, will he, Grandfather?" said Duncan.

"Och, no, lad." The duke shook his head emphatically. "Gaisgeach is not the horse Claymore is, and though there is no better horseman in the land, Ian MacGillivray weighs nigh on sixteen stone. 'Tis a heavy burden for even

Gaisgeach to carry. No, Duncan, Claymore will win the day. I know it."

Alison scarcely heard her grandfather's words, so intent was she on watching Ravenstoke and Mull. The marquess's face was expressionless, revealing no sign of excitement or nervousness. He was speaking to Mull, who was nodding in reply. Suddenly Ravenstoke looked over and met her gaze, a questioning expression on his face. Alison fought an impulse to look away and regarded him closely.

"Allie, doesn't Claymore look splendid?"

Alison looked down at her youngest brother. "What?"

"Claymore. Doesn't he look splendid?"

"Aye, he does," murmured Alison. When she looked back at Ravenstoke, she found that he was gone, having ridden off to join the others at the race's start.

As he brought his horse alongside the others, Ravenstoke cursed himself for being a fool. He knew that agreeing to ride in the race was sheer folly. Indeed, the marquess considered himself a very competent horseman, but he had little experience racing. How could he have let himself be talked into it? he wondered.

And if that were not bad enough, Ravenstoke told himself, he had allowed himself to be caught in a far more important trap, that of marriage to Deborah Willoughby. The marquess looked over to see Alison once again, but could not find her in the crowd. She had met his gaze with an expression that had brought acute pain to his heart. How she must despise him and, indeed, how else could he expect her to feel? He undoubtedly deserved the misery that had befallen him.

The bay gelding moved nervously beneath him, and the marquess was forced to turn his attention to the matter at hand. He steadied his mount and stroked the animal's neck. Ravenstoke then looked about him, seeming to note his competition for the first time. He saw Ian MacGillivray several horses down from him in the envied pole position. MacGillivray grinned at him scornfully and the marquess glared in return.

Ravenstoke then looked around to find Andrew Murray

and Claymore, and noted that the big chestnut horse and
his young rider were some positions down from him.
Andrew was having some difficulty keeping his mount
under control and was unaware of Ravenstoke's scrutiny.

Turning to look once more into the crowd, Ravenstoke
searched again for Alison. He did not find her but instead
saw Deborah and the other London guests. Deborah's
attention was focused upon Lord Ensdale and the two of
them were laughing merrily. The marquess directed a
black look at them, but they were oblivious to him. He
could only frown and concentrate once again on his horse.

The sharp report of a pistol announced the beginning of
the race. Ravenstoke's horse shied at the sound and made
a bad start while MacGillivray's Gaisgeach hurled into the
lead. The marquess cursed and urged his bay gelding
onward at the heels of just about every other horse in the
field.

It did not take the bay long, however, to catch up, and
the marquess deftly handled his mount, weaving past the
other horses until finally there were only two ahead of
him. In the lead was Gaisgeach, thundering across the
ground as if the devil were on his heels. Some lengths behind was Claymore with Andrew atop him. The big chestnut stallion was running well and his long strides would
in no time bring him alongside MacGillivray's black.

Ravenstoke continued to urge his steed on and the
gallant bay responded valiantly, mustering every inch of
his strength to narrow the distance between himself and
the two leaders. The marquess was now unaware of
anything but the race and the horse beneath him. He was
riding as he had never ridden before, his whole being
propelling his horse forward. He must overtake MacGillivray, Ravenstoke demanded of himself and his horse. He
must!

The baronet cast a brief glance backward and was
unhappy to see the distance between himself and Claymore narrowing rapidly. His backward glance also revealed the remarkable fact that another horse was coming
swiftly upon him. Another quick look confirmed the
identity of the horse and its rider, much to Sir Ian's
dismay. The Englishman was only a few lengths behind
Claymore, and Gaisgeach was tiring. MacGillivray

shouted a Gaelic expletive and spurred his horse merci-
lessly.

Andrew Murray had been holding Claymore back,
knowing well that MacGillivray would push Gaisgeach as
hard as he could and suspecting that the black stallion
would weaken. As they turned the curve that headed into
the final stretch, Andrew gave the big chestnut his head
and Claymore galloped wildly forward. In seconds he was
neck and neck with Gaisgeach and then the chestnut
surged ahead, leaving MacGillivray and his mount behind.

Sir Ian shouted another curse as Claymore passed him,
and furiously applied his whip to Gaisgeach's flanks. The
black struggled to overtake Claymore, but was nearly
spent by his efforts. Ravenstoke saw Claymore take the
lead and noted with great satisfaction that Gaisgeach was
faltering. He urged his bay gelding onward and the plucky
steed took the challenge eagerly. They were soon upon
Gaisgeach's heels and ready to make the move forward.

MacGillivray saw Ravenstoke's horse coming up behind
him. He veered his own horse into the path of Ravenstoke, forcing the marquess to swerve his bay gelding
sharply to the right to avoid a collision.

"Damn you!" cried the marquess as his horse broke
stride, misstepped, and nearly fell. The bay managed to
recover and at Ravenstoke's further urgings set out to
overtake MacGillivray again.

Ravenstoke's horse made a courageous attempt, but
MacGillivray's maneuvering had given the baronet more
than enough time. Ian crossed the finish line more than
five lengths behind Claymore, but well ahead of Ravenstoke's bay.

The crowd cheered loudly for Claymore, and Andrew
beamed at his moment of triumph. Alison tried to appear
elated at her beloved Claymore's victory, but the race had
terrified her. She knew well that Ravenstoke had only
narrowly averted disaster. For a brief moment she had
feared that his horse would fall, and the idea that he might
be killed had filled her with unspeakable horror. As she
took her grandfather's arm and Duncan's hand and made
her way to Claymore and Andrew, Alison watched the
marquess. Ravenstoke seemed somewhat shaken, although he was trying hard to appear calm.

Alison was barely aware of Andrew receiving his trophy amid the accolades of a delighted crowd. She thought only of Ravenstoke and kept her eyes glued to him. She watched him dismount and start to make his way out of the crush of people. Alison broke away from her grandfather, knowing well that the delighted duke would hardly notice her absence, and followed after Ravenstoke. Weaving through the throng, she caught up with him at the edge of the crowd.

"Lord Ravenstoke?"

He turned around and regarded her in surprise. "Lady Alison?"

"Are you all right?"

The marquess noted the concern in Alison's enormous blue eyes. "Yes. I am fine. I must congratulate you on Claymore's victory. He ran a good race."

"It was you who ran the good race, my lord. If you were not the horseman you are, you might have been killed. Och, MacGillivray! How could he have done such a thing!"

Amazed and touched by Alison's solicitude, Ravenstoke smiled. "It was nothing. No ill came of it."

"I was so relieved that you did not fall."

"Oh, there you are, Ravenstoke!" Lord Ensdale's languid voice called to them and they both turned toward it. Ensdale approached with Deborah on his arm. Behind them were Lady Willoughby and Fenton. "Ah, Lady Alison," continued Ensdale, "you are to be congratulated."

"Your horse won quite handily," said Fenton Willoughby. His aunt directed a disapproving look at him, but Fenton did not seem to notice. "Dashed fine horse. I daresay he would do well anywhere."

"Thank you, Mr. Willoughby."

Deborah smiled at Alison. "It was such an exciting race. And Lord Ravenstoke did very well, too, don't you think?"

"Yes, he did," said Alison.

"Better if you had won, old man," said Ensdale. "But then, you did show us you could sit a horse, and right adequately, too. Had that dreadful fellow MacGillivray not behaved so ungentlemanly, you might have taken second. But then, what does it signify if you are second or third? Being first is what matters. Is that not correct, Lady Alison?"

"Not to me, Lord Ensdale." Alison directed a cool look at that gentleman and then continued. "Do excuse me. I must rejoin my family. Good day." Taking care not to look in Ravenstoke's direction, Alison hurried off.

22 It was not until evening that Alison, her brothers, and her grandfather returned to the castle. Andrew and Duncan were in high spirits, as was the duke, and they could talk of nothing else save Claymore's victory. Alison was uncharacteristically silent, but the male members of her family were so engrossed in discussing the race that they took little notice of her.

"It was a great day for the Murrays," said the duke as they entered the drawing room.

"Aye," said Andrew, sitting down on the sofa and grinning. "I think Claymore did well for us."

"And so did you, lad." The duke sat in his armchair and regarded his grandson fondly. "Och, Ian was not even close to you."

Duncan nodded enthusiastically. "Claymore is a great horse. Gaisgeach cannot touch him."

Andrew nodded. "And after all the bragging Ian did about Gaisgeach, I must say I was glad that he discovered who the better horse was."

"And I hope you discovered what sort of man Ian MacGillivray is," said Alison, speaking for the first time.

"What do you mean by that?" replied Andrew.

"Is it not clear to you, Andrew? Ian nearly caused a terrible accident. Lord Ravenstoke might have been killed."

"Alison, I think you mistake what happened," said the duke.

"Aye." Andrew nodded. "A horse race can be dangerous. You must not blame Ian."

"You did not see what happened, Andrew Murray. It was very clear that Ian turned his horse directly into Lord Ravenstoke's path."

"Now, lass, I saw the race, too, and I am not so certain that that is what happened."

Alison turned to her youngest brother. "Duncan, you did see it, did you not?"

Duncan nodded. "It is as Allie says. I saw it clearly."

"And why is it that no one else seemed to think Ian did anything wrong?" Andrew shook his head. "Everyone was discussing the race and no one saw fit to say a word against Ian."

"Of course not. There are few who would speak against MacGillivray, and fewer still who would speak for Ravenstoke."

Andrew shook his head. "In truth, Alison, I grow weary of you talking against Ian. He is my friend."

"He is a friend to all of us," said the duke. "And fond of you he is, too, my girl. MacGillivrays and Murrays have always been allies."

Alison shrugged. "I can see there is no point in saying anything more. I pray you will excuse me. I am very tired and wish to go to my rooms."

"Good night, lass." The duke and his grandsons watched Alison leave the room and then his grace turned to Duncan. "I think you had best retire, too, Duncan. The hour grows late."

"Could I not stay up a little longer, Grandfather?" The duke's expression told the youngest Murray that the matter was not open for discussion and Duncan obediently took his leave.

Now alone with Andrew, the duke frowned. "I do wish your sister would think more kindly of Ian."

"Aye, but she has always disliked him."

"And do you know why?"

Andrew looked thoughtful. "I suspect it is his reputation she dislikes." The young man grinned. "He does love the ladies."

"Och, he is more the man for it. And Alison is a woman who could keep a man in tow if any woman can. It is time your sister married, Andrew, and Ian MacGillivray would make her a fit husband."

"That he would," agreed Andrew. "But she would not have him, sir. My sister is too much against him. Indeed, I never saw her favor any man save for . . ." The young man hesitated.

"Save for?"

"Ravenstoke." The duke frowned and Andrew continued. "It was very fortunate that he is engaged to be married. Och, I know, Grandfather, that you think well of the Englishman, but I daresay I would not want him for a brother-in-law. Aye, I was very glad to hear of this Miss Willoughby. I only hope that Ravenstoke and she will be wed soon and that they will stay very far away from Scotland."

His grace seemed to ponder this. "That would be for the best. There is little fondness for Ravenstoke here. He would do better in England. Let us hope that your sister will soon come to her senses and appreciate a man like Ian."

Andrew nodded but knew very well that it was quite unlikely his sister would ever change her mind about Ian MacGillivray.

Ravenstoke entered his bedchamber tired and yet very much agitated. It had been a very trying day, and the difficulties of being in a horse race and nearly avoiding a collision had been nothing compared to the difficulty of getting through the rest of the day.

Seeing Alison Murray briefly after the race and then going back to Glenfinnan in the company of Deborah and the others had been hard to bear. Dinner had been quite dreadful that evening. Ensdale and Deborah had been in the happiest of moods, and Ravenstoke had found their laughter and gaiety most annoying. Even Lady Willoughby, who was at most times glum, had been excessively cheerful, a fact Ravenstoke had noted with irritation.

The marquess was tremendously depressed. He had suffered through dinner in silence as best he could. When Miss Willoughby had announced she wished to play cards after dinner, Ravenstoke had begged off, suggesting the others do as they wished. He had then spent the rest of the

evening sitting sullenly in an armchair, watching his
fiancée and the rest of his guests play whist.

It had seemed an eternity before the guests had reluctantly announced it was time to retire and Ravenstoke was
able to proceed to his rooms. He found Mull in the
bedchamber readying his night things. "There is no need
for you to stay up any longer, Mull. Go on to bed."

Mull regarded his master with a worried look. He had
never seen the marquess so dispirited. "Are you feelin' all
right, m'lord?"

"I am fine. I am very tired." The marquess sat wearily
down on his bed.

"I should think you would be, m'lord. 'Tis hard work
sittin' atop a race horse."

Ravenstoke nodded. "And it is work I shall in the
future leave to others. I nearly broke my neck out there."
The marquess frowned. "Perhaps it would have been
better if I had done so."

Mull directed a shocked look at his master. "M'lord!"

Ravenstoke smiled. "I was only joking, Mull."

"I do not appreciate such a jest as that, m'lord."

The marquess smiled again. "Go on to bed, Mull."

The worthy servant nodded, but seemed reluctant to
leave. "Good night, then, m'lord," he said finally, and
started for the door.

"Jack?"

"M'lord?"

The marquess stared reflectively at Mull. "Do you think
there are persons who deserve to be miserable?"

"Indeed there are, m'lord," said Mull. He paused for a
moment and then continued, "But your lordship is not
one of them."

Ravenstoke smiled. "Thank you, Mull. Good night."

When the servant had gone, the marquess rose from the
bed and paced across the room. He thought of Alison and
the look of concern that had been on her face as she had
spoken with him after the race. "Am I mad?" Ravenstoke
said aloud. "How could I even think of marrying Deborah?"

Pacing once more across the room, he stopped in front
of the window. Of course, he could not marry Deborah
Willoughby. Hang his word as a gentleman and hang the

marriage contract! He would break the engagement, and no matter how costly or how scandalous it would be to do so, he did not care. He would marry Alison Murray or he would marry no one.

Having thus made such a momentous decision, his lordship experienced a tremendous feeling of relief. He glanced over at the mantel clock, noting the late hour. No, it was certainly too late to inform Miss Willoughby of his decision, but he resolved to do so at first opportunity.

Ravenstoke thought then of Alison and a smile came to his face. He knew she still cared for him and he loved her so very much.

Much .heartened by his decision and his thoughts of Alison, Ravenstoke smiled. Then, thinking that the next day would be perhaps the most important of his life, he began to prepare for what he expected would be a very restless night of sleep.

Sir Ian MacGillivray arrived at Dornach Castle very early, much to the surprise of the butler MacPherson, who admitted him. MacPherson noted that Sir Ian seemed unusually agitated, and when told that none of the family had yet risen, MacGillivray scowled and informed the butler that he would wait. He wished to see the duke and would do so as soon as his grace would receive him.

Knowing that the duke usually rose at daybreak and spent the early-morning hours reading in his rooms, MacPherson hurried up to see if his grace was still in bed. Finding him up and about, MacPherson informed the duke of the early visitor.

"Here at this hour?" His grace was dumbfounded.

"Aye, your grace, and ill-tempered he seems."

"Well, I shall see him in my sitting room. Bring him up."

When the butler was gone, his grace reflected that Sir Ian was behaving rather strangely. He was not an early riser. Indeed, one of the few criticisms the duke knew that could be rightly leveled against the baronet was that he kept London hours. It must be a matter of some importance to bring him to Dornach Castle so early in the morning.

"Duke, good morning to you," said MacGillivray, entering the duke's sitting room.

"Ian." The duke gestured toward a chair. "Sit down, lad."

MacGillivray did so, but then leaned forward in his chair. "You must wonder why I came so early. By God, I do not often make calls at this hour, but I have been thinking lately a good deal about Alison. I am not a man to delay action once I have set my mind to it, so here I am. I wish to ask for Alison's hand in marriage."

This abrupt statement did not seem to surprise his grace, who nodded solemnly. "I might have known. I am well aware that you are fond of her."

"Fond? That I am. And I shall make a good husband for her. Alison needs a strong man and a tight rein. And I shall not be unreasonable in terms of the marriage settlement."

His grace rubbed his chin thoughtfully. "I must say, Ian, that I have expected you would one day offer for Alison. Indeed, I could wish for nothing more than the union of Murray and MacGillivray. But there is a problem."

"A problem, Duke?"

"Aye. The problem of the girl herself. I shall not force her to have a man she does not want. It is for Alison to decide."

"Then I should like to see her at once."

"Well, man, 'tis very early. But I shall see if she is up. You had best go to the drawing room and wait."

MacGillivray nodded and, after shaking the duke's hand, left the elderly man. The duke, still in his dressing gown, made his way toward Alison's rooms. To his surprise he found Alison in the corridor. She was dressed in her riding habit and evidently on her way to the stables.

"Good, you are up."

"Good morning, Grandfather. Is something wrong?"

"Not in the least. Ian MacGillivray is here to see you."

"Now?"

The duke nodded. "Aye. He is in the drawing room. He wants to speak with you."

"What ever for?"

"Can you not guess, lass?"

Alison regarded her grandfather with a horrified look. "No! He has not come to make an offer for me!"

"Aye, that he has."

"And what did you tell him, Grandfather?"

"I told him that I'd not force you against your will to marry him. But I do wish you to see him, Alison. You must give him the courtesy of hearing him."

"You cannot think I would ever consider marrying him?"

"I think you could do far worse than Ian MacGillivray, lass. And it is time you married. I wish to see you with bairns of your own before I leave this world."

"Oh, Grandfather, that is a very long time off."

"I'd not be so sure of that, my girl. I'm an old man, and who knows how much longer God will give me? That is why I would see you settled. Aye, and Andrew, too, although he is still a boy. Promise you will be civil to Ian. Listen to what he has to say. Do this for me."

Alison nodded reluctantly. "Oh, very well. I shall do so, but do not think there is anything he could say to me that would change how I feel."

These words seemed to satisfy his grace, who smiled and, taking Alison's hand, squeezed it affectionately. Alison placed a quick kiss on the old man's cheek and then left him and went to the drawing room.

"Ian?"

MacGillivray rose as she entered the room. He towered over her and looked huge and bearlike. "Alison. That was quick, lass."

"Grandfather said that you wished to speak with me."

"Aye, I do. And did he tell you why?"

Alison nodded. "Ian, I do not want you to take offense at my words, but you know we do not get on and never have. I have no wish to marry you. Indeed, I cannot understand why you would trouble to ask me."

To her surprise the big man did not seem in the least upset at her words. "I suspected that you would refuse me at first."

"At first? I shall always refuse you. Truly, Ian, you must seek your wife elsewhere. And there are many who would be happy to be Lady MacGillivray. Choose one of them."

"I have chosen you, Alison Murray. You're the only lass fit to be wife to me and mother to my children. No, my girl, it is you I shall have."

"But I have already told you my answer."

MacGillivray smiled. "Och, I know you bear no love for me, or at least that is what you think now. I tell you, lass, once we are wed, that will change."

Alison was growing impatient with Sir Ian and irritated with his refusal to accept her answer. "I think we have said all there is to say, Sir Ian."

"Have we? I think not. Do you intend to live here all your life? Do not forget that you are very nearly on the shelf. Perhaps you should reconsider my offer."

Alison's blue eyes flashed dangerously. "Ian MacGillivray, I should prefer to die an old maid than marry such a man as you. Good heavens! Why, only yesterday I saw you nearly kill Lord Ravenstoke in your effort to stop him from besting you in the race."

"So it is still the Englishman? I suspected that."

Alison looked startled. "He has nothing to do with my feelings for you."

"Doesn't he?"

"He does not! Indeed, it does not signify in the least that it was Lord Ravenstoke. You acted abominably yesterday! You are an unscrupulous ruffian, Ian MacGillivray!"

To Alison's considerable astonishment, MacGillivray only grinned and then, to her horror, pulled her to him and fastened his lips upon hers, kissing her brutally. When she was finally able to extricate herself from his grip, she gasped and then attempted to strike him hard across the face. He caught her hand. "Admit it, lass, that was to your liking, and 'tis only a promise of things to come."

"You villain!" Tears of rage came to Alison's eyes. "How dare you! Get out! Get out!"

"I will, Alison, but I'll be back. Think well on my proposal." Then, grinning once more, he hurried out of the room.

Alison resisted her urge to take up the heavy glass vase sitting on the table and hurl it after him. She tried to calm herself. How could anyone be so despicable? And how could her grandfather think she should consider MacGillivray's offer? She sat down on the sofa, furious at the baronet.

Moments later her grandfather and Andrew appeared in the drawing room. "So you sent Ian on his way, then?" said the duke.

"Aye, and I wish that I could have murdered him."

"Och! Whatever happened?"

"Grandfather, Ian MacGillivray is the most insufferable man. And he is also the most empty-headed if he thinks I would be impressed with his ungentlemanly behavior."

"Ungentlemanly?" Andrew regarded his sister in surprise. "What did he do to so upset you?"

"He asked for my hand in marriage and would not accept my answer. And then . . ." Alison reddened. "He kissed me."

"Och, lass, what can you expect? You are a lovely woman and Ian a hot-blooded man who loves you," said Andrew.

"Loves me?" Alison laughed derisively. "He loves no one but himself. How can you stand up for him?"

"Calm yourself, my girl," said the duke soothingly. "Do not be so upset. Give yourself time."

"Time? I need no time!" Alison directed an exasperated look at the duke and Andrew and then fled the drawing room. She rushed out to the stables and saddled Claymore herself. Then, mounted on the chestnut stallion, Alison galloped across the moorlands, hoping to get as far away from Dornach Castle as she possibly could.

23   When he awakened in the morning, Lord Ravenstoke was surprised to find it was past ten o'clock. He rose from bed and looked out the window. The sky was clear and the sun was shining brightly.

Ravenstoke continued to stare out the window, reflecting that this would be a most important day for him. First, he would inform Deborah of his decision and then he would hurry off to see Alison. Although it might have been expected that his lordship would dread his impending conversation with Miss Willoughby, he smiled and seemed to look forward to it.

Coming downstairs and entering the dining room, the marquess expected to find his London guests assembled there. Discovering the room empty, he called one of the maids and asked where the others might be.

"They went oot, m'lord," answered the servant.

"Out?" Ravenstoke regarded the woman in some confusion.

"They took the carriage, m'lord. The young lady said they needed some air and would be back in time for luncheon."

"Damn," muttered the marquess, extremely irritated. Why would Deborah get the idea to go off on this of all days? The maid regarded him curiously. "That will be all," he said. The woman bobbed a curtsy and went off to the kitchen.

Ravenstoke frowned as he paced across the dining

room. He had hoped to quickly conclude his business with Deborah and then be on his way to Dornach Castle. He wanted desperately to see Alison and set things right with her, and the idea that he would have to sit there waiting for Deborah to return galled him.

The marquess started toward the library, but stopped. He would go to Dornach Castle and see Alison immediately. Ravenstoke called to a servant to fetch his cloak and hat, and was soon on his way to Dornach Castle.

It was not long before he arrived at the castle door and was admitted by Bob MacPherson. "I should like to see Lady Alison."

"I am sorry, m'lord, but her ladyship is nae here."

"Not here?" Ravenstoke frowned. "Where is she?"

"She went off riding, m'lord."

"Damn," muttered the marquess.

"Lord Ravenstoke?"

His lordship looked up to see Duncan Murray standing in the entrance hall and he smiled. "Good morning, Duncan."

"Good morning, sir. No one is about save for myself. Grandfather and Andrew went to the village and Alison is out riding."

"That is what your man has told me."

Bob MacPherson was eyeing Ravenstoke with keen interest and was rather disappointed when Duncan informed him that his services were no longer required. "Would you care to come in, Lord Ravenstoke? It is so good to see you, sir."

"Very well, Duncan." Ravenstoke followed his young host into the drawing room and sat down on the sofa. Duncan followed suit.

"You did a bang-up job in the race, my lord. If Ian had not forced you over, you'd have been second, and second to Claymore is very good, don't you think?"

His lordship smiled. "Indeed, it is."

The boy nodded. "Alison and I thought Ian acted very badly, but Grandfather and Andrew did not. They are fond of Ian." Duncan sighed. "I used to think him a fine fellow, but now agree with Alison. He is a disagreeable bully. I do not blame Allie for not wishing to marry him."

"Did he ask for her hand?"

"Aye, this morning. Andrew told me all about it and he thinks she is daft to refuse him. I should not like him for a brother-in-law." He looked over at Ravenstoke. "Pity you cannot be my brother-in-law, sir."

"You mean you would not object to my marrying Alison?"

"Indeed not, sir. Mull told me you are a good sort of fellow."

Ravenstoke repressed a smile. "That is kind of Mull."

"And then, you are related to Prince Charles Edward," Duncan continued. "Aye, sir, you would make a dashed good brother-in-law. I wish you were not marrying that other lady."

"But I am not marrying her."

"You are not?"

"No. And since I see that I have your approval, young man, I shall endeavor to convince your sister that I would be a fit husband."

Duncan's freckled face lit up. "Truly, my lord? Och, that is wonderful!"

"But I shall have to find her first. Do you know where she might have gone?"

Duncan pondered the question. "There is one place that Allie might have gone. Daingneach Dubh."

"Then I shall go there and find her. Thank you, Duncan."

Duncan escorted the marquess to the door and smiled at the eager way his lordship mounted his horse and rode off.

Alison Murray stood near the ancient castle ruins, looking out at the sea and listening to the cries of the gulls. She ran her hand along the weathered stones of the castle wall and frowned as she reflected how dreadful it was to feel so depressed amid such beauty. Alison sighed. How was one to feel after a proposal of marriage from Ian MacGillivray?

She shook her head distastefully. It was so abominable that her own grandfather and brother Andrew could see nothing wrong with the man. Indeed, they thought him a fine marriage prospect and doubtlessly felt her to be an unreasonable female.

Alison walked slowly along the wall and thought of Ravenstoke. It was useless to try and stop thinking about him, she had decided. One day perhaps she could do so, but not now.

Claymore, who had been grazing nearby, neighed suddenly and Alison started. Looking past the horse, she saw a rider approaching some distance away. When she recognized Ravenstoke, Alison was filled with conflicting emotions.

What was he doing there? she wondered. Alison watched Ravenstoke intently, her mind confused. What would she say to him? She watched him scan the horizon and fix his eyes upon the castle ruin. He then headed toward her, deftly directing his horse up the steep hillside until he arrived on top.

Alison stood there motionless as he pulled his horse up beside her. "Alison, I had hoped you would be here."

"How did you know . . .?"

"Duncan told me you might be here." Ravenstoke dismounted and dropped the reins of his horse. "I wanted to talk with you."

She turned away from him. "I cannot think what we would have to say to each other, Lord Ravenstoke."

"But there is something I must say to you. Please, Alison, look at me."

She turned toward him, trying valiantly to fight the tears that were welling up inside her.

"I love you, Alison. I cannot live without you."

Alison's blue eyes regarded him imploringly. "Stop. Say nothing more."

"No, I must. Good God, Alison, how could I ever have thought I could live without you? How could I have thought I could marry Deborah Willoughby and disregard my feelings for you? I was mad, Alison. I cannot marry her."

"But you are engaged."

"Damn the engagement! It is you I want, only you! Will you marry me, Alison?"

Alison hesitated only a moment. "Oh, Ravenstoke!"

She threw herself into his arms and hugged him tightly. "I do love you!"

He did not reply but covered her lips with his own, kissing her gently and then with increasing fervor. She responded eagerly, returning his kiss with an ardor that delighted him. When they finally parted, the marquess smiled. "How I adore you!"

She smiled in return and then ecstatically kissed him again. "Och, I was so miserable, and now I have never been so happy!"

"Nor have I, my darling. Then, you will have me?"

"Och, Ravenstoke, of course."

He regarded her with mock seriousness. "You may wish to think the matter over. I understand this is not your only offer of marriage today."

Alison laughed. "So you know about that? Well, my lord, perhaps I am hasty and should reconsider."

He encircled her waist with his arm and pulled her to him once again. "You had better not, my girl."

Alison smiled up at him and was soon once more lost in his embrace.

Some time later an elated Ravenstoke returned to Glenfinnan. He found Mull in the entry hall. "Mull, are Miss Willoughby and the others returned?"

"Aye, m'lord. Miss Willoughby is in the drawing room."

"Good."

Ravenstoke strode briskly toward the drawing room, eager to tell Deborah the engagement was off. "I must speak with you, Deborah," he said as he flung open the doors and entered the room.

The marquess stopped abruptly, surprised at the sight that greeted his eyes. Reclining on the sofa was Deborah Willoughby in the arms of Lord Ensdale. They sprang apart, jumped to their feet, and looked guiltily at him.

"Good God," said Ravenstoke. "What is the meaning of this?"

"Oh, Robert!" Deborah's pale face reddened in acute embarrassment, but Ensdale stepped forward, a defiant expression on his face.

"It means, Ravenstoke, that Miss Willoughby is not going to marry you. It is me she loves and she has agreed to be my wife."

Ravenstoke looked over at Deborah, who nodded her head in confirmation.

"And do not think, sir, that you can hold her to the marriage agreement," continued Ensdale. "We hope you will be decent about it and release Miss Willoughby from her obligations. And do not blame Deborah, Ravenstoke. It is I who must bear your displeasure."

Ravenstoke stared incredulously at them both for a moment and then burst into laughter, much to the astonishment of Deborah and Ensdale. "Bear my displeasure, Ensdale? By God, you have my eternal gratitude."

Deborah looked insulted. "You are acting most ungentlemanly, Robert. A gentleman would have had the decency to feign disappointment."

"As you feigned affection for me before we became engaged? In truth, madam, we are well rid of each other. I wish you both all the happiness in the world. I expect you will all be returning to London as soon as possible?"

"Indeed we shall!" exclaimed Deborah, furious at Ravenstoke's response. "I shall be only too glad to leave this horrible place."

"Do ask my servants for any help you need. They will be very glad to assist you with your packing. Now, do excuse me. I must go." Ravenstoke then hurried out the door, leaving Ensdale and Deborah standing there in the drawing room.

24 Allie, you're back!" Duncan Murray hurried excitedly over to his sister as she entered the drawing room. "Did Lord Ravenstoke find you?"

Alison smiled. "He most certainly did."

"Then, you were at Daingneach Dubh?"

"Aye."

Duncan found his sister exasperatingly closemouthed. "Tell me, Allie, what happened?"

To the boy's surprise, his sister leaned down and caught him up in an exuberant embrace. "Oh, Duncan, I am going to marry Lord Ravenstoke!"

"I thought as much," said Duncan matter-of-factly.

"You did?" Alison pulled away from her brother and regarded him curiously.

He nodded. "I told Lord Ravenstoke that I was not opposed to the idea, and he seemed glad that I approved."

Alison laughed. "I am certainly happy that you gave him your permission."

Duncan grinned and Alison hugged him once again. They both then sat down on the sofa. "You will not have to live in London, will you, Allie?"

"Och, I don't think so. Ravenstoke loves Glenfinnan too well."

"Good," said Duncan. "And if you do go to London, I shall go, too. I fancy I should like to see it."

"That is good of you, Duncan," said Alison with a fond smile. "Indeed, I would not think of venturing so far without you."

Duncan started to reply, but they were interrupted by the appearance of Bob MacPherson. "Angus MacKenna is here tae see the duke, m'lady. I told him your ladyship and Master Duncan were the only ones home and he asked tae see ye."

"Angus MacKenna? Is he not one of Sir Ian's tenants?"

"Aye, m'lady, and he says it is an urgent matter."

"Then, we should see him, should we not, Allie?"

"Certainly, Duncan. Do bring him here, Bob."

"Aye, m'lady."

MacPherson returned shortly with Angus MacKenna. He was a short wiry man with black hair and pale-blue eyes, and he looked extremely agitated.

"Is something the matter, Mr. MacKenna?" asked Alison.

"Aye, m'lady. Sir Ian MacGillivray is evicting Hetty Munro frae her cottage. The poor old woman. She is near eighty and nae well. I thought his grace might speak tae Sir Ian."

"The duke is in the village."

"Aye, Bob MacPherson told me that. There is little time, m'lady. Even now Sir Ian and his men are on the way. They mean tae burn the old woman's cottage."

"Burn her cottage?" Alison regarded MacKenna in disbelief.

"Aye, she would nae leave and he told her that when he came back, 'twould be tae torch her house."

"Good heavens! Well, Mr. MacKenna, you must go to the village and tell his grace and my brother Andrew. They will come as soon as possible. I shall go there myself and see if I can stop Sir Ian."

" 'Tis good o' ye, m'lady. Mayhap Sir Ian will listen tae ye. Do ye know where the old woman lives?"

"I know," said Duncan. "I have been there several times. I shall go with you, Allie."

"Good. We should hurry, then. I shall do my best, Mr. MacKenna. Now, do find his grace and Lord Culwin."

MacKenna nodded and rushed off. Alison and Duncan

followed, hurrying to the stables, and were soon mounted and on their way toward MacGillivray's lands.

Lord Ravenstoke smiled as he rode toward Dornach Castle and wondered at his good fortune. Certainly, it was hardly surprising that his fiancée preferred another man to him, but he had not expected Miss Willoughby would wish to break the engagement.

A laugh escaped the marquess as he thought of Deborah and Ensdale. It seemed, he reflected, that he had misjudged her. He had thought Deborah cared only for wealth and position, but now she was choosing a husband of lesser rank and inconsequential fortune. Ravenstoke smiled again as he thought of Deborah's mother and suspected that Lady Willoughby would not be very happy with her daughter's decision. Well, at least he was free of them all and Alison Murray was to be his wife. He was, he told himself, the luckiest man in the kingdom.

Ravenstoke turned his thoughts to Alison's family and wondered how the duke would respond to the idea of an Englishman in the family. Of course, the marquess knew very well that Alison's hotheaded brother Andrew would not like the idea. Well, it did not signify what Alison's family thought of the match. They would be married and that would be that.

Arriving for the second time at Dornach Castle, Ravenstoke was again admitted by Bob MacPherson, who dourly informed him that no one was home. "You mean Lady Alison is not here?"

MacPherson nodded. "Aye."

"And where has she gone?"

"She and Master Duncan went tae the cottage o' Hetty Munro."

"They are paying a call?" Ravenstoke regarded the butler strangely. He could not imagine Alison going off on a social call when she knew very well he was returning to the castle as soon as he had settled the matter of his engagement to Deborah.

" 'Tis nae a social call, m'lord. Her ladyship and Master Duncan went tae stop Sir Ian MacGillivray frae evicting the old woman."

"Sir Ian? Good God! Where is this place? I must go there at once."

MacPherson explained how he might find the cottage and the marquess hurried out the door and to his horse. He did not like the idea of his beloved Alison having anything to do with MacGillivray. Once mounted, he galloped off in the direction MacPherson had told him.

Angus MacKenna was in such a great hurry to reach the duke that he pushed his roan mare harder than he had ever done before. It was not long before he arrived at the village pub, and jumping down from his horse, he breathlessly raced inside.

Locating his grace and Andrew at a table on the far side of the room, MacKenna made his way through the crowd of men. "Your grace! Glad I am tae find ye here!"

The duke and Andrew looked up in surprise at the obviously distraught man. "Angus MacKenna, what the devil is wrong?" said his grace.

MacKenna's exclamation had caused all heads to turn toward the duke's table and everyone listened expectantly for his reply. " 'Tis Sir Ian MacGillivray, your grace. He is going tae burn the cottage o' Hetty Munro! Ye must stop him!"

"What the deuce are you talking about?" Andrew eyed MacKenna in disbelief.

" 'Tis true, Lord Culwin. She hae nae paid the rent and Sir Ian says he must make room for sheep. But she is an old woman and sick, wi' nae place tae go. Even now his men are on their way. Ye must act quickly!"

"Are you sure of this, man?" said the duke. "I cannot believe it of Ian."

"Nor can I," said Andrew. "It is pure fustian. Ian would never do such a thing."

"Would he not, m'lord?" An elderly man stepped up to the duke's table. "He has done worse in his time."

"What?" The duke looked startled. "Peter Gowan, what do you mean?"

"I mean, your grace, that there are many things Ian MacGillivray hae done tae make his people fear and despise him. I can tell ye many a tale. Only a month ago he forced James MacLeod frae his land and hae him cruelly beaten. And was it because MacLeod was a bad farmer and could nae pay his rent? Och, nay, it was because MacLeod would nae let Sir Ian hae his way wi' his young daughter."

"I have heard enough, old man!" Andrew jumped to his feet. "I'll not have such calumnies spread about Ian. If what you say is true, why have you not come to the duke before this?"

"Because I hae been a coward, young Master o' Dornach. We hae all been cowards." There was a murmur of assent from the onlookers.

"Aye, we hae! Peter Gowan speaks the truth." A young man now stepped forward and addressed the duke. "Your grace, we all fear MacGillivray."

The duke regarded the man, who was one of his own tenants, in surprise. "Robby MacDonald, you are not Ian's man. If what Gowan said is true, why did you not come to me?"

"Och, your grace, knowing how friendly ye are wi' Sir Ian, I dared nae speak out. I dinnae think ye or Lord Culwin would take my word over a gentleman like Sir Ian MacGillivray."

Andrew looked at the faces around him. "Then all of you say Gowan speaks the truth?"

The men nodded and another one spoke. "Ye dinnae know me, your grace, but my name is Fraser. I hae heard many rumors about Sir Ian MacGillivray, and what is true I can nae say for certain. I do know that wi' my own eyes I saw the man turn his horse into Lord Ravenstoke's at the Dornach Fair. Some said it was an accident, but I know otherwise." Fraser shrugged. "It seemed few cared whether it be accident or nae, since it was the English laird who was nearly killed."

Andrew looked once more at the men around him and could see by their expressions that they were telling the truth. He had known that Ian was a hard man, for he had upon occasion witnessed his rough treatment of servants. Andrew suddenly remembered one incident in which an enraged MacGillivray had viciously kicked his groom. At the time Andrew had excused his behavior, attributing it to drink. Indeed, perhaps he had always been too eager to overlook MacGillivray's faults, refusing to believe the worst of him. Andrew frowned, realizing that Alison had been right about his friend.

"There is little time," said Angus MacKenna. "Your grace, ye must hurry tae stop Sir Ian. Lady Alison and Master Duncan hae already gone there."

"What?" cried the duke. "Alison has gone there?"

"Aye," said MacKenna.

"Don't worry, Grandfather," said Andrew. "I shall go. I can be there quickly."

"Then hurry, lad. Take the swiftest horse in the village. I shall follow in the carriage."

Andrew nodded and rushed from the room.

Duncan Murray knew well the way to Hetty Munro's cottage and he and his sister lost no time in getting there. Alison and Duncan pulled up their horses as the house came into view. There was Ian MacGillivray standing outside the cottage beside the diminutive figure of Mrs. Munro. He was shouting at her and the elderly woman was weeping piteously. Two of MacGillivray's men were busily tossing Mrs. Munro's belongings out of the cottage onto the ground.

Alison exchanged a glance with her brother and then the two of them galloped toward MacGillivray. "Ian!" shouted Alison. "Wait, please!"

The baronet was surprised and not at all happy to see Alison and Duncan ride up. Alison jumped down off her horse and hurried to Ian. "Surely you cannot mean to put the old woman out!"

"Well, now. And what are you doing here, lass?"

"I'm here to speak for this poor woman."

"Bless you, lass," said Mrs. Munro, wiping her eyes with a corner of her apron and looking gratefully at Alison.

"Ian, do allow her to keep her cottage."

"Alison, my girl, I cannot allow every penniless old hag in the Highlands to live on my lands. By God, I have not seen any rent from her since that worthless son of hers took himself off to America. Who told you of this? I shall have his head."

"That does not signify in the least, Ian. I did hear of it

and shall think you the most heartless of men if you leave Mrs. Munro homeless."

MacGillivray grinned. "Well, lass, I have made up my mind. It is my land, and 'twill be better as pasture for sheep than home to an old crone. Cameron!" Ian shouted to one of his men.

"Aye, sir?"

"Light the torch and bring it to me."

"You cannot mean to burn her house!"

"I can and I will." His man handed MacGillivray the lighted torch.

"You must reconsider, Ian." Alison regarded him imploringly.

"I would reconsider, my girl, if you have reconsidered my offer."

Alison frowned. "No, you cannot think I would ever agree to marry you."

"I thought as much. Now, stand aside, all of you."

"Nay, sir! 'Tis my home all these years." Hetty Munro rushed toward Sir Ian, but he shoved her aside. The elderly woman would have fallen had Alison not caught her.

"Keep her away or she will come to harm. I warn you." Ian started toward the cottage, torch in hand.

"No!" Duncan Murray hurled himself at MacGillivray. "You cannot do this!" The boy attempted to grab the torch, but Ian slapped him hard, sending Duncan sprawling.

"MacGillivray!"

Ian looked up, startled to hear a masculine voice, and found Ravenstoke there, mounted on his bay horse. There was an expression of cold fury on his face that even MacGillivray found a trifle unsettling. "Ravenstoke! What are you doing here? This is my land and you are not welcome on it."

"You miserable ruffian! If you hurt that boy, I warn you, you shall pay dearly for it."

Alison had by this time run to Duncan's side and found her brother badly shaken, but seemingly all right. She knelt by his side and glared at MacGillivray. "How could you!"

Ian ignored her words and was intent upon Ravenstoke. "I shall pay dearly? Do you threaten me, Ravenstoke?"

"I give you fair warning. It is more difficult to face a man than a boy."

"A man?" MacGillivray laughed derisively. "You? You must be joking."

Ravenstoke dismounted and stood before the big man. "I am not joking in the least, MacGillivray. I suggest you put down that torch before someone is hurt."

"You dare tell me what to do?" MacGillivray grinned unpleasantly and then called to one of his men, handing him the torch. "I have long thought what a pleasure it would be to meet you like this, Englishman." He placed his hands on his hips belligerently. "When I am done with you, Ravenstoke, you will wish you had never been born."

Alison watched this exchange with a horror-stricken expression. MacGillivray easily outweighed the marquess by fifty pounds and she suddenly feared for Ravenstoke's life.

The marquess, however, seemed remarkably calm. He took off his hat and tossed it to the ground and then his well-cut coat.

The baronet fixed a malevolent smile upon Ravenstoke. "I shall enjoy this, Englishman."

"Perhaps," murmured the marquess, raising his fists in a boxing pose.

MacGillivray threw back his head and laughed. "God, you are ridiculous." Then, without any warning, he lunged toward the marquess, flinging his beefy fist at Ravenstoke's head.

The marquess deftly dodged the blow and then, with lightening precision, planted a hard right to MacGillivray's midsection. The big man gasped in pain and surprise, and Ravenstoke leapt back. Sir Ian muttered a Gaelic epithet and raised his fists menacingly. He then hurled his arm forward with such force that had the blow landed properly, it might have felled an ox. Luckily, the marquess sidestepped neatly and MacGillivray, caught off balance, fell heavily to the ground.

Picking himself up quickly, the baronet faced Ravenstoke once again. The mocking look that had been on his face when they had started to fight was now replaced by an expression of rage.

Alison clutched Duncan and watched fearfully as Mac-Gillivray approached the marquess. Ravenstoke watched his adversary intently as the big man started to draw his right arm back. Then, suddenly, the marquess struck, directing a blow that connected sharply with MacGill-ivray's chin. Sir Ian's face had barely enough time to register his shock when Ravenstoke's second blow hit him in the stomach and knocked him over.

"Have you had enough?" The marquess stood over MacGillivray, his fists poised.

The baronet did not speak, but looked up groggily at the marquess.

Ravenstoke called to MacGillivray's men. "Get him out of my sight!"

The two men eyed Ravenstoke with astonishment and then obediently got Sir Ian to his feet.

"God in heaven! What is going on here?" Andrew Murray pulled his horse up and jumped down. "Alison, are you and Duncan all right?"

"Oh, Andrew!" Duncan ran to his elder brother. "Did you see him? Did you see Ravenstoke?"

"Aye." Andrew nodded. "By my honor, sir, you did that nicely." He looked over at Sir Ian, who was leaning heavily on his men.

"Ian! Then it is true that you were evicting a poor widow?"

"It is true," cried Duncan. "He was going to burn the cottage down. I tried to stop him and he struck me. That is when Lord Ravenstoke fought him. It was glorious!"

Andrew shook his head. "I did not want to believe you capable of such a deed, Ian, but this day I have heard much ill said of you. It seems I have been blind. But for the sake of our friendship I am willing to hear your explanation. What do you have to say in your defense?"

MacGillivray rubbed his jaw and winced in pain. "I say to you, Andrew Murray, that you and all your kin can go straight to the devil! I'll have naught to do with any of you from this day forward." The big man then shouted at his men in Gaelic. They hurried to fetch their horses, and after assisting a still-groggy Ian MacGillivray onto his horse, the three of them rode off without another word.

"Oh, Ravenstoke!" Alison ran to the marquess and threw her arms around him. "I was so worried about you."

"Do you have so little faith in Mull's tutelage, madam?" He grinned and, pulling her close, kissed her firmly on the lips.

"What is the meaning of this, sir?" cried Andrew in astonishment. "Alison, have you lost your senses?"

Alison smiled at her brother. "I think I have."

"Lord Ravenstoke, I demand you release my sister."

"Be careful, Andrew," said Duncan with a grin. "You saw what happened to Ian."

"Calm yourself, man," said Ravenstoke. "I am going to marry your sister. Oh, I know the idea won't please you, but you had best become accustomed to it."

"Marry her? But you are engaged!"

"My former fiancée would not have me," said Ravenstoke, directing a grin at Alison. "Your sister shows less judgment, it seems."

"Aye," said Alison, regarding him fondly. "That I do." She then looked over at Andrew, expecting his disapproval. She was surprised when he only smiled.

"No, Allie, I will say nothing against the match. I have been very wrong about Ian and I fear I have also been wrong about you, Ravenstoke." Andrew offered his hand to the marquess, who shook it warmly.

"Bless ye, m'lord, and Lady Alison," cried Hetty Munro tearfully. "Bless ye for what ye hae done for a poor woman."

Ravenstoke had nearly forgotten the elderly woman in the excitement, and he smiled kindly at her. "Do not worry, Mrs. Munro. You must leave this house, but we will find you a home on Glenfinnan land."

"Och, thank ye, m'lord," said Mrs. Munro, again dabbing her eyes with a corner of her apron.

Alison placed a comforting arm around the old woman's shoulders. "Don't worry. Everything will be fine."

"Look!" cried Duncan suddenly. "It is Grandfather's carriage."

They turned to watch the vehicle approach, and when it came to a halt, Andrew opened the carriage door and assisted the duke down. His grace looked at his granddaughter and, noting her radiant expression, seemed relieved. "Alison, I would ask if you are all right, but I can see very well that you are."

"I am indeed," said Alison, hurrying over to her grandfather and giving him an affectionate hug.

Duncan ran to them and said excitedly, "Grandfather, you should have seen it! Ravenstoke thrashed Ian soundly, and richly he deserved it for striking me and trying to burn poor Mrs. Munro's cottage!"

The duke looked at the marquess. "It seems I am once again in your debt, sir."

Ravenstoke smiled. "I am glad of that, for perhaps it will make you look favorably on the request I wish to make of you."

"Request?" said the duke.

"Indeed, sir. I would like to request your granddaughter's hand in marriage."

"Marriage?" repeated his grace. "But I thought—"

"You thought I was engaged to Miss Willoughby," said Ravenstoke. "I was, indeed, but the engagement is broken. It is your granddaughter I wish to marry." The marquess looked over at Alison, who smiled, and then he turned to the duke. "I hope you have no objections, sir."

"He would not have any objections, Lord Ravenstoke," interjected Duncan.

"That is for his grace to say, Duncan," said his lordship, looking toward the duke.

"Indeed so, young sir," said his grace with mock severity. "I need no young cub answering for me. And how can you be so certain I would not object, my lad?"

Duncan looked a trifle surprised. "Why, Grandfather, you could not refuse to allow Allie to marry a man who is Prince Charlie's cousin."

They all laughed heartily. "Right you are, lad," said the duke, glancing at Alison. "It is what you want, my dear?"

She nodded. "Aye, Grandfather, with all my heart."

"Then you have my blessing." The duke shook Ravenstoke's hand and then kissed Alison. "Let us go home at once," he said. "This is cause for celebration."

"Aye," said Duncan enthusiastically. The boy looked over at Mrs. Munro, who had been watching the proceedings intently. "And what of Mrs. Munro? She cannot stay here."

"Of course not," said the duke. "You must come with us to Dornach Castle, Hetty."

"Aye," said Alison. "We will have someone come and get your things." Mrs. Munro murmured her thanks and Duncan led her to the carriage and helped her inside.

"We must go, then," said the duke. "Alison, will you ride with us?"

"If you don't mind, Grandfather, I should prefer to ride Claymore back."

"And I shall escort her," said Ravenstoke.

The duke directed a knowing look at the marquess. "Very well," he said.

"And I shall ride with them," said Duncan.

"You shall ride with us, young man," said the duke. "In the carriage with you."

Andrew smiled. "I shall ride in the carriage, too, Allie, unless you prefer my company."

Alison laughed and kissed her brother on the cheek. Andrew then tied his horse and Duncan's behind the carriage and followed the duke into the vehicle. Duncan jumped in after them and, as the carriage started off, waved merrily at Alison and Ravenstoke.

They waved back and watched the lumbering vehicle make its way along the road. Alison turned to the marquess. "Duncan seems very happy."

Ravenstoke caught her up in his arms and pulled her close. "It is I who am happy, my darling," he said, and before she could make a reply, he kissed his Highland lady soundly.

About the Author

Margaret Summerville grew up in the Chicago area and holds degrees in journalism and library science. Employed as a librarian, she is single and lives in Morris, Illinois, with her Welsh corgi, Morgan.